Enemy Planet – Son of Wolf
by Paul Lentz

This is Book III of *The Stuff of Life* Tetralogy

Ty Ty Press, Peachtree City, Georgia
Earth Analogue III

iv

Other books by the author:

"On Ty Ty Creek: Sweet Potato Pie, Moonshine, and other Southern Traditions"

"The Stuff of Life"
Book I"

"Enemy Planet: House of Wolf"
The Stuff of Life: Book II

"Holy Fire"

"The Cry of the Innocents"

Upcoming books:

"Three Planets" (Working Title)
(The Stuff of Life, Book IV)
2020

Books are available on Amazon.com.

https://www.amazon.com/author/paullentz

For information about
all books check
www.PaulLentzAuthor.com

Dedication

To the wolves, and those
who would be children of wolves.

TABLE OF CONTENTS

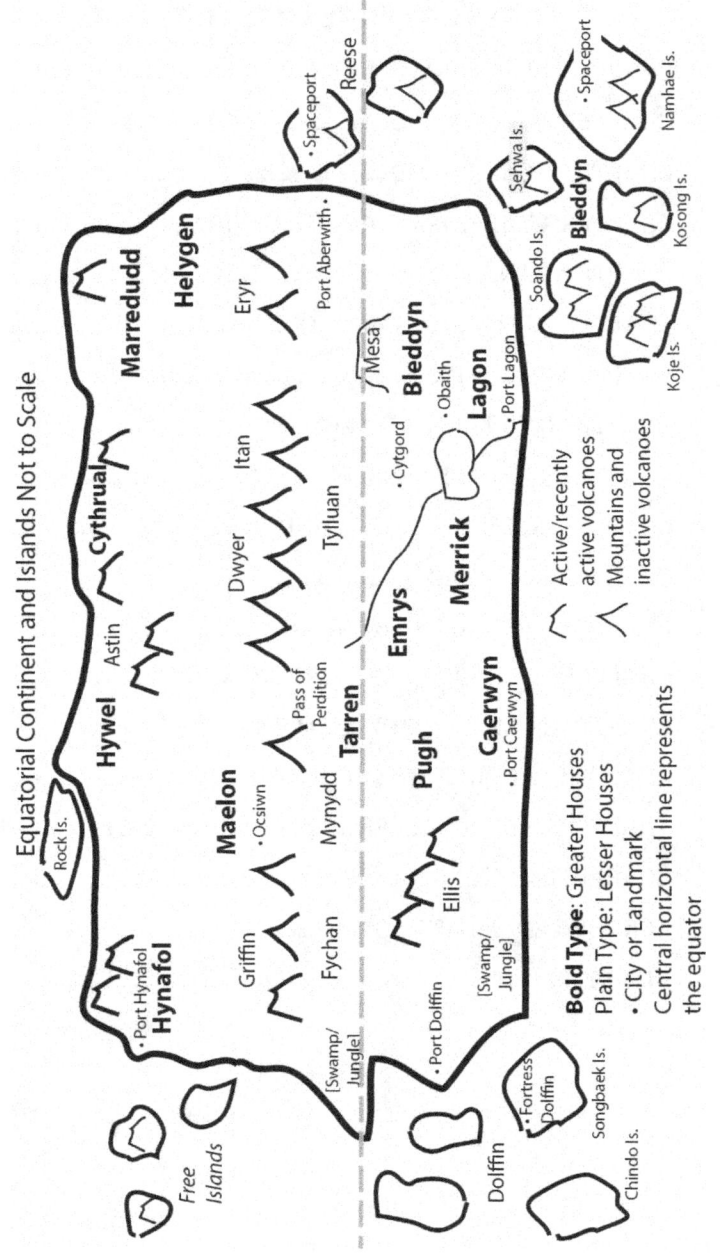

Equatorial Continent and Islands Not to Scale

Bold Type: Greater Houses
Plain Type: Lesser Houses
• City or Landmark
Central horizontal line represents
the equator

Λ Active/recently
active volcanoes

Λ Mountains and
inactive volcanoes

Marredudd
Helygen
Eryr
• Port Aberwith
Cythrual
Hywel
Astin
Itan
Dwyer
Tylluan
Mesa
Bleddyn
• Obaith
Lagon
• Port Lagon
• Cytgord
Merrick
Emrys
Caerwyn
• Port Caerwyn
Pugh
Tarren
Pass of
Perdition
Mynydd
• Ocsiwn
Maelon
Fychan
Ellis
Griffin
[Swamp/
Jungle]
Hynafol
• Port Hynafol
Rock Is.
[Swamp/
Jungle]
• Port Dolffin
• Fortress
Dolffin
Dolffin
Songbaek Is.
Chindo Is.
Free
Islands

• Spaceport
Reese
• Spaceport
Namhae Is.
Bleddyn
Sehwa Is.
Soando Is.
Kosong Is.
Koje Is.

x

CHAPTER 1 BIRTH AND DEATH

"The boundaries which divide life from death
are at best shadowy and vague."
– Edgar Allen Poe, Earth Analogue III

The first assassins strike when I am six days old. My family and I are in the Council Chamber where my father, Gens and Patriarch of the House of Wolf, elevates me in front of the Council of Thirteen Houses, names me Garreth, and declares me to be his son. Father is holding me in his outstretched arms when three would-be assassins stand in the benches behind us. Two fire energy weapons before Telor, my Brother-plus-twenty, and Nana, my Nurturing Mother, return fire and kill them. Daggers wielded by people loyal to House Bleddyn kill the third.

That is what I was told.

One hundred eleven years and several assassination attempts later, I am helmsman of the corvette *Cardis* of my father's fleet when a starship of the Adversary attacks and destroys the *Cardis* except for the bow section which holds the command crew. We are tumbling through space and facing death when I feel someone enter my mind. *Who are you?* I ask.

I am Kendrick. I am on the Founder ship beside you. We can rescue you. Who are you?

1

I am Garreth, Son of Bleddyn and Helmsman of the Corvette Cardis of the House Bleddyn Fleet. Is your ship the one that destroyed mine?

Yes, I'm afraid so. But you fired first. I detect seven infrared spots. Are there seven of you? Is your captain among them?

Yes. There are seven of us on the bridge, including the captain. He will kill himself and us rather than allow us to be captured. I think of the ancient directive – "Leave no companion behind; never become a captive."

What if it's not capture, but rescue?

I don't know.

A few moments later, Kendrick returns to my mind. *My captain says if you and your crew offer your parole, we will treat you as guests and we will do everything possible to return you to your people. He says we are subject to the authority of others and bound by universal constants which may make it difficult, perhaps impossible. We promise we will try.*

"Captain, a message from the Adversary ship." I gesture to my console as if the message came from there. Even in the face of death I keep my telepathy secret. I relay the message to the captain who rejects the offer. I watch him set the auto-destruct timer. "You have ten minutes to say your farewells," he announces.

I feel a jab in the back of my neck. I turn and see Barri and Betsan through a haze. They catch me and carry me from the bridge. Captain sees them, and I dimly sense his approval. Deryn is waiting at a hatch. He and Barri strip off my jumpsuit and the slippers we wear aboard ship and shove me into a life pod.

"There is only one undamaged life pod," Betsan says. She looks away. I see her pressing buttons on the console. "The pod will seek the star we were approaching. It may take millennia to reach it. This is a long shot, but it's the best chance you have." She looks over her shoulder, turns, and disappears. I hear the clang of the pod door closing and the thump of ejection. Moments later, I feel the death of the captain and my friends Betsan, Barri, Deryn, and the others. The pod's computer puts me into cold sleep.

I am asleep as the pod seeks first the star and then a stable orbit to occupy and perhaps survive. The hemocyanin in my blood plus two fish glycoprotein genes spliced into my DNA keep my cells from rupturing in the near absolute zero temperature of space. Other spliced genes protect me from cosmic radiation. Nothing can protect my brain from quantum fluctuations or from random sparks in atoms triggered by the pod's power supply. They energize memories that flash among my brain cells like electrons in a frozen superconductor – one memory triggers another until the energy fades. I am in cold sleep, but sometimes, I dream…

4

CHAPTER 2 GLINT

An electron drops from one orbit to another, releasing a quantum of energy that flashes from cell to cell. In my sleeping brain, a memory forms of days after Spring Stormtime when thralls repairing damage to the gardens of Fortress Bleddyn are silent observers of a game of hide-and-find.

I won a valuable token and am a prime target for the Seeker. I look for a place to hide when a hand snakes from a patch of reeds and a voice calls, "Garreth! There's room here."

It is a boy new to our play. I duck between the reeds, and squat beside him.

"Shhh," he warns.

I hear the Seeker. He is an older boy and his footsteps are heavy. They approach. I shiver with mock fear. The Seeker's footsteps turn away.

"He's here!" the boy beside me calls, revealing our hiding place. "He's here!" The Seeker parts the reeds and cries, "I claim the token!"

I tell no one about the betrayal. It is my fault. The new boy's Gens swore to my father, but we are too young to take an oath. I do not tell this story to Brother-plus-twenty Telor or to Father, but other companion-playmates learn of it. Those older and who understand the politics of the Res Publica say nothing. Only one speaks to me.

"I will never betray you, Garreth." It is Glint, a cousin, son of my Uncle Madox and of Second Rank of House Bleddyn. Glint and his father are visiting my home, and Glint is new to our play. I see a boy my age, a little taller than my 100 cm and a little heavier than my 16 kg. Like me, he wears a black jumpsuit with orange and gold stripes on the sleeves – House Bleddyn colors. Our jumpsuits are bare of other insignia. We will not wear house patches until we are older and take blood-oath to my father.

I see the promise in his face and return it. "Thank you, Glint, I will never betray you. I think we both need someone we can trust."

Father is not immune to my wolf-puppy eyes and I convince him Glint should remain and become one of my companion-playmates.

~~~~~

A few days before Spring Stormtime of my eighth year, Glint runs to our room, babbling his excitement. "We will visit Namhae Island tomorrow!"

Namhae is Glint's home. The volcanic island off the eastern coast holds our shipyards and spaceport. Two starships, a corvette and a colony ship of House Bleddyn's fleet will launch in three days. Colony ships are rare. They are big and expensive.

The wind from the sea carries salt evaporated from spindrift that stings our faces when we leave the shuttle. Glint's father, my Uncle Madox, greets us and escorts us through the

6

ships. I watch Glint's eyes light with pride when his father speaks and my father, the Gens, listens intently. We meet crewmembers of the two ships, including pilots for the swarm of fighters carried in the corvette's belly and crew members of the two caravels for exploration, science missions, and defense.

The fighters are small – long as shuttlecraft, but narrow and sleek. They are heavy with weapons and armor, leaving little room for pilot and copilot in their couches.

"What if you need to pee?" I ask a pilot.

His answer does not reassure me and I decide I do not want to be a fighter pilot.

The caravels are large, with quarters for crew and laboratories where scientists can work. They are big enough to have artificial gravity and real toilets.

Uncle Madox takes us through the caravel's laboratories. "These are our best DNA sequencers," he says. "It's a wonder the crew of the *Kobaya* learned what they did with the equipment they had."

I know the *Kobaya*. It is the caravel that escaped when the Adversary destroyed its mother ship, sparking our war with them. After we walk through the engine room, I turn to Father. "Caravels don't have stardrive."

"The *Kobaya* did not," Father says. "The crew established a position at one of the libration points of an outer gas-giant planet and its sun, then entered cold sleep. I sent the closest starship. If the Adversary does not find them and some accident does not befall, we will rescue them in a few centuries. Caravels built since then have stardrive."

Father sees me shudder, and says, "Space is vast and unforgiving, but also exciting and wonderful. The crew of *Kobaya* knew the risk and accepted it."

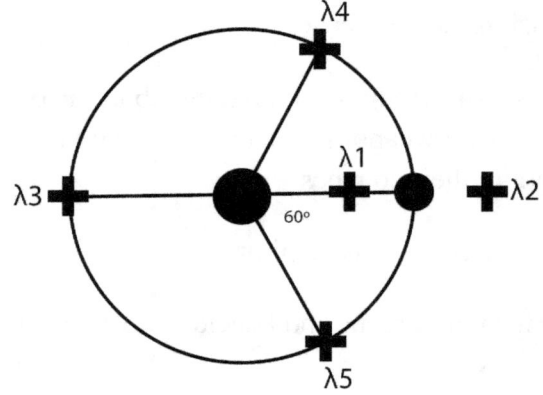

Libration Points (Lagrangian Points or Stable Points) in a two-body system (sun & planet or planet & large moon). Points λ4 and λ5 are stable without expending energy. A ship that drifted slightly away from one of those points would be pulled back into equilibrium.

They went to sleep without knowing if they would ever wake. I think I do not have the courage of Kobaya's crew.

I have seen corvettes, but am not prepared for the colony ship. It is a globe many times larger than the corvette, and rests in a cradle. Uncle Madox leads us to a window overlooking a vast space where cold-sleep chambers hold five thousand people already asleep, to be wakened when a suitable planet is found.

"Why so many people, Father?"

"Five thousand is the number required to have the knowledge, skills, and training we believe necessary to survive on a new world."

A chill runs through me. They will be on their own for millennia. Will they remember World? Will they stay loyal to the blood of my house? Will they survive?

Father anticipates my questions. "A cousin commands this mission. The crew and colonists are of-the-blood. They will be in contact with us and other colonies with our faster-than-light comm system. We will not forget them, nor they, us."

Uncle Madox's communicator chimes. He holds it to his ear. After speaking quietly, he tells Father the launch will be delayed until evening of the next day, and invites us to stay overnight at Fortress Namhae. He and Father walk away, but Glint tugs my hand.

"We have hours and hours before dark," Glint says. "And the tide is low."

"Why does that matter?" I ask.

"Because we can reach my secret cave only at low tide. Come on, they're not watching us."

Glint pilots a two-person floater down the sheer cliff walls on the south side of the island to the coast. Low tide has exposed a sandy beach and the entrance to a cave. I see the mark on the rocks where high tide will cover the cave entrance. Glint lands the floater on the beach and leads me into the cave.

The cave floor rises; the walls are smooth and curved but rubble from the ceiling litters the floor. We unclip lights from our utility belts and climb. After a while, the cave levels and walking becomes easier. Glint searches for something. He stops, reaches into a hole in the wall, and pulls out a wooden box filled with colored rocks and shells.

"Treasures from my childhood," he says, and blushes.

He is naming the creatures that once lived in the shells when the air pulses and our ears pop.

"What happened?" I ask.

"A wave! A wave beat against the cave opening and pressed the air. But it can't be! The tide hasn't turned."

My ears pop again. "Maybe we should leave."

Glint closes the box and stuffs it into the hole. We hurry down the tunnel, but the scree is loose and we must be careful not to start a slide. Perhaps we are too cautious, for our descent is slow. We have not reached the entrance when we see water filling the cave below us.

I remember my lessons on weather and realize what happened. "A storm. An early spring storm created a tidal surge. Low pressure and wind lifted the water. We're trapped. We need to climb higher."

Glint and I climb to the highest part of the cave to escape the rising water. We turn off our lights to save power and perhaps to hide our fear of the rising water. The storm gets stronger. Thunder shakes the rocks and our bones.

"Garreth, I betrayed you. I led you into danger," Glint says. I hear his voice over the thunder.

"No," I call over the sounds of the storm. "It is not betrayal. You did not expect this." I tell him about the time I was nearly killed by lightning while dancing on the battlements. I don't think this makes Glint feel better.

~~~~~

We are tired and hungry but mostly thirsty when soldiers with underwater breathing masks and air tanks reach us. They find us because waves beat the floater against the rocks and set off its crash beacon. The soldiers carry us to the entrance, where the water receded enough to open the cave to the air. Our fathers are waiting when the soldiers carry us into cold wind and rain.

Father's face is dark and his lips are tight with anger. Before Glint and I may bathe or change clothes, we face him alone. Our wet clothes stick to our skin, and we shiver. I wonder why Glint's father is not present and if Father will administer High Justice. He could execute Glint for putting me in danger. I promised never to betray Glint. This means I must defend him.

"You knew the approaching storm delayed the launch," Father says.

"Only that the launch was delayed, Father," I reply. "We did not know about the storm, and were never in danger, even after the storm—"

"You did not know you were not in danger," Father snaps.

I remember my oath to Glint – I will never betray you. It gives me courage to reply. "No, Father. I was excited to see the cave. If I had refused, Glint would not have taken me there. He is not responsible—"

11

"Your name, Garreth, means brave and modest," Father interrupts me, again. "Do you understand the difference between brave and foolish?"

This is the lesson he wants us to learn. I look at the floor, and then into my father's eyes. "It is the beginning of understanding, Father."

"Glint?" Father asks.

"It is the beginning of understanding, Your Grace."

Does Father believe we learned a lesson? Will he punish us? The answer to both questions is 'yes.'

"You will return to Fortress. You will not witness the launch. You will do nothing except attend training until twenty days past the end of Spring Stormtime. You are restricted to your rooms, schoolroom, and dojo. No games, no floaters, no horses, nothing. Do you understand?"

"Yes, Father."

"Yes, Your Grace."

Father waves his hand to dismiss us.

~~~~~

Lightning from a summer storm flashes through the windows of the dojo. My mates and I face older companion-guards. We practice two-person kata, learning how to attack and defend against a bigger opponent. The flow of the exercise breaks when Glint yells, "That hurt!" He sweeps his opponent with a low kick, knocking him to the mat. Glint stands over the man with his fists pressed together in challenge.

The rest of my companion-students are too surprised to move. Teacher steps in. "Relax, young one. It is an exercise. The time for challenge will come." His words calm Glint, whose face and body relax. Teacher leads him away.

The Challenge

~~~~~

Glint returns to our room just before supper. He is wearing a vambrace like mine. I know what it means. Because of his anger, the vambrace will inject drugs to calm him and to focus his attention, but Glint sees only what he thinks is an honor. I wonder how much I should tell him about the vambrace.

"I wish my father were here to see this," Glint says. His eyes move from his vambrace to mine. "It is an important step in our lives. One of many you and I share."

I see something in his face, something he wants to say but dares not. I push my thoughts through Telor's teachings, through Father's stories, through the lessons in my books, and through the drugs in my own vambrace.

Brotherhood. He wants to ask for brotherhood but he cannot. I am of higher station. Only I can ask, and I should not do so without Father's permission. "You want brotherhood," I whisper.

"I may not say it," Glint says, "lest you think me froward."

Father says law and custom are for those who cannot think for themselves. This gives me courage to speak. "Then I will say it. Glint, will you swear brotherhood by our blood?"

A year ago, on Glint's eighth birthday, his father brought Glint to Fortress Bleddyn and took Glint to swear fealty with my Father. Glint received a dagger like mine, with the wolf head. The daggers we exchange tonight are identical. No one but Glint and I will know of the oath.

~~~~~

For millennia, the Res Publica gathered in the days before Fall Stormtime to celebrate the harvest and, if stories whispered among children are true, for older brothers and sisters to select mates. Today, the gathering is a festival of friendship and solidarity. Relatives and people from allied houses crowd Fortress. Guests who traveled all night arrive at dawn.

It is the tenth month of my tenth year. Glint and I rush through breakfast. We pat our pockets to be sure we have coins for treats and run through the south gate of Fortress to the greensward. My companion-guards anticipate our speed and split their forces. Some are outside the gate, waiting for us. They laugh when I pout because they have caught me. I laugh, too, and promise not to tease them too badly.

Booths along white gravel paths offer food, trinkets, toys, games of chance and skill, and more. The customers are members of the Res Publica. Thralls who operate the booths call and cajole passers-by. A parrot perches on one thrall's shoulder. An illusionist performs for a gaggle of delighted children whose parents drop coins into a cup. Other thralls wander through the courtyards playing musical instruments. Near the central fountain, two jugglers toss back and forth a hundred – or at least a dozen – crystal rods that flash and glitter in the sunlight. In one corner, an acrobat does a handstand five meters above the crowd; her only support is a pole held by her partner on the ground. A tightrope reaches from one corner of the square to another and a trio of equilibrists walks back and forth, performing daring feats when they pass.

Glint and I wander through the booths offering games, food, and trinkets. We debate whether to try a game of chance or find more pastries when a thrall wearing a particolored baldric steps from a booth toward us.

Glint stiffens, and cries out. "Assassin! He has a weapon!"

Two of my guards push us behind them while two others tackle the thrall. The people around us step back, then move closer when the threat passes. One of my guards searches the thrall and pulls an energy pistol from deep inside the man's garments. He stares at the pistol and then at Glint. "How did you know?"

I feel the paralysis that seizes Glint's body. He cannot answer.

A voice from the crowd cries. "He's a demon! He saw what he couldn't see."

The crowd hushes, but only for an instant. "He knows things he can't know!" someone cries.

"He sees things that are hidden," says another.

"He is a demon," comes a softer voice. Someone repeats that accusation, loudly.

"He can control our minds!" That is the final accusation.

I know what this mean. If Glint is a demon, he is dead. Demons are executed without appeal.

Two of my guards hold Glint to the ground and bind his arms and ankles. Someone calls Father. He and Glint's father, Uncle Madox, approach. Cousin-Lieutenant Fender, commander of my companion-guards, reports to them.

I see the pain in Uncle Madox's face and in Father's when he orders Glint removed. Glint will be executed. Father has no choice. This is a law even he must obey.

The festival is over for me. Bright colors fade to muted shades of gray. Music becomes a dull drone. Accompanied by my guards, I re-enter Fortress. When I reach the family quarters, I dismiss my guards and return to my rooms.

Sani – the thrall who was my tutor – once told me it was okay to cry when faced with great sorrow. I did not cry when I learned Sani was dead. However, on this night I cry myself to sleep. I wake the next morning with my heart filled with hatred for what was done to Glint and fear it might happen to me, because I know I am a demon. I hear whispers from my companions and my teachers. The whispers are not in my ears but in my mind. How long can I keep this secret? Will I slip the way Glint did? Will I be discovered and killed?

I am alone with my sadness and fear. Brother Telor comes to my room, but I don't let him in. He is the only one I might confide in, but I am afraid he will betray me if I tell him what I am.

The next morning, Father summons me. I must be very careful what I say so he will not suspect I am a demon. I must be careful not to find in his mind an answer I couldn't know.

Father speaks without saying *good morning*. "Garreth, I am sorry. Glint was your friend. I know you were sworn brothers. He was my nephew. His father is my brother. I..." Father runs out of words. It is the first time I have seen this happen.

I keep my voice brisk and, I hope, impersonal. "Thank you, Father. I cried for Glint last night. I used all my tears. It is past, although I will hate that law as long as I live."

~~~~~

I am eighteen and in my last year at Academy when the Tactical Officer summons me. The sun has not risen; I stifle a yawn that would earn punishment if Tac saw it.

"Your father interrupts your training," Tac says. He is of unaligned House Lagon and is more puzzled than angry.

"Gens Bleddyn requires your service on a mission. A shuttle will—" Tac's communicator chimes. He glances at the screen. "A shuttle landed on Pad Three. It will take you to your destination. You will learn more then."

His words are a dismissal. Should I be frightened? Excited? I wonder while I run to the shuttle pad.

17

~~~~~

Morning the next day, I walk the streets of Sangtae, an eastern-coastal city on the Southern Continent. I wear a mercenary's cammies, armor, and boots. My cammies have no house insignia. An energy pistol is at my waist and a slug rifle rides over my shoulder. A saber joins a plain dagger and the grace knife at my belt. I am qualified with all these weapons, but that does not give me a lot of confidence.

The weather is cool. Sani told me seasons on the Southern Continent are mixed up and more violent than on the Equatorial Continent. The weather can turn into a storm with no warning.

The fishing boats and wharves of Sangtae remind me of our port on Kosong Island, from which our trading ships sail westward to allies on the Equatorial Continent and southward to the Southern Continent. Opposite the wharves, stone buildings line the street. Chandlers who sell ships equipment and supplies display hempen rope, block and tackle, sails, and barrels. Shingles with icons for fish, bales of hemp or wool, and other trade goods hang from warehouses. Members of the Res Publica and thralls fill the cobblestone streets of this city. The thralls step aside when I approach and avoid my eyes. Unlike the thralls I grew up with, I sense fear and hatred.

The Res Publica carry weapons. Mercenary guards accompany those whose clothes suggest they are prosperous. My mission is to contact someone. I do not know who it will be – even if he or she will be Res Publica or thrall. I was told someone would recognize me. Will this person be an ally, or must I be suspicious? I open my mind, searching for danger and for this unknown contact.

18

I walk the main street along the wharves and quays until I see a boy standing in the street twenty meters in front of me. He wears mercenary garb. He stares at me. I return his stare and understand. He is my brother-cousin Glint. He has changed, but it is he.

I promised never to betray you. My life is in your hands. Glint speaks into my mind and reminds me I swore the same oath. I sense both fear and courage in his thoughts.

I promised never to betray you, I say with my mind. *Until death, I promised. Where have you been?*

Glint walks toward me. He smiles, and I know he hears my thoughts. "Come, there's a safe place we can talk."

We talk with our mouths about inconsequential things while thoughts flash faster than I can keep up. Glint understands and slows his thoughts.

Your father's agents removed me from the Harvest Festival and reported my death. They took me to the hospital on Sehwa and changed me – my face mostly, but they also cut six centimeters from my leg bones to make me shorter. I'm surprised you recognized me.

I think about the games we played, the danger we faced together in the lava cave, the floater races, games of hide-and-find, and the nighttime hours we spent whispering in the dark. *How could I not recognize you?*

I share these memories and I feel Glint's happiness.

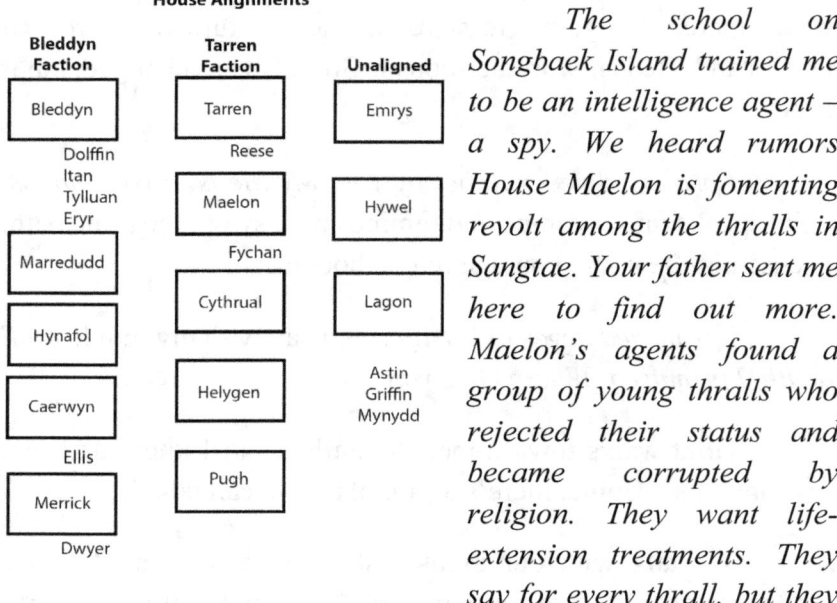

The school on Songbaek Island trained me to be an intelligence agent – a spy. We heard rumors House Maelon is fomenting revolt among the thralls in Sangtae. Your father sent me here to find out more. Maelon's agents found a group of young thralls who rejected their status and became corrupted by religion. They want life-extension treatments. They say for every thrall, but they mean for themselves.

This does not surprise me. Life extension has been a source of conflict since the Res Publica created the process one hundred-forty millennia ago. It's a poorly kept secret no thralls receive life extension, except a few favored bed warmers and courtesans – and those only in Greater Houses Tarren and Maelon. Father would not do this; other Greater Houses and the Lesser Houses do not have the technology or resources to do it.

How many? Who are they? Who are their leaders? Who are the House Maelon agents? My mind bubbles with questions.

This memory stick holds information. Take my hand.

I do what he asks. We walk hand-in-hand like close friends while we whisper. It is easy to do this. Glint is the first of my companion-playmates I invited to my bed.

Glint presses the memory stick into my palm. When we release our hands, the memory stick is in mine.

Come, Glint says. *Here is a café where we will be safe. We have time, and you need to know more.*

The staff and most patrons of the café are thralls. A waiter brings us hot drinks.

Will you ever come home? I ask Glint.

No. I feel his sadness. *Your Father ordered my seed preserved. The hospital will modify my DNA and I will join a starship crew. He wants people with my skills among the stars to—*

Glint's thoughts stop. His fear washes over me and I see the source. A man who appears to be a mercenary enters the café. He scans the room and then turns toward our table. Before he takes a second step, I see his intention.

Energy pistols operate at the speed of light, but the speed of thought is faster. I fire first. The man's head vanishes in a cloud of blue blood.

You may leave Sangtae sooner than you expect, I say to Glint. The staff and customers of the café who are not frozen in their seats fall to the floor and huddle beneath tables.

My communicator buzzes. I read the tiny screen. A shuttle has landed. I pull Glint from his chair. I take the would-be assassin's energy pistol from his dead hand and hurry Glint toward the door. *While you were staring at the body, I signaled for pickup. They're expecting only me, but they will take you, too. You cannot stay here.*

I failed my mission, Glint sends. I feel his disappointment, but more so, his fear.

I open my mind to Glint. *You found another piece of the conspiracy. Don't you see? He was sworn to House Helygen. It's not just Maelon fomenting revolution. They're in league with Helygen. House Tarren is the link between Maelon and Helygen. Helygen agents discovered you were spying on them and hired the mercenary. You will receive credit for these discoveries.*

~~~~~

The shuttle crew accepts my orders. "Land on the battlements. There. You will never speak of this mission to anyone. In my father's name."

I have never used Father's authority this way, but the pilot-commander's acknowledgment assures me I did the right thing. He and the three crewmembers will bury the knowledge of the mission and any curiosity about the nameless passenger.

Telor is the only person who meets the shuttle. He takes us unseen through back halls and secret passages to Father's den. Father's mind is cloaked. I cannot sense how he feels or what he is thinking. His face gives nothing away. It seldom does. "Explain," he says to me, not Glint.

"Father, this memory stick contains proof of House Maelon's plot. More important, my brother-cousin Glint foiled an assassin, and found in the assassin's mind proof that House Helygen is part of the conspiracy."

Father knows there is more, but he does not press me. He gives the memory stick to Telor and dismisses Glint and me.

~~~~~

"You did not betray me; you saved me," Glint says. "You put your promise above duty. You lied to your father."

"No call of honor requires me to say you are not dead. The Council wrote the law that telepaths – demons – must be destroyed because they are afraid of stories written to frighten children. They were wrong; I am right. There is no call of honor for me to take credit for uncovering Helygen's involvement. Father knows I lied to protect you. He will agree I did the honorable thing. I did not betray you or our house."

Three days pass. Father restricts Glint and me to my quarters: bedroom, small dining room, and schoolroom. They are empty of all but us. Then, Father summons Glint. I am not included in the invitation. When Glint returns, I feel his sadness.

"I do not think we will meet, again. Your father sends me to hospital for a new disguise. Then, I will return to Sangtae. We exposed the plot; now we must put it down." Glint smiles. "I hope they don't make me any shorter." I know he accepts his role, but I see agitation and a little fear.

From within the breast of his jumpsuit, Glint draws a dagger. It is the one he and I exchanged years ago when we swore brotherhood. Despite the danger to himself, he kept it hidden. He jabs his arm. I watch the blood flow. "My blood is your blood until death," Glint says, and then adds, "Until forever."

The last two words are not a traditional part of the oath, but I understand. I jab my arm and repeat his words – all of them. We exchange daggers and jab our arms again. I know this is the last time I will see Glint. I think he knows this, too.

CHAPTER 3 CHILDHOOD

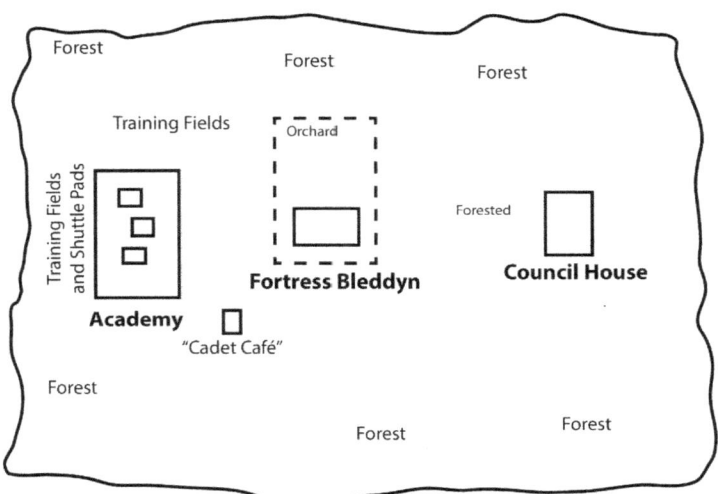

Not to scale. The three elements (Academy, Fortress Bleddyn, and Council House are separated by about 20 km. The mesa on which they sit slopes steeply on all sides to forested land broken by farm fields.

Fortress Bleddyn is a castle more ancient even than our family – the House of Wolf. Fortress, Council House, and Academy share a mesa anchored deeply within World. From our fortress, House Bleddyn rules over hectares of farmlands and forest, over rolling hills and deep river valleys, over the towns and villages of house members and thralls, and over the Eastern Islands that were our first home. On a sunny day a few days after my third birthday, Telor, my eldest brother and mentor, takes me to the battlements.

Winter Stormtime is past, but spring still hides. Most of the trees are bare, but spots of green – Telor names them gymnosperms – appear among the forest. Most of the land looks gray and dead. In the far north, mountains with snowcapped glaciers rise to meet the sky. Southward lie forests and fields turned in anticipation of spring. The innocent green of winter wheat sprouts in some fields, getting a jump on warmer weather.

Telor pulls my attention back to Mesa and points to the west. "Those buildings are Academy—"

"That's where Sisters Bethan and Delwyn and Brothers Daffyd and Guffudd are," I say. "Can we see them?"

Telor chuckles. "No, Garreth. Academy is twenty kilometers away, but they will come home for Spring Stormtime. Come, we will go to the Keep."

"Keep what?"

"The Keep is the tallest and strongest tower in Fortress. In olden days, the family and retainers would retreat there if enemies overran Fortress. Now, it's a museum."

My legs tire climbing the steps of the Keep and quiver before we reach the top, but I do not complain so my brother does not think I am weak. The windows in the highest room are narrow. They are too high for me to see anything but sky until Telor lifts me.

"The windows are arrow slits. They are just wide enough for an archer to shoot through," Telor explains.

From the eight arrow-slit windows, I can see all of Fortress. Telor tells me which buildings hold my bedroom and playroom and which hold the library and Father's den. He shows me the gardens, brown with winter, and the greensward outside the south wall where games and festivals are held.

To the east is Council House. Telor tells me about my elevation in front of Council – and the assassins. "We will go there soon for your sister Alaw's elevation."

~~~~~

Garreth's Siblings

Telor Brother+20
Llywelyn Brother+18
Bethan Sister +15
Delwyn Sister +12
Guffudd Brother +9
Alwen Sister +6
Rodric Brother +3
Alaw Sister -3

Nana, my surrogate and Nurturing Mother, takes my hand and leads me from the shuttle into the Council Chamber where Father will elevate Alaw and declare her his child-of-the-blood. Thirteen high-backed chairs sit behind a long table on a raised platform at one end of the room. They are for the Gens of the thirteen Greater Houses. Benches line the other three walls. This chamber is where assassins tried to kill me and Father when he elevated me. I look around for other assassins. They are not here. Only fear creates the memory. Nana takes me to a bench where other members of my family gather, surrounded by guards.

When it is time for Alaw's elevation, Nana takes me to stand beside Father. Actually, I stand beside Brother-plus-three Rodric, who stands beside Telor who stands beside Father. Brother-plus-eighteen, Llywelyn, the heir, sits in Father's chair on the dais. Alaw's surrogate stands on Father's other side. When the ceremony starts and Father lifts Alaw in his hands I need to pee. I grit my teeth until the ceremony is over and Nana leads me away. When we reach the toilet, I cannot pee and realize the feeling came more from nervousness than need.

~~~~~

There are still patches of snow on the mountains when Telor takes me to the stables.

"This horse is yours," he says. My eyes open wide and my heart sings. From the battlements I watched others riding these animals. I begged Telor to let me, but he said I was too little.

My horse is a reddish-brown, darker than my own skin. Her mane is black, like my hair. She stands a meter-and-a-half tall at her shoulders. I am one meter tall – the right height to ride her. Telor makes this a teaching moment. He thinks he has my attention, but my eyes are on the horse.

"Artificial selection," Telor says. "Horse and cattle breeders practiced it for millennia. It can create significant changes in a few generations. Since our civilization began two hundred millennia ago, we created a new breed of horse. Ancient horses were smaller than wolves are, today. They had three toes on each leg. The toes splayed out when they walked and made them well suited to the swamps and grasslands where their ancestors lived. We needed horses to run on the rocky trails of our mountains. We bred a new species of horse we call Dawn Horse.

28

They have a single toe with a hard hoof and can run along mountain trails. They are much bigger than their ancestors who still live in the wild. Artificial selection took only a dozen millennia. Natural selection, driven only by random mutations, isolation, and competition for resources takes much longer, often a hundred millennia or more."

Telor chuckles, and punches my shoulder to get my attention. "You will someday learn how important this is." Then he shows me how to tend the horse and put on her tack.

I name my horse Rhiannon after a woman warrior in the stories Telor tells me. After I show I can keep my seat, Telor allows me to ride her freely. Freely, except he and my companion-guards who lie on military floaters hovering above and following me.

~~~~~

A rocky outcrop rises steeply on the right. Telor's floater is behind me. Rhiannon is not afraid of floaters; their flight is silent. However, she is afraid of the snake warming itself in the sun in the middle of the trail. The snake coils and buzzes. Rhiannon shies and scrapes her flank and my leg against the rock wall. The heat of Telor's energy pistol flashes past me. The snake is ash, and Rhiannon is trying  to buck me off. I pull hard on the reins and press my legs into her sides. Telor must have jumped from his floater because he is standing in front of me. He grabs the bit and forces Rhiannon's head down. The bucking stops, but my heart is racing. And my leg hurts.

I see the blue of my blood mix with Rhiannon's red blood. Moments later, Telor pulls me from Rhiannon's back and wraps my leg in a bandage.

"You will be all right. So will Rhiannon," Telor says. "Your wound and hers look much worse than they are." He signals for one of the two-person floaters.

"Telor, Rhiannon's blood is red."

"Yes. And I will explain. For now, lean on me and walk to the floater."

I am proud Telor doesn't carry me like a child, but allows me to walk, although with help, like an injured soldier.

I have been to the infirmary many times for exams and to be bandaged for cuts and bruises. The windowless rooms are deep inside Fortress. The walls are white; the lights, bright. Telor takes me to a room with shelves full of bottles and stranger things. The medico, a cousin, smears something greasy on my wound, wraps my leg in a new bandage, and gives me a jab in the arm. "An antibiotic ... something to keep you from getting sick."

He gives me candy like he does after every visit. I take the candy, but wonder if I should have accepted it. Candy is for children, and I no longer want to be a child.

~~~~~

"You said you would explain." I remind Telor when we reach my room.

30

"Explain why your blood is blue and Rhiannon's blood is red," Telor says. "Blood carries oxygen from the lungs to other parts of the body. In your blood and the blood of our species – the Res Publica and the thralls – hemocyanin, a copper-based chemical – carries oxygen. In the blood of Rhiannon and the beasts of the field and forest, hemoglobin, an iron-based chemical, carries oxygen. Thousands of millennia ago, during a long glacial period, hemocyanin-based blood became a survival trait. Our ancestors changed from iron-based blood to copper-based blood. The genes for hemocyanin won the skirmish, even though we still have the genes for both hemoglobin and hemocyanin blood.

"Our blood has no color until it comes in contact with oxygen. Then, it turns blue. Your horse's blood turns red when it comes in contact with air. When we say 'of-the-blood,' we mean more than family and house relationships. We mean the hemocyanin-based blood, which separates us from the beasts of the field."

I don't understand about blood and oxygen, and those hemo-things, but I understand what it means to be of-the-blood. I am of-the-blood; Rhiannon is not.

~~~~~

I am five in the year boys and girls my age come to live at Fortress and play with me. They are members of House Bleddyn or of houses sworn to my father, Gens Bleddyn. We play together and attend class together. Not every class, though, because Father and my tutors, Telor and Sani, give me individual attention.

When we are alone, Telor tells me which of my playmates are of-the-blood of House Bleddyn and which are of-the-blood of houses sworn to my father.

31

When I seem puzzled, he explains this new meaning of of-the-blood. "If they have Father's blood, or our grandfather's blood, or our great-grandfather's blood, they are blood of House Bleddyn."

"Like my aunts and uncles and cousins?"

"Many of them. Some are of-the-blood through marriage or adoption."

"What about Nana?"

"Nana is Daughter-of-the-blood of House Caerwyn and a member of House Bleddyn because she is your surrogate. We select carefully those who will be surrogates. You know what that means, don't you?"

"Yes. Father's seed was combined with Mother's egg and implanted in Nana. She gave birth to me. I nursed at her breasts and she is my Nurturing Mother." I say words Telor gave me, but I really don't understand them all.

I understand what Telor said about blood, though. House Bleddyn is strong. We have many members-by-blood and many members-by-marriage whose children become members-by-blood. Father encourages marriage to members of subordinate and sworn houses. Blood is the ultimate bond of loyalty.

~~~~~

Sani is the only thrall I am close to. I have seen thralls all my life. It is easy to recognize them. Their skin is pale, unlike the bronze skin of the Res Publica. Their hair is white and worn short. My hair is black and long. It will not be cut until I am older.

I am accustomed to thralls who serve in the kitchen and dining room, who make my bed and lay out my clothes, who clean Fortress, and who bear burdens. It is easy to ignore them. They are silent and never speak unless I give an order. They stand aside and bow when I pass through the hallways with Nana and my guards.

Sani is different. He is trusted to be alone with me and my playmates. Somehow, this is important.

On a warm summer afternoon, Sani gathers my companion-playmates in the library. When he speaks, we listen closely because his stories are always fun.

The Saber-tooth Cat
and the Wolf

A great saber-tooth cat, the biggest and most powerful of beasts, ruled the forest and the savannah. One day he sent word he was sick unto death and summoned animals to receive gifts before he died. The goat went into the cat's den. Then a sheep entered. Before the goat or the sheep came out, a calf went in to receive his gift from the Lord of Beasts. After a while, the cat went to the mouth of his den where he saw the wolf.

"Why do you not come in to receive your gift?" the cat asked the wolf.

"I beg your pardon," said the wolf, "I saw the tracks of animals who visited; and while I see many footsteps going in, I see none coming out. Until the animals who entered your den come out again, I prefer to wait in the open air."

"What did you learn?" Sani asks.

"Do not trust saber-tooth cats," one of my mates says.

"Don't go into caves," Ceirois says. "That's what the den must have been. And caves are dark and scary."

"Goats, sheep, and calves are stupid. Wolves are smart," I say, and fold my arms across my chest.

Sani listens to other thoughts. "Those are all good answers. The lesson of the story is, *it is easier to get into the enemy's hands than to get out again.* When you go into danger, you should always have an escape plan. Think on this."

<p align="center">~~~~~</p>

In the summer of my fifth year, Telor brings strange clothes to my room. White pants and jacket, but no boots or sandals. Telor always has a reason for his demands, so I dress while he explains.

"This is a gi. It allows easy movement, but is reinforced to withstand the intense actions involved in *Jaryeondo*, and—"

"In what?" I interrupt.

"*Jaryeondo*. It is from the ancient language and means 'self-training-way.' You will learn both physical and mental discipline."

Telor shows me how to lap the front panels of the jacket across my tummy. He stands behind me and pulls the belt to the front and ties it, allowing the loose ends to dangle. Then, he leads me to a room he calls, "dojo." It is a large room with polished wooden floors, stone walls, high ceiling, and clerestory windows. The high windows face south, giving a constant light.

Telor teaches me a new bow – stiff, from the waist with legs straight and arms held close to my side. A man enters the dojo. He wears a white gi, but his belt is black. I make the new bow.

I think I will learn all sorts of attack and defense, but Teacher makes me stretch my body. "You will hurt yourself more than your opponent if you cannot control your body," he says. Teacher shows me how to stretch parts of my body I've never stretched before. By day's end, Teacher shows a beginner's stance, and demonstrates a series of movements he calls *kata*.

The next day, my companion-playmates join me in what is now my dojo. My mates and I do the stretching together. After stretching, Teacher demonstrates kata while his assistant beats a cadence on a drum. Then, Teacher shows us several punches. If we get off balance, Teacher corrects us, gently but firmly.

After two months of lessons, I think I know everything. Telor and Teacher do not agree. Teacher takes me aside after dismissing my mates. "There are many skills left to learn. Here is one. Close your eyes. Stand perfectly still," he says. "Imagine the wood of the floor is water and you are standing on it."

I am barefoot, the floor is cold, and it is easy to imagine I am standing on water. Teacher whispers to me. The wood seems to soften. My feet become part of it. Teacher tells me to keep my eyes closed and imagine myself skating along the floor, like an ice skater on a frozen lake. "Keep your eyes closed. Move silently," Teacher demands.

I obey and pretend I am ice-skating on the moat which Father fills in winter for that purpose. I cry out and open my eyes when Teacher grabs me before I run into a wall. "I did it?" I ask. "I really did it!" I exclaim.

Both Telor and Teacher are pleased, but caution me not to become too confident. "You moved swiftly and silently. It is an important skill, but hubris – overweening pride – may be a stronger opponent than your enemy."

~~~~~

Harvest Festival brings cousins and allies to Fortress Bleddyn. Children fill the playing fields. My companion-guards press closely, but not so much I cannot join the sport and the play.

A teammate kicks the ball to me. I spin and kick it into the goal, scoring a point in a game of footy. I take the required time-out, pour water over my head and shake it from my hair. Then I hear the sharp smack of flesh meeting flesh. I turn to see a taller boy facing a smaller one. The smaller boy's cheek bears the mark of a hand, certainly the hand of the taller boy. They are not siblings. From their house crests I see the bigger boy is Dolffin; the smaller, Hynafol.

Not a good situation – a fight between allies. The taller boy raises his hand, again. Before he can act, I step between the two boys and grab the taller boy's wrist. "I do not want my brothers fighting, especially at a time of celebration." I release his hand.

"Who are—" the aggressor snarls, but closes his mouth when he sees the crest on my jumpsuit and my companion-guards who have moved bedside me.

"Garreth," he spits. "You are Garreth. You hide behind your name and your guards. You would not challenge me otherwise."

Challenge? I hesitate only for a second. He knows the old custom. When I seized his arm, I challenged him. We are children, so we may not use weapons, but I could be hurt.

"I hide behind no one. I know the old custom. If you accept my challenge, I will take you to the dojo where my name and my guards and my father will not protect me. But first, your name."

The boy's eyes narrow. "I am Deryn of House Dolffin."

I turned to the smaller boy. "And you?"

"Derog of Hynafol."

"Derog will be referee and witness. No one else will be admitted to the dojo." I say and watch Derog's eyes widen. He is proud of his role, but also frightened.

My guards do not want to leave me in the dojo with only the two boys. "It is a matter of honor," I say to Lieutenant Fender. "Honor, valor, loyalty, and the greatest of these is honor."

Her understanding beats back her fear of my father. She salutes and leads the other guards from the dojo. Before the lock snaps, I turn to face Deryn. He is stronger and heavier than me. I can't let him grapple me. We take our places and bow to one another. Deryn rushes toward me, arms extended.

I step to the side and strike his forearm with the edge of my hand. I aim for his wrist, but miss. We both step back. We have taken the other's measure. I think I am ahead. Deryn does not agree.

"A weak strike, hah!" Deryn taunts. His voice echoes from the dojo's stone walls. He waits for my reaction. His mistake. I step back drawing him toward me. When his right foot is off the ground, I sweep the left from under him. He lands on his back, hard. I jump and land on his thighs. I hook my ankles under his shins to lock myself in place and strike with clenched fists just below his sternum. The bundle of nerves there fires and paralyzes his breathing. His legs bend. I feel his knees against my back and I feel his desperation. He pushes his feet hard against the mat and flings me off. I stand and turn to face him.

He has fallen back onto the mat. Before I can strike again, his mouth opens but his chest is not moving. Deryn is not breathing. That is wrong!

I kneel beside the boy, pinch his nose with one hand, press my lips over his, and puff two breaths into his lungs.

Deryn gasps. His breath rasps in his throat. He is breathing.

I offer my hand to help Deryn up, but he only stares at me.

"Haven't you ever been hit there?" I ask. "It's a common blow."

"Yes, but not that hard. You saved my life."

"But only after nearly killing you. I ask forgiveness."

Deryn's eyes flicker from side to side. "I ask you and the little one to forgive me. I was angry because of a spilled drink. Not a good reason to bully someone smaller. You beat me fairly. Now I will be known as a bully beaten by a boy half his size." He tightens his lips into a thin line.

"I'm a little bigger than that," I say, and grin. Then I hold my face emotionless as I have seen Father do many times. "We will forgive one another, and we will speak of this to no one," I say to both boys.

"You mean it, don't you?" Deryn asks. I see confusion in his eyes.

"Yes, and I mean we should not be fighting. Our houses – mine, yours, and Derog's – are allies. May we at least try to be friends?"

Deryn accepts my hand and stands. "I am an ass."

I laugh, and smile so he knows I am not laughing at him. "No, an ass is a plodding beast. I saw you at footy. You do not plod; no one could catch you."

I turn to the smaller boy. "What do you say?"

"Thank you for standing up for me." He turns to Deryn. "I'm sorry I bumped you and made you spill your drink. I was watching the parrot. I'm the smallest of my family and want to have friends who are bigger than me."

Deryn grins. "You can count on me." He looks at me and sees my nod. "On both of us."

We three return to the festival for more games and lots of treats. At nightfall, Deryn and Derog return to their families and Telor summons me to the library. "You disappeared. Lieutenant Fender said only you were in the dojo and it was a matter of honor."

"She was correct. I challenged a boy; we settled the challenge and are now friends."

Telor realizes I will say no more. "I will answer Father's concern and ensure he is not angry," he says.

~~~~~

Summer showers soak the greensward and forest. The ground is soggy and humidity is high enough to make breathing uncomfortable for bodies evolved in the cold, dry air of a long glacial age. Lessons will be indoors, today. After breakfast, Sani takes my companions and me to my schoolroom. A battle computer projects a map under the floor. Today, the map is the Equatorial Continent, which stretches west to east eight thousand kilometers from Port Dolffin to Port Aberwith. The Western and Eastern Islands add more than a thousand kilometers. My playmates and I fight many battles on the floor. I want to play battle-games and decide to be bored when Sani tells us today's lesson will be geography.

"The Equatorial Continent and the Southern Continent were once joined," Sani says. "They separated when the underlying tectonic plates floated apart."

The map on the floor changes to match Sani's words.

Ceirois, who was sitting on Sehwa Island, giggles when it slides away and she finds herself sitting on Fortress Merrick.

Sani smiles at Ceirois's reaction. "Many vast, open lands on the Equatorial Continent are swamps, rain-shadow deserts, and undeveloped savannah. Even today the continent drifts northward. It runs over the tectonic plate to the north and pushes it into the molten core of World. This creates the northern volcanoes."

Schoolmates sitting along the northern shore flinch when volcanoes erupt beneath their bottoms. They giggle, either because it is fun or to cover their surprise.

~~~~~

The day is warm and the wooden floor of my dojo is slippery with sweat. My mates and I practice kata to a drum's cadence while my companion-guards watch. When we complete a series, we pause. The door opens and Delwyn – my Sister-plus-twelve – and one of her mates, Soosong, enter. The drum stops.

"Garreth, would you like to practice with Soosong and me?" Delwyn asks.

Of course, I do. I am always happy to play with my brothers and sisters and their friends. "Yes, Sister. Please?"

Delwyn steps back. Soosong offers her hand and I take it. For the next hour, Soosong and I and my mates rehearse *Jaryeondo* kata. I think I surprise Soosong by how high I can kick, how fast my hands move, and how focused I am.

When the drill ends, I take Soosong's hands. "Thank you for teaching me. Will you always teach me?"

My plea in these words, that she always teach me, is a heritage from Geraint, an ancient teacher. I ask her to be a mentor, a person of trust and responsibility. I hope she knows this and will not refuse me. Delwyn understands what I did. I see her eyes widen and I sense her approval.

Soosong understands, too. She completes the ancient litany, but brooks no nonsense. "I will forever teach you. Now, we will work on low block. Your elbow must touch the opposite arm."

I spread my legs and extend my left arm in front of me and across my body. I fold my right arm with elbow pressed firmly into the left arm and fist under my left ear.

After several trials, I complete the form to Soosong's satisfaction. A chime signals the end of training. I thank Soosong for her lessons and say, "My name means 'brave and modest.' What does Soosong mean?"

"Soosong is a name associated with bastardy," she says. "Your brother and sister call me Soosong because it is the name with which I enrolled at Academy. But they do not speak it with the contempt others use."

"I knew you were a bastard," I say, without thinking. "Kind of like Telor."

Delwyn blanches. I hear her suck in her breath. I've done something wrong. Soosong's smile overcomes my fear. "No. Your father recognized Telor. Mine never recognized me. We will move to the next form, tomorrow, if Delwyn agrees."

I understand she is not angry with me, but that I will learn no more about her name.

~~~~~

I find Telor in the library and ask him what it means to be a bastard, and why he isn't.

"Do you remember when we talked about what it meant to be of-the-blood of a house, and why you are of-the-blood of House Bleddyn?" When I nod, he asks, "Have you seen the horses, cattle, and other animals on our farms coupling to create offspring?"

"Yes."

"Humans can create offspring that way, too."

"I suspected that after I saw my own penis rise and, later, to produce what I learned to be my seed."

Telor stares at me for a moment. "Garreth, sometimes I forget how clever you are."

"I have good teachers."

"Lust more than logic often drives young men. Father created me the natural way with a daughter of House Marredudd. He recognized me and our grandfather elevated me in front of the House. Had he not done this I would be a bastard."

Something in Telor's thoughts worries me, but he dismisses me before I can ask. Outside the library, my guards meet me and escort me to the medicos.

After the medicos repeatedly harvest my seed, I understand what Telor means by *lust*.

~~~~~

Soldiers who are cousins-by-blood and sworn to my protection accompany me everywhere. They graduated from Academy and are assigned to the Home Guard. They carry weapons – swords, energy pistols, slug rifles, and other things they keep hidden. I make them uncomfortable when I ask to hold the weapons, to use them, but I may not. I may use only wooden practice swords and pretend-weapons that buzz and shoot light at their targets.

One hundred fifty millennia ago, House Bleddyn claimed Mesa and named itself guardian of the place where Fortress Bleddyn, Council House, and Academy stand. We defined safe-passage lanes for floaters and shuttles and said we would attack anyone outside the lanes. The other houses objected at first. Today, it has become *status quo* and no one challenges us.

44

Ten years have passed since the last overt attack on House Bleddyn when a single fighter tried to strafe the Harvest Festival. Our missiles destroyed it before it reached Mesa. Today, our watchers are vigilant and Father always keeps the War Room staffed. It is only later I learn what happened.

~~~~~

The duty controller reported to his commander. "Sir, unknown floater approaching from the west. Drifted out of an Academy safe-passage lane. The friend-or-foe radar transponder is not reporting. I would guess, foe."

"Launch alert floaters to intercept; follow proportional response rules. What else is out there?"

The controller put a new display on the main screen. "Two registered shuttles leaving Academy for exercises. They're in lanes. A dozen Academy floaters in their safe areas. And Garreth Bleddyn and his guards and mates. They appear to be playing hide-and-find among the trees four kilometers south of Mesa."

"Alert floaters launched," another controller said. "Armed with rocket grenades. Intercept in three minutes."

"Sir, the unknown changed direction. It is now between Garreth and Fortress ... turning toward Garreth."

"Missile batteries, destroy the floater," the commander ordered. "Notify Garreth's guard commander."

~~~~~

I hear the explosion the instant Cousin-Lieutenant Fender scoops me up and runs toward Fortress. Other guards grab my playmates or draw energy weapons and scan the sky. A shuttle meets us before we reach Fortress. Floaters circle overhead. My guards and the shuttle crew babble; I listen closely. They think my playmates and I were targets of an attack. When I hear them, I am afraid I will never be allowed to play in the forest again.

Father meets the shuttle on the battlements. I am careful not to show any fear or nervousness when I walk down the ramp and bow to him. He gestures and I follow to his den. The fear I felt from Lieutenant Fender returns. I bite my tongue and clench my fists and the fear goes away – at least, it no longer sits in the front of my mind. Father moves behind his desk and tells me to stand across from him.

"Do you know what happened?"

I feel tightness in my tummy and decide it is nervousness and not fear. "Yes, Father. Someone tried to attack Fortress or me. No one is sure. The defenses worked. And my companion-guards over-reacted."

"Better over-reacted than failed to protect you," Father snaps. Then, his voice slows. "Were you afraid?"

"Not until Lieutenant Fender grabbed me. I knew she was afraid, and that made me afraid. But I didn't know what she was afraid of."

"A good answer, Son. An unknown floater turned from a safe-passage lane and did not have a radar transponder. Lieutenant Fender was ordered to remove you from danger. She didn't know, herself, what to be afraid of."

46

"Telor was right," I say. "He taught once we understand danger we should not fear it, but spend our energy finding a way to conquer it."

"I'm sure that's not what he said."

"No, Father, he said, 'All we have to fear is fear itself.' Then he made me think what it means. May I still play hide-and-find in the forest?"

"You are not afraid?"

"No, Father."

"Then you may play in the forest. I will ensure Lieutenant Fender knows."

~~~~~

The Harvest Festival heralds the approach of Fall Stormtime. Even though I must stay in Fortress during the storms, I look forward to Fall Stormtime because I know Soosong will visit and continue training me. I stand on the battlements when the shuttle carrying Delwyn, Daffyd, and their friends lands. I look for Soosong, but she is not there. When I ask Daffyd, he tells me Soosong has something else to do. I am not happy with his words and I do not think Daffyd is happy, either. There is something in his mind – images of Soosong and feelings of fear. I cannot make sense of them and they trouble me.

Before stormtime ends, I learn Gens Tarren, our enemy in vendetta, is dead and House Tarren has a new Gens. I hear Daffyd whispering to Delwyn. They say something about Soosong. When they realize I am listening, they stop. "Garreth, it's not polite to listen to people's secrets."

47

"I didn't know it was a secret, and I wasn't listening. You were talking."

Delwyn laughs. "You are right, but it is secret and you must never speak of it."

I'm not sure what I'm not supposed to talk about but I know, somehow, I will never see Soosong again.

CHAPTER 4 THE HORMONES OF PUBERTY

I lie in the unadulterated darkness of my life pod, the darkness I do not see or sense until a hadron – the proton or neutron in an atomic nucleus – disintegrates, releasing the binding energy of three quarks, and triggers another memory.

Today, only Telor watches me arrange my forces for battle. My carved, wooden toy soldiers wear the leather armor of two hundred millennia ago and carry pikes. I place them on the floor where the computer projects a map of the Southern Continent. I lay down a measuring stick and place my soldiers, their feet touching the stick, exactly ten centimeters apart, in *ilja-jin* – one-line formation.

I place Number 14 when Number 5 falls. I stop, pick up Number 5 and put him back exactly halfway between Numbers 4 and 6. I move to 15, 16, and 17 until Number 5 falls again. I stand him in his place, precisely halfway between Numbers 4 and 6. I continue: 18, 19. Number 5 falls again. I raise my hand and smash it onto Number 5. My blood covers Number 5. I am fascinated by the blood that drips onto the floor. It is bluer than the sea. I...

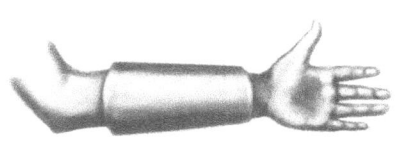

Vambrace

... I wake. Father stands at my bedside. A bandage wraps my right hand; a vambrace wraps my left forearm. All the older boys and girls wear a vambrace. It is part of their uniforms; a badge of maturity. I am no longer angry with Soldier Number 5, and I am proud I am old enough to wear the vambrace. It means I am no longer a child. It is an important step in my life and a key to open new training. The fingers of my right hand protrude from the bandage. I stroke the vambrace with them and look at Father. I do not understand his expression. It is neither the way he shows pleasure when I perform well nor the way he shows disappointment when I fail.

"What is wrong, Father?"

"Nothing is wrong." Father pauses to think. "We mark progress from childhood to adulthood in many ways. Your dagger and grace knife, your vambrace, entering Academy. It is time for supper. Do you feel strong enough?"

"Why would I not, Father? I only hurt my hand."

~~~~~

After supper, Father takes Telor and me to his den. "Garreth, you believe the vambrace is a sign of maturity. What is its function?"

"It is part of a soldier's armor," I say, confident in my knowledge. "I will have more armor when I am older, but now with the vambrace I am a soldier."

Father corrects me. "This vambrace contains sensors that monitor your health. It injects medicines when needed." Father tells me I may not take it off except for bathing. I must insert my arm every fifth morning into a device to replenish the medicines.

When he says *medicines*, I hear *drugs*, and am afraid. There is something Father is not telling me.

~~~~~

Another Harvest Festival is over and Fall Stormtime rages. Telor watches my mates and me set up soldiers on the floor of the schoolroom. The measuring stick leans against the wall. I do not think I will need it. I have been wearing my vambrace for five months, and my mates are over their jealousy. I do not tell them about the drugs which make the vambrace a sign of weakness, not strength.

I march half my soldiers to the battle grid when a ball rolls through the formation, scattering the soldiers. I jump up and clench my hands. Alaw, my Sister-minus-three, who is chasing the ball, sees me and freezes in fear.

I feel something wash through me. I am no longer angry and I don't know why I was angry. I grab Alaw and hug her. "Come, Alaw, you won the battle with the Giant Ball Attack! You must join our side! But it won't be so easy next time."

Alaw giggles. She knows there is no such thing as a giant ball attack, but she is happy I invited her to play.

~~~~~

After playtime, I follow Telor to the library. "Telor, what happened to me when Alaw's ball knocked over my soldiers?"

Telor does not hesitate and I believe he is telling the truth. "As Father said, your vambrace monitors your blood and injects medicines to keep you in balance, to calm you."

51

"It didn't just calm me; it made me forget." I become angry until something washes over me and I am not angry. "I don't like how it makes me feel. And they are drugs, not medicines!" I get angry again. The vambrace gives me more of the drug. I struggle to hold my thoughts and my anger.

"When you are angry or afraid, your body creates a chemical that triggers the vambrace to release a counter-chemical into your blood."

"Make it stop, Telor, please?"

"I cannot. Everyone wears a vambrace from about age nine or ten until about age sixteen. It is the law. Your vambrace may need adjusting. I will take you to the medico tomorrow."

~~~~~

The medico's room smells of chemicals; it is cold and lights reflect brightly from white walls, cabinets, and tables. When I was little, the medico gave me candy after every visit. The vambrace makes me feel grown up even though I know about the drugs. I hope he doesn't give me candy, today.

Telor tells him I am reacting too strongly to the drugs.

The medico shrugs and takes a device from his pocket. It is five centimeters by two centimeters, and less than two centimeters thick. He places it against my vambrace. I am startled when it buzzes and lights flash. He looks at a small screen.

"What is that?" I demand.

"Everyone calls it a buzzer," he says. "It lets me check and control your vambrace. You are receiving several drugs."

I'm glad he calls them drugs and not medicines.

"One is a fast-acting stimulant to help you focus. A longer-acting stimulant helps keep the focus. These drugs may make you angry. You also receive a drug to calm you when you get angry."

"I'm getting one drug because another drug makes me angry? That's really stupid."

"It's not stupid," Telor says. "The drugs have side effects, but what they do for you is more important than what they do to you."

The medico fiddles with the buzzer and presses it against my vambrace again. "I reduced the doses of two of your drugs. They will still affect you, but not as strongly."

He doesn't offer candy, but I am not happy.

~~~~~

My companions are in the dojo. Telor wants me there, but I demand we talk. "I want to know more about the vambrace and the drugs. Why does everyone wear one?"

Telor gestures for me to sit. "Like all of our species – both the Res Publica and the thralls – your body creates chemicals that affect your brain and your body. They are part of our evolutionary history. When we were living in hunter-gatherer bands among animals much faster and stronger than us, the chemicals were important to survival. Adrenaline, for example, triggers a *fight-or-flight* reflex that moves blood to your muscles.

"When you reach puberty, your brain turns on other chemicals, hormones, including testosterone in boys and estrogen in girls. These chemicals create imbalances. The drugs in your vambrace correct those imbalances so you can concentrate and not harm yourself or others. After a few years, the body settles down.

"Adrenaline made you angry with your toy soldier, so you smashed him into the floor. You were angry with Alaw yesterday. If the vambrace hadn't given you a drug, you might have smashed her like you did the soldier. You are strong and trained in *Jaryeondo*. You could have killed her. Is that what you want?"

Telor frightens me, but only for a moment until a drug takes control. "No, I would never want to hurt any of my brothers and sisters. But I want to feel. I want to feel angry, just not hurt anyone. I want to feel afraid, but not too much. The vambrace makes it so I can't."

"Only for a few years. When your hormones settle and you learn self-control, medicos will remove your vambrace. That is all I may say."

'May say' … 'can say.' I see the difference. Telor is telling the truth, but he is also hiding something. It's the same as lying.

I'm not happy with Telor's answers, but I thank him – and resolve to do without the drugs, to take charge of my feelings and myself.

~~~~~

Telor has access to Father's business and to Father's oversight of me. It's easy to learn Telor's computer password. I am nervous when I use it to search his files. I learn my vambrace holds enough drugs for ten days. I will let the drugs in my vambrace run out. I want to know how I will feel without them.

It is easy to steal a buzzer from the infirmary – they are on countertops, in drawers, and in pockets of white jackets hanging from wall hooks. It is easy to understand how they work. I program the buzzer to reduce the drugs to zero, and press it to my vambrace. I will put my arm into the charger because Nana or Telor watch me. But the charger will not add any drugs. Now, I must wait for the drugs to run out.

~~~~~

I think the drugs run out on the ninth day. My thoughts are clear. Colors look brighter, sounds are crisp, and my mind speeds through my plans. I also feel jittery and it is hard to complete the simplest tasks.

On the eleventh day, my instructor calls me out during *Jaryeondo*. I get angry with him, but seize my anger, squeeze it into a corner of my brain, and slam a door on it. It's still there, seething below the surface, but I don't strike out.

That afternoon, I play a battle game with my mates. The computer follows my command to position my ships. I want them in *chang sa jin*, the long snake formation. Stupid computer put them in *ilja-jin*, the one-line formation, just the opposite. I gave the wrong command, and my anger kicks in. I calm myself with a mantra learned from an ancient book: 'First, I will discipline myself, turn my anger or fear into energy, and use the energy to help others. First, I will discipline myself, turn my anger or fear

55

into energy, and use the energy to help others.' I repeat this until I am calm.

It is too late to change the battle formation, and I lose to a mate two years younger. I push away my anger and smile when I congratulate him on the win and later when I give him my dessert. I see his delight, and something else. He didn't think I would honor the bet. What did he feel when I did? Gratitude? Loyalty? Whatever he felt, I created a bond. Perhaps the mantra paid off.

I have no trouble falling asleep, but my dreams are vivid and frightening. I wake with bedcovers soaked in sweat. Enough! I take the buzzer from where I hid it and reset my vambrace. The next morning, when I put the vambrace in the charger, I feel the drugs burn through my body. I hate them, but I must accept them.

~~~~~

When I was younger, Nana or Telor put me to bed. I did not want to sleep and often lay awake. Even now, when the lights are off, my eyes open to search the darkness looking for answers I cannot find. Tonight, I think about a battle game I played this afternoon.

My mates and I exercise in the dojo all morning and play hide-and-find in the gardens after lunch. We are tired, but Telor sets a battle game on the floor of the playroom. We know that pleading tiredness would earn us another session in the dojo, delay our supper, and maybe cost us our desserts.

The computer displays a naval battle set among the islands on the southeast coast. I take command of one force; Ceirois, the other. The computer hides the opposing forces from each commander. I send out swift scout ships, the pinnaces slung from

56

davits on the stern of larger ships. I know Ceirois will do the same. "Hug the coastline," I order the coxswains. "When the adversary spots you, retreat slowly and draw them into a trap."

I don't know how I know Ceirois sees my scouts before I see hers. I don't know how I know she will order her forces to sail behind an island and from there flank my main force. Reaching into the wisdom of *The Book of Proverbs*, I change the positions of my ships and capture Ceirois's flagship.

Ceirois is not happy. "How did you know?"

"A lucky guess," I say. "The island was too good a shelter for you to pass up. The winds, the tide, the current. It all came together." My voice holds confidence I do not feel. *How did I know?* I wonder.

~~~~~

I wait until Telor accompanies Father to Council and break into Telor's computer again. At first, I learn only what Cousin Medico said. Two stimulants, to keep me alert and focused. Another drug is a blocker chemical to slow my neurons creating the chemicals they use to talk to each other– and makes me feel foggy. It also keeps me from getting angry.

Then, I find a message from the medico to Telor. "I added melatonin to Garreth's regimen at the Gens direction." What is melatonin and why did Father order it?

I look up melatonin. The body creates that hormone. It helps people sleep and calms hyperactive children. It's different from the anger-blocker chemical. I wonder why the vambrace doesn't put me to sleep at night. It has melatonin, and could, but it doesn't. What is the melatonin for? Just another drug to make me foggy, I guess.

On the first night after Telor returns I ask, "Telor? Why does my vambrace give me melatonin?"

Telor laughs. He sees his laughter makes me angry, but I cannot stay angry for long. The drugs won't let me. He stops laughing. "Garreth, I laughed because I never thought of giving you melatonin, even though you are always hard to put to sleep. You demand story after story, game after game, until I have to pretend to be sleepy before I may turn out your light.

"I promise to ask why you're getting melatonin. Now, will you go to sleep, or must I—"

"I'll be good," I say. "But I won't forget your promise." And I won't forget you lied to me. Telor hasn't told me an untruth, but he told me less than the truth, and he taught me this was the same as lying. He knows why I am getting melatonin.

CHAPTER 5 ANCIENT WEAPONS

Wars are fought with weapons
but are won by soldiers.
— Karmet, in *The Book of Proverbs*

≈≈≈≈≈

Except at night when I am in bed I am surrounded by people – Telor, whom I love; my Nurturing Mother, Nana, whom I love; and guards sworn to my father and to me. I do not love my guards and sometimes I am angry with them, but Father orders me to obey them. The best of times is when Father takes me away from these people and speaks only to me.

"Father," I ask, "why may I not play without guards? Why is someone always with me? Why are so many cousins—"

"Garreth!" Father says, and laughs. "You are full of questions."

His smile disappears and I am afraid he is angry with me. "Come here," he says, and takes me into his lap. I think I am a big boy, but I delight in this closeness.

"We have enemies among the other Greater Houses," Father says. "They seldom attack directly, but through mercenaries or through agents of Lesser Houses who are loyal to them."

"Then I must learn to fight and to kill," I say.

"You are learning, Garreth. Every day your lessons and exercises bring you knowledge."

"But I don't have a sword or a gun!" I stick out my lower lip and widen my eyes.

"Garreth, you are not a wolf-puppy. Your tricks may work on Nana, but not on me. You will have a sword and a gun when you are ready."

Father pauses to think. He removes his dagger from its sheath, pricks his arm, draws blood, and then holds the dagger toward me, hilt first. "Garreth, accept this gift. Use it with honor, valor, and loyalty to House Bleddyn and to the Res Publica."

My eyes become big when I take the dagger. A wolf's head caps the hilt. The blade is forty centimeters long. The sharp edges catch and condense the light. I recognize the oath. Father watches me prick my arm with the dagger and respond with the Soldiers Oath.

"Father, I swear always to live by honor, to be valorous in battle and loyal to you, to my house, and to the Res Publica." I am not sure what all those words mean, but I know they are important.

"You will have a belt and sheath for your dagger later today. The Arms Master will teach you to fight with a dagger. Remember the Council Edict that no thrall may touch a weapon on penalty of death."

The Council holds the memory of our war with the thralls, even after two hundred millennia. Are they so afraid they still deny thralls weapons? Are we so wrapped in the past we cannot see beyond it?

~~~~~

A few days later, I am in my schoolroom puzzling over one of Telor's naval battles. He set the battle in the distant past before we exhausted World's reserves of fossil fuels, in a time when coal-fired steam engines powered warships. Today, wind and sails propel our surface ships. For this battle, I do not have to compensate for the uncertainty of the wind, only for the minds of the enemy captains.

"Telor, this is a waste of time," I say. "No one has steam-powered ships, only sail."

"Do you think your floater and our shuttles are powered by magic? Do you think our starships explore the galaxy with sails?"

Fleet locations when battle game begins.

* Garreth's Fleet

• Enemy Fleet

Soando Is.

Koje Is.

His challenge silences me. I believe that is what he meant to do and think carefully before answering. "No, Brother. Electricity created by wind and water mills and stored in batteries powers floaters and shuttles. Nuclear fission powers our starships. All the ships on the oceans of World are driven by sail. Why?"

"Both tradition and an agreement among the houses," Telor replies. "The Council outlawed fission reactors except in starships. Batteries cannot power surface ships." He turns to his book and I return to the battle game.

When the game re-starts, my fleet of eighty-two ships anchors in the strait between Koje and Soando Islands. The strait is a tidal bore. Waves and current are treacherous, even for an experienced sailor. The tide will turn, soon. I must move my fleet out of the strait. East or west? I am unsure.

The enemy decides for me. I spot six enemy ships steaming into the strait from the west. They see my fleet, turn, and retreat. This chance to destroy enemy ships is enough for me to order my fleet to weigh anchor, move west, and pursue. When we reach open sea, lookouts report the entire enemy fleet of 51 ships lies ahead in a tight *ilja-jin* – one-line formation. I have the larger fleet, and order my ships into *chojeom*, focal-point formation, and steam toward the enemy.

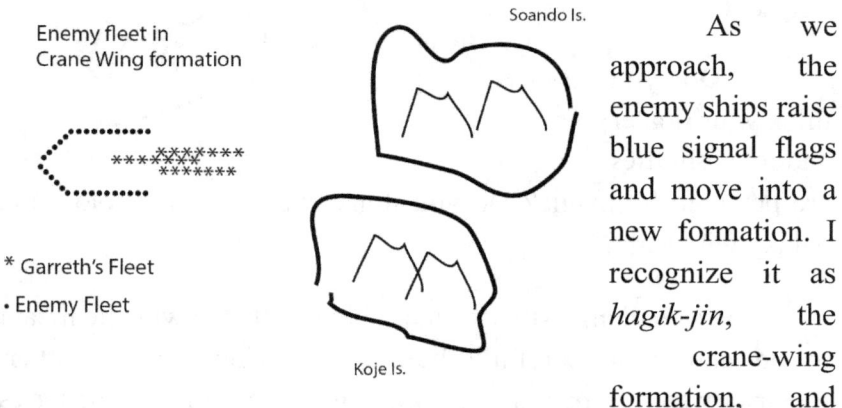

Enemy fleet in Crane Wing formation

Soando Is.

* Garreth's Fleet

• Enemy Fleet

Koje Is.

As we approach, the enemy ships raise blue signal flags and move into a new formation. I recognize it as *hagik-jin*, the crane-wing formation, and believe the enemy commander will be at the center. It is too late to change my strategy. I send orders for ships to fire at will and to disperse left and right so they will not be in range of cannon from both of the crane's wings. I order my flagship and two battleships to steam directly toward the enemy flagship.

The enemy raises green signal flags. His ships close the wings of the crane, exposing my ships to cannon from both port and starboard. Two heavily armed ships, hidden until now, move from behind the enemy flagship and fire on me and the ships closest to me. In only minutes my entire fleet is burning, listing, or sinking.

The computer chimes to announce I lost the game, and the ships disappear from the floor.

Telor looks at me over his book. "Well?"

He wants me to explain how I lost. "It is easier to fight a battle with wind and sail," I say. "I understand the wind. I understand what a sailing ship can and cannot do. I did not know how fast the enemy could react, how fast his ships could maneuver to change formation. If this battle were between sailing ships, I would have won. I had the wind at my back, but it made no difference with steamships. I do not understand steamships, and the computer's commander is smarter than me."

Before Telor can ask another question, I blurt, "Why do we not have fission generators except in starships?"

"You will learn how to fight with steam-powered ships and fission-powered starships, and to anticipate the tactics of enemy captains. But not today. Come, and I will answer your question."

I sit on the floor in front of Telor's chair. Telor sets aside his book. "Millennia ago, our people discovered nuclear fission, the chain reaction that splits atoms of an isotope of Element 92 to create incredible heat. Today, we control the reaction and use the heat to power our stardrive. An uncontrolled reaction creates a tremendous explosion, one great enough to destroy Fortress, Academy, and Council House."

Telor presses keys and an image forms in the air. It is a town, set in a savannah, surrounded by fields and pastures. Without warning, the computer creates a flash and a roar. I watch a cloud burst upward, rolling high in the air to form a mushroom cap. When the cloud disappears, nothing is left of the town, only a crater two thousand meters wide.

"That was a single weapon, Garreth. Its fuel was made in a nuclear fission reactor that powered the fortress of House Kaetween—"

"There's no such house," I interrupt.

"Not anymore," Telor says. "The attack by Kaetween on Lagon was devastating. The radioactivity from a single weapon was so damaging the remaining houses banded together and annihilated House Kaetween. No one from that house survived. It was erased from history. Council amended the Charter to prohibit nuclear fission reactors and weapons."

"But you said we have fission reactors in our starships. And what's radioactivity?"

"Fission reactors on starships were a later exception. And shipyards and spaceports are isolated on eastern islands – ours on Namhae; Tarren's on one of Reese's islands," Telor replies. Then, he explains what radioactive fallout is. "If there were an accidental explosion at the shipyards, prevailing winds would carry the radiation out to sea."

What Telor says about radioactivity is almost as frightening as the image of the explosion.

~~~~~

When he gave me a dagger, Father warned me of the Council edict prohibiting thralls from touching a weapon upon penalty of death. I learn "weapon" means different things to different people. The Council's definition of weapon is "anything that could cause harm," including a kitchen knife. Since Father and everyone else employs thralls in the kitchens, at least part of the edict is ignored.

Sani and I are in the garden, sitting on a bench at the edge of a stream when I ask him about this. "How do you hunt without weapons? Traps and snares are fine for hares, but they are not enough for a mastodon or a saber-tooth cat. I see the claws of a large cat on your necklace."

I have given Sani a dilemma. He takes a moment to think. "Garreth, the Council's edict that thralls may not have weapons does not say what a weapon is. And rightly so, because anything can be a weapon in the hands of the trained warrior you are becoming."

I puff with pride when he speaks and almost miss what he says next.

"The rocks at your feet could be a weapon."

I look at the rocks and try to imagine how one could be a weapon. I could throw rocks at someone. I could hold a heavy rock in my hand and strike someone. I might find a sharp rock and—

"A page in a book could be a weapon," Sani interrupts my thought. "You once got a paper cut from a book. In the hands of an assassin, a piece of paper could cut your throat."

I look at the book Sani holds and am afraid. He sees my fear.

"Garreth, I am sworn to your father and to you. You need not fear me."

I feel the truth in what he says. However, my dreams that night are troubled.

~~~~~

Sani answers my question more fully the next morning.

"Garreth, you asked how we take game. We do use traps and snares. The Council's rule against weapons applies only to the lands of the Res Publica. On the Southern Continent, we use weapons for hunting. These weapons fall short of slug rifles and energy pistols. This," he says, showing me a Y-shaped thing in his hand, "is a reshot." He picks up a pebble, puts it into the pouch of the reshot, and pulls the pouch against the resistance of two elastic bands. When he releases the pouch, the pebble flies through the air and splinters the limb of a small tree.

Before the day is over, Sani shows me how to use the reshot and something he calls a bolas – three balls of steel tied together which he spins once around his head and releases to wrap around a sapling. If it had been my throat, I would be dead.

Atlatl and spear

Over the next months, Sani teaches me to make my own reshot and bolas, and an atlatl to extend the range of a spear.

~~~~~

I released my bolas to wrap around a tree when Sani drops the weapons he is holding and kneels. I feel his resignation and something else. Pain in his knees, but he ignores the pain because he knows he will be dead in an instant. I turn to see Father.

Father surprises Sani and me when he touches Sani's elbow and urges him to stand. "Sani, you have been part of this family too long for such ritual. Please, stand."

Father picks up the spear. "From where did this come? Surely, it is not something Garreth made."

I reach Sani and Father and put myself between them. "From the museum, Father. I … I borrowed it."

Father smiles for an instant and I know Sani and I are not in trouble although I don't understand why. "This spear is too long for your arm and that atlatl. We will find you one more your size." He looks around the garden. "And a place more suited to your training."

He turns to Sani. "Garreth will become a soldier. He is well along the path, thanks to your training. His knowledge of these … devices … will serve him. Garreth, you will not always have energy pistols and slug rifles. Pay close attention to what Sani teaches you."

Before I can recover from my shock, Father is gone. The next day, Sani takes me to a part of the forest I've not visited. Trees and brush thickly screen a glade carpeted with low grass. The glade is fifty meters long and twenty wide. Targets are set at one end.

"Your father reserved this place for your training and prohibits others from entering because of the danger they might face." Sani smiles. "You may practice with all the … devices."

~~~~~

Summer heat penetrates Fortress Bleddyn. In the afternoons, storms rage, each outperforming the last with bolts of lightning and hailstones. Father and Telor are at a Council meeting. Many of my playmates went home for Summer Stormtime. I am bored, but that is easy to fix. It is also easy to elude my guards.

Early in a morning, before the summer thunder storms start, I take my bolas and reshot and go to the special place in the forest where Sani taught me how to use them. I have not been here since stormtime began. The straw targets are in disarray, so I make the trees my targets. They become enemies, advancing toward me. My slug rifle and energy pistol are exhausted. The other soldiers in my element are dead. I, alone, stand between the enemy and my house. I shoot pebble after pebble from my reshot, but the enemy still advances. I shoot my last pebble; my only weapons now are bolas, dagger, and grace knife. I take the knot that joins the three strands of the bolas in my right hand and raise my left to wipe sweat from my eyes. I hear a thud and feel something strike my vambrace. I sense someone in the forest, near me.

Startled, I drop my left arm. A man breaks through the trees and rushes toward me. He has a dagger in his hand. Danger! Enemy! I look into his eyes and see my death. I must act before the vambrace numbs me. My thoughts go no further. I spin the bolas once and let fly. My aim is good. The bolas wraps around his legs and he falls. He sits up to untangle himself. He glares at me. I still see my death and draw my dagger and throw it. The blade buries in his stomach. In an instant, I reach him. He releases my bolas and grabs his dagger. His eyes blaze with death. I dance away from his blade. Before he can stand, the narrow blade of my grace knife slides through his throat. Blood pumps from a heart that does not know it is dead and spurts onto my hand and arm.

He is dead, and my guards are running toward me. I turn to face them. My heart is pounding; my throat is dry. The glade becomes dark. I sway. How did they get here? Where were they? Why can I not stand? Why can I not see?

Cousin-Lieutenant Fender, the commander of my guards, does what no person except a close relative may do – she grabs me before I fall and hugs me. "Shhh," she speaks for my ear, only. "Breathe."

The drugs from the vambrace calm me until I can see and my heartbeat slows. The vision of my death is gone from my mind. I hug Lieutenant Fender. "Thank you." She knows what I mean. She kept the others from knowing I almost disgraced myself by fainting.

Her voice becomes sharp when she resumes her role as soldier and commander. "We cannot leave you alone for a minute before you are in trouble. You were killing trees, but you found a better target. What's that on your vambrace? Don't touch it! Sergeant, call for a medico and a forensic team."

The medico arrives on a floater. A shuttle follows, and then another and another. Medicos, soldiers, and thralls swarm through the forest. Someone wearing gloves removes the dart embedded in my vambrace. Medicos examine the body of the man I killed. *Killed.* Father's shuttle arrives from Council House. Telor is with him. I am confused, and although I admit it only to myself, frightened. And sick. My stomach …

Telor hands me a water bottle. "Drink this. You've been in the sun for hours and you didn't bring water." I understand. He is protecting me, hiding my weakness from the others.

Father puts his hand on my shoulder. "We interfere with the investigation. Come." I follow him to his shuttle. The trip to Fortress is quick and quiet. Too quiet.

When we reach Fortress, Telor takes me to my rooms while I shower and put on a jumpsuit and sandals.

People are waiting in Father's den when Telor and I arrive. Father, Cousin Medico and Cousin Fender – now very much Lieutenant Fender – soldiers, and a woman in a white coat are seated at the Privy Council table.

When Telor and I are seated, Lieutenant Fender speaks. "We tracked Garreth into the forest and established a perimeter. I failed to examine the interior of the perimeter. A man was already there.

"He fired a dart from a weapon using compressed air. There was no energy signature to trigger our sensors. By chance, Garreth raised his arm as the man fired, and the dart struck Garreth's vambrace. The man ran toward Garreth, who tripped the man with his bolas, threw his dagger effectively, and killed the man with his grace knife."

Lieutenant Fender stands and raises her hand in salute. "Your Grace, I acknowledge my failure. You hold my life."

"Yes, Lieutenant, I held your life since you first swore to protect Garreth. I also took an oath to you. By those oaths you will

House of Wolf Clan Salute

71

continue with honor to command Garreth's guard detail and you will recommend his punishment for going into the forest alone."

Punishment. I feel my face darken when blood rushes from it. If Father sees this, he ignores it and gestures to the woman in the white coat.

"Your Grace, the dart held a drug, but not something deadly. It would have put Garreth to sleep. We cannot know how much drug was present initially; if the dart were full, the drug would have knocked out an adult. A jumpsuit might have blocked the dart; however, Garreth, as usual, was wearing only loincloth and sandals."

"Thank you." Father turns to a soldier. "What do we know about the assassin?"

"Nothing, Your Grace. He does not exist. He is not on any house roll nor is he registered with the mercenary central computer. He may be from the Free Islands. Our information points to a professional assassin who carefully studied his target. The man was in position near Garreth's training range, suggesting he had good intelligence about Garreth and the land around Fortress. He may have hidden in the forest for days or longer. We are looking for weapons and supplies he might have cached nearby."

When Telor takes me back to my room, I ask him how I overcame the calming drug. "If the vambrace injected it, I would not have been able to attack the man and I would have died."

"Yes, you would have died. This is another reason you must not slip away from your guards. You were waging an imaginary war against the trees. Your adrenaline level was high for a long time. The vambrace took that to be normal and reduced the dose of the calming drug."

Telor shows me my dagger, which I left at the scene. It is dull with the black of dried blood. "Father ordered this dagger placed in a trophy case in the Great Hall." Then he hands me another dagger, bright except for a dark stain on the point. "This is father's blood. He wishes you to carry this new dagger as if it were offered in ritual."

I accept the new dagger, knowing it marks another milestone in my life. I have killed someone. I have taken a life. I will never be the same. I prick my arm with the dagger and watch my blood mingle with Father's. Father was right to do this. I am whole, again. Although I have killed, I am not burdened by that death, and I know I may have to kill again to protect my house or myself. I know if I am called upon to do this, I will be able.

Telor turns out the light and leaves. I find it hard to fall asleep, and when I do, blood and death fill my dreams.

~~~~~

I sit up and push the covers aside. It is the deepest hour of night. What wakened me?

The door opens. It will open only to family, and I'm not afraid until the figure silhouetted in the doorway speaks. "Your punishment begins now. Boots, jumpsuit. You may bring your reshot and bolas. Five minutes until I drag you out." It is Cousin-Lieutenant Terrwyn, commander of Father's Praetorian Guard. His voice is harsh.

Four and a half minutes later, I scamper behind Lieutenant Terrwyn, trying to keep up with his long-legged stride. My punishment is to be with the Praetorians? "Sir? Where are we going?"

"First lesson. Don't question me," he snaps.

"Yes, sir."

He rushes me into a shuttle. Two soldiers grab me and strap me in a jump seat between them. The door closes. I feel the surge of acceleration.

A screen drops from the ceiling. Lieutenant Terrwyn uses images to describe and plan the mission. "An unknown enemy seized Fortress Soando. There were forty-two adult members of House Bleddyn present when the attack began. We do not know how many survive. Our task is to retake the fortress with minimum casualties among the hostages and ourselves. A secondary goal is to capture at least one attacker for questioning."

What about weapons? I have my dagger and grace knife, which are always with me, and my bolas and reshot. The soldiers wear utility harnesses with energy pistols, grenades, ammunition, and extra charge blocks. I want to ask what weapons I will carry, but I know not to ask questions.

"Elint satellites report radar is active. We cannot approach the fortress in the shuttle. There is a blind spot in the radar on the southeast corner of the island, where this basalt protrusion blocks it. Normally, radar on Koje and Kosong cover that spot. The Gens ordered them shut down. We will approach at wave height and land on the beach."

"We will climb the rock face, then proceed through jungle to the fortress. I will assess and provide additional instructions. Markham, you and Warner will equip Recruit Garreth Bleddyn with armor, climbing gear, and utility harness. Now."

The two soldiers beside me retrieve equipment from under the seats. They strip off my jumpsuit. Before I realize I am naked, they dress me in a soldier's armor. A real vambrace replaces the one with drugs, which would keep me from reacting to danger and make me calm in the storm of battle. These soldiers expect me to face danger. They would not remove the vambrace otherwise.

The utility harness holds ammunition only for a slug rifle. I understand. It is the only weapon I am qualified in. The slugs look real. So do the energy pistols the others wear. These are not laser-tag weapons. They are not paintball rounds. This is real – or am I asleep and dreaming?

Minutes later, Markham and Warner – I still don't know which is which – add climbing gear to my harness. Carabineers, cams and nuts, pitons, a wall hammer, and rope.

I know when we cross from the mainland to the water between the continent and our islands. The pilot dives the shuttle. The ride becomes bumpy when the AG-drive reacts to the waves. A soldier passes through the shuttle, offering energy bars and bottles of water. He makes me take two bottles and hooks one to my utility harness. I get the message. This is real. This is real. By Camalos, this is real! I don't know whether to be proud or frightened. I would rather be proud than frightened, but I have trouble separating those feelings.

I do not know how much time has passed before the pilot announces our landing.

"Check your harness, check your weapons." Lieutenant Terrwyn commands and then sets the example by checking his own. There is a bump when we land. The soldiers unbuckle from their jump seats, stand, turn, and move toward the open ramp. Each takes a slug rifle from a rack. I follow their lead. Terrwyn sees me with a slug rifle but says nothing. I've done the right thing. I jump from the shuttle and land on a strip of sand at the base of a hundred-meter vertical escarpment.

The ramp closes and the shuttle departs, skimming eastward at wave height. Soldiers uncoil rope and climb. Markham and Warner rope me between them. "You have climbed before. We depend on you for our lives, as you depend on us," one says. I decide she is Markham. "Yes, ma'am."

The climb is not too hard. Markham is above me and sets pitons in cracks in the rock. I only need to follow her. At one point, she is unsure of a piton and tells me to set one near it.

Without warning, one of Warner's pitons pops out. He falls, pulling the rope between us taut. I lose my grip on the rock and swing. I am hanging above Warner facing a deeply concave section of rock. The face of the escarpment is at least three meters in front of me. The only thing holding me is the rope between Markham and me. Warner, who is below me, grabs the rock, and presses his body into it. Actually, that is a good first response, but he can't get past it.

I kick my legs and swing back and forth. After a few swings, I get close enough to the rock to grab a crevice. I set two pitons and tie Warner to one and myself to the other.

Warner is still frozen. I will get no help from him. The beach and my death are nearly a hundred meters below. I am hanging over eternity.

"Is your rope to me secure?" Markham calls.

"Double secure."

"And the rope to Warner?"

"Attached to two pitons."

"Then," she calls, "cut the rope holding you to the rock and put your arms across your face."

I know what she is asking me to do. When I cut the rope, I will swing like a pendulum away from the rock and then back. I might smash into the rock. The rope might break. Markham might not be strong enough to pull me to safety. There are so many ways to die; there is only one way to live.

I look at Warner, pressed tightly into the rock; he is whimpering. I cut the rope. It is secured to pitons. If Warner loses his grip, he won't drop more than a meter. I cut the rope holding me to the pitons. I swing and hit the rock, bounce and spin. I hit the rock a second time but get a handhold before I bounce away. I pound in a piton, hook myself to it, and climb. Soon, I am beside Markham. Without thought, we hug each other with our free arms. There is a catch in my voice when I speak. "You saved my life. Thank you."

Markham shrugs and says my own courage saved me. I don't agree. I also know we don't have time to discuss it. We need to rescue Warner. Markham and I set new pitons and prepare to rappel to him. Before we reach him, others of the element climb to Warner. Two rope themselves to him and start climbing.

At the top of the basalt spur the element regroups. We leapfrog over the plateau. I am still partnered with Markham, who tells me when and where to move. Warner stays in the rear.

In less than two hours, we reach Fortress Soando. Lieutenant Terrwyn signals a halt. "Intelligence from the War Room," he announces. "The people who took the fortress claim to be without house – bastards, although they don't say that, who demand recognition as a house with a base at Soando. They threaten their hostages, which they say are thirty-seven. They say they regret the deaths of five.

"Their true number is unknown. Their skill and weaponry are unknown. Their training and organization are unknown. I believe we will be most effective in close combat. Keep your slug rifles but be ready to exchange them for energy pistols, swords, and daggers."

I feel my companions' tension and watch them check their equipment again.

Built millennia ago, the fortress's defenses are no match for modern equipment and determined soldiers. We use our climbing gear to scale the curtain wall. We pour over the battlements and run to the towers. We attack and move down the stairs. I see one of my companions fall, a dagger through his heart. Markham thrusts her sword through the killer, and the body

78

splatters on the stone floor forty-five meters below. A pebble from my reshot hits an enemy's forehead. He falls sixty meters. I think he is dead before he hits the floor.

Lieutenant Terrwyn faces the surviving enemy and declares them prisoners of House Bleddyn. The battle took less than an hour.

We gather the prisoners in the courtyard where Father's shuttle lands. Telor is first off. He rushes to me. When Telor reaches me, the rows of dead bodies and the shackled prisoners flicker and disappear. I realize this is a teaching story. The ascent of the cliff and storming the fortress were real, but the enemy forces were holographic projections. Father takes Lieutenant Terrwyn and me into his shuttle where Lieutenant Fender is waiting.

Father does not look at the others before asking me, "What did you learn?"

I am prepared. "Father, I learned that protecting me is not easy. I learned I can kill to protect my house, my companions, or myself. I learned my guards are much more than guardians. The attack in the forest taught me House Bleddyn is truly at war, and I may be a target. I learned to trust my guards. Father, I could have died today."

Father's face is immobile. I don't know if I am in trouble or not.

"Yes, Garreth, you could have died. You could have died when the assassin attacked you in the forest. Warner is the best climber in the company. He knew you could save yourself if you didn't lose your head. You risk much, Garreth. Please remember, brave and modest."

I also learn we have some incredible training simulations and wonder when I will get to be in another one.

~~~~~

Spring Stormtime of my seventh year halts outdoor training. The wind is strong and the weather, unpredictable. Rain and hail pelt the roof and windows; wind whistles through the crenels of the battlements; lightning flashes among the clouds and thunder shakes even the thick stone walls of Fortress.

Fortress and the lower caverns fill with people who live on our estates. We give shelter to the thralls who are farmers so they will survive to continue their service to us. Others shelter on our islands. The caverns below Fortress are crowded and the kitchens are open day and night. The sails of the windmills are tightly furled; the only power comes from turbines in the rivers.

The weather excites me and I am not afraid of it. During a break in the storm, I slip away from Nana and my guards, and climb the stairs to the highest turret of the Keep. A door opens to my hand. I push it aside, walk down a narrow passage, and stand on the battlements, naked to the storm but for sandals and loincloth.

The rain and wind stop, but I know this will not last. My arms and legs tingle, and I feel their fine hairs rise. I see sparks dancing on the tip of a metal rod pointing from a merlon to the sky. In my exhilaration and ignorance, I do not know what it means. I spread my arms to embrace the storm until Father grabs

80

me from behind and drags me into the passageway as lightning strikes the battlements, blasting the merlon into powder.

Father is shaking. I have never known him to show fear, but that is what he feels. He holds me tightly and strokes my hair.

"It is time," he says, "for Sani to teach you about weather … and lightning."

The next day, Sani takes me to the battlements. We can see the sky for kilometers in every direction. He describes the clouds, gives them names and tells me what weather they bring. With the help of two thralls, I release a balloon carrying instruments to measure temperature, humidity, air pressure, and wind speed.

"Tomorrow," Sani promises, "we will visit the laboratory where scientists receive and analyze the data from balloons and satellites."

~~~~~

Sani always wears long pants, a shirt with long sleeves, and a wide-brimmed hat. When outdoors, he seeks the shade. I wear only loincloth and sandals. I revel in the sun, dancing in the rays that warm my skin.

"Why do you not dance in the sun?" I ask Sani.

"The sun would burn my skin," Sani replies. "If I get too much sun or too often, I might develop a disease of the skin that could kill me."

"Why?"

"Because my skin does not have the melanin that gives your skin its bronze color and protects you from the sun."

"Why?" I have learned no matter what Sani says, he always has an answer to *why* – until I reach a question that makes him uncomfortable.

"Because my people evolved on the Southern Continent, which receives less sunlight than the Equatorial Continent."

"Why?" I ask. "I mean, why do you get less sunlight?"

"Do you know about World's orbit around the sun?" Sani asks.

I remember my lessons. "World's orbit is an eccentric ellipse and requires 590 days to complete one year. World's axis is tilted at 37 degrees. The tilt and the orbit cause the seasons and stormtime at the equinoxes and solstices."

"Very good," Sani says. "And it answers your last *why*. When it is summer in the southern hemisphere and the South Pole points toward the sun, World is farthest from the sun in its elliptical orbit. The Southern Continent never gets much sunlight, even in summer. Our bodies and yours need sunlight to create a chemical important to life. This continent and its islands, the home of the Res Publica, girdle the equator. Over millennia, the melanin in your skin increased to protect you from too much sun. Southerners have light skin to allow more sun to penetrate to create the chemical."

We are the same species. That was one of Telor's lessons. Yet we are different in this way. And the difference is only the color of our skin and because my people lived near the equator and Sani's people lived near the pole. We are more alike than different.

84

CHAPTER 6 RITUAL OF CAMALOS

Daffyd and Delwyn graduate from Academy just before Winter Stormtime. Tonight, the first night of stormtime, the Great Hall is open only by invitation. It is the largest room in Fortress and when we celebrated the elevations of Alaw, my Sister-minus-three, and Macca, my Brother-minus-six, thousands of people filled the hall. Today, for the Ritual of Camalos, when new soldiers swear to Father and to House Bleddyn, only forty people are present. Lieutenant Fender, the commander of my guards, is one. I am not surprised to see Master Sergeant Rhingyll, commander of the Mountain Company. He will watch the new soldiers take the oath and blood daggers on their arms, looking for those who might be candidates for his company.

My Brother- and Sister-plus-twelve, Daffyd and Delwyn, are among the candidates. Even though they are family and of-the-blood, they will take the oath. Telor says they do it to set an example for the others.

Today, a score of Academy graduates, young men and women, stand at attention at the foot of the thirteen steps leading to the dais. The steps represent the thirteen Great Houses. Father stands atop them to symbolize his power and position, although we never talk about this.

My brother-plus-eighteen, Llywelyn, the heir, stands at Father's right. Telor stands beside Llywelyn. More of my elder siblings and I stand with them. Alaw, Sister-minus-three, stands with me. This is the first time I am not the youngest and at the end of the line. I am responsible not only for myself, but for Alaw. I hold her hand and hope she will not wiggle too much.

 This is also the first time I wear a house uniform. It is like the members of the Home Guard – black with gold and orange stripes on the sleeves, but now bearing the house crest – *an escutcheon or, a wolf, proper, couped* – a snarling, gray and black wolf's head with a red eye and tongue on a golden shield.

I stand silently and watch Father speak to the assembled soldiers. "Honor, valor, loyalty," he says. The soldiers, my siblings, and I expand these words to the Soldiers Oath. "We swear always to live by honor, to be valorous in battle and loyal to Gens, House, and the Res Publica." The words echo from the vaulted ceiling.

Father stands by a table that holds twenty daggers, each with a wolf's head atop the hilt. The soldiers climb the steps, one by one. When a soldier reaches him, Father takes a dagger from the table and pricks his arm, drawing blood. He hands the dagger to the soldier who pricks his or her own arm, sealing the oath with blood.

Then, the soldier steps behind Father. One by one, the soldiers, holding their blooded daggers, complete the ritual and stand behind Father.

"Father offers trust by allowing newly sworn, armed soldiers to stand behind him with naked daggers," Telor tells me later.

I understand what he says, but know Telor and Father are hiding something.

~~~~~

After the ceremony, I ask Father why we call it the Ritual of Camalos.

"Camalos was a warrior of our house in ancient times. We invoke his name because it draws us to a common story. Do you understand?"

"I think I do, Father. Like blood, the stories bind us."

Father smiles briefly and I know he is pleased. "The words and stories we hear as children impress themselves on our minds. They create our beliefs and our understanding of our world, house, and culture. Do you remember when I punished you for teasing a thrall child about the color of his skin?"

My blush brightens my face. "Yes, Father. I only repeated what I heard. It was a joke. You told me even jokes can create evil in our mind and that words can wound. Then you spanked me so I would remember. And you made me apologize."

I giggle at the memory of the thrall child's parents when Father and I arrived, alone and unarmed, at their home. When Father explained our errand, I saw their love for their child and they saw Father's love for me. I apologized to the young boy and I learned thralls aren't as different from the Res Publica as I once thought.

Father interrupts my memory. "Remember, your name has a meaning and a prophecy. Garreth was a soldier both brave and modest. Those words are important to you and to House Bleddyn."

Father abruptly changes the subject. That is his way. "What is the purpose of a grace knife?"

"To administer a deathblow to a wounded comrade rather than leave him or her to be captured. To kill an enemy so he might not recover and fight again. To take one's own life rather than be captured or if disgraced."

"And what do you think of those things?"

"Karmet orders us to fire upon an enemy when one of our own is captured even if it causes the death of our mate. It is better to be dead than become a hostage. He also tells us to crush enemies because they can avenge themselves of lighter injuries but of more serious ones, they cannot. Therefore, the injury ought to be such that the victor does not stand in fear of revenge."

"Do you forget part of Karmet's words?"

I must have looked puzzled, because Father says, "Karmet's aphorism is, 'Men ought to be well treated or crushed.' Remember, Garreth. Both brave and modest."

Father's expression is inscrutable. That is also his way.

~~~~~

On the day after the ritual, my companions and I go to the dojo shared by Delwyn and Daffyd. During the years they were at Academy, it was empty except during stormtime. Now, it will be

88

an important training ground for my siblings, companions, and me.

Three of Daffyd and Delwyn's friends are part of their team. Delwyn is the only one who wears a short sword. When I ask her why, she says, "So when I encounter an adversary, I can get close enough to see death in his eyes." Sometimes my sister is a little frightening.

Daffyd announces our first training will be on the firing range with slug rifles. Ceirois, my only mate more curious than me, asks why we bother with slug rifles when we could use energy rifles.

"A good question," Delwyn says. "Energy rifles require heavy charge packs for each five shots. Slug-packs of the same size and weight hold forty slugs. Also, an energy rifle's beam becomes diffused in air, especially humid air. A slug rifle has greater effective range than an energy rifle of the same size. In the hands of a trained soldier, special slug rifles can place a slug in a spot the size of a silver coin at a distance of 3.5 kilometers."

Delwyn's explanation rings in our minds, and we are eager to pay attention to Daffyd's instructions.

~~~~~

Before classes begin the next day, Telor summons me to the War Room. He stands at the Senior Controller's position and points to a satellite view. I recognize House Marredudd's hardwood forests. They are burning. Marredudd's territory is the largest place where hardwoods grow, and the wood is important for our surface fleet of sailing ships. House Marredudd maintains these forests carefully, allowing enough natural fire for germination and to clear underbrush to prevent bigger fires. The dozens of fires now are not natural.

"What happened?" I demand of Telor. "Why—"

"What and why are questions for later. The question now is what can we do to help Marredudd," Telor says and tells me to sit at a console. "Watch and learn," he adds, and then turns to issue orders to the controllers.

Despite the efforts of House Marredudd and their allies, the fires devastate the hardwood forests. I listen to Gens Marredudd and Father on a comm circuit. "It will be at least twenty years before new trees are mature enough to harvest," Gens Marredudd tells Father.

"What help may we send to replant the forest?" Father asks.

Gens Marredudd thanks Father, and explains it will be more than a year before the seedlings are ready. She and Father agree that members of our Home Guard will help during late summer next year.

~~~~~

My mates and I are playing a war game when Father comes into the room. His eyes sweep over the maps, the model war machines, the holographic images of sailing ships projected onto the floor, and of starships into the air above. Father's path takes him through the image of a three-masted, square-rigged corvette. Telor switches off the computer and the ships disappear.

Father sits in Telor's chair and gestures us to sit facing him. He points to five islands projected on the floor – Sehwa,

Namhae, Soando, Koje, and Kosong. "Long before the Conquest Era, House Bleddyn governed only these five islands and the surrounding islets. House Reese claimed two islands to the north. House Dolffin claimed four islands to the west. The Free Islands northwest of the continent were the home of pirates. Other houses lived on the continent. We had not yet discovered the Southern Continent or its people, the thralls.

"Houses grew larger, and we did not have enough land for our children to have their own farms and homes. Much of our continent is steep mountains or swampy jungle. The need for lebensraum – living room, land – drove voyages of exploration. House Bleddyn and other houses sent ships on these voyages. We found the Southern Continent. The Southerners discovered us at the same time and began raiding our islands and trading fleets. The problem became so great, the houses assembled an army to make war on the Southern Continent."

"But Father, you said our people wanted more land. Wasn't that the real reason for the war?"

"That was the reason the houses united to fight the war. The Southerners' raids were the excuse for war. Do you understand the difference between *reason* and *excuse?*"

"Yes, Father. We wanted to conquer the Southerners to take their land. War to stop their raids was an excuse."

"You are correct. The need for land was the ultimate cause for war. The attacks on our fleets and ports were the proximate cause, the match that ignited the fire. Instead of preparing for war with the Southerners, House Tarren sent assassins against the other houses. Enough of the assassins succeeded that Gens

Triumph Tarren seized control and declared himself ruler. It was the only time the Res Publica had a king.

"It took House Bleddyn and our allies more than two millennia to mount a challenge to King Triumph. We assembled our supporters and forced him to swear to a Compact giving control of the war to a Council of Houses. House Tarren has hated us ever since."

Father sits silently for several minutes. We dare not interrupt his thoughts before he dismisses us. "You are precocious children, but you are children. That is enough history for today."

~~~~~

My mates and I rush to the dojo. Today, we will learn to use sabers. At first, Delwyn does not allow us to practice with one another. "You would teach each other bad habits," she says. "Later, you will hold mock duels, but not until you perfect your form."

We pay closer attention after Delwyn speaks of duels. Children's duels will be only for score. We will wear padded clothing and masks to cover our faces. It is bad form to strike below the waist or above the neck. Delwyn and Daffyd tell us Academy cadets use heavier sabers than ours, and they don't always wear padding. They make us swear never to tell anyone before they share stories of forbidden duels that led to injury and death.

~~~~~

Delwyn gathers us in a semi-circle on the wooden floor of the dojo. Daffyd's voice is barely more than a whisper and we lean forward to hear him.

92

"More than thirty millennia ago, two sons of allied Houses Lagon and Helygen and a daughter of House Maelon were assigned to the same element at Academy. The boys swore brotherhood under the ancient tradition."

Daffyd chuckles. "At twelve years old, they didn't think a girl might come between them."

Delwyn's snort interrupts Daffyd and brings a few giggles from the girls.

Daffyd tries not to smile. "By the time they passed puberty and their vambraces were removed, the boys' attitude about girls changed, and they became rivals for the daughter of House Maelon. The rivalry spread to the schoolroom, the athletic field, and the dojo. No longer comrades, they became enemies. Their animosity found its way into everything they did. Eventually, it became too great and one called the other to the field.

"There were no Academy restrictions on energy weapons, then. The boys agreed to duel for the girl's favor with energy pistols – and to the death.

"Energy pistols of the era were like ours in some ways. The pistols used a crystal of corundum. What is that?"

"Aluminum oxide," Elfyn, one of my mates, answers. "It's also a gemstone." Elfyn's family is a sept of House Hynafol. They are miners of volcanoes where World's intense heat and pressure separates minerals and creates gemstones.

"You are correct," Daffyd replies. "Our energy pistols use crystals to create coherent light—"

"What is that?" Ceirois interrupts.

"The light from an energy pistol marches in lockstep, the way soldiers march during the Changing of the Guard," Daffyd answers. "Since the light is marching together, it is more powerful than the light on your utility belt.

"Our pistols can fire five bursts of coherent light before they exhaust the charge pack. The boys' pistols could fire only once. If that shot were not effective, the two boys would resort to swords and daggers."

Daffyd's listeners shiver at this. I do not. Telor told me this story. Both boys missed with their energy pistols. Some historians think it was deliberate, and the boys wanted to face one another with steel. Daffyd does not say this. Perhaps he doesn't want to give us ideas.

"The two boys fought with sabers until the boy from House Helygen broke the other boy's blade. Before the second boy could draw his dagger, the first executed a perfect flèche, daring but deadly if successful. The boy lifted his left foot and shifted weight into the thrust. The saber pierced the second boy's breast. He died instantly."

Daffyd finishes the story. The girl did not wed the victor, and the duel shattered the amity between the two boys' houses. House Lagon withdrew into itself and to this day remains neutral in the feuds and vendettas of the Res Publica.

~~~~~

Father often stands on the balcony that surrounds the floor of the dojo and watches our mock duels. One day, he summons me to his den. "War is something more than a duel on a large scale," he says. "In what way is this true?"

His eyes search my face. My stomach quivers under his gaze. Then, I laugh. "You quote Karmet, Father, but reality will trump philosophy every time."

Father frowns, but before he can speak, I say, "Karmet wrote that victory comes from motive plus power. In children's duels, the only motive is points. The consequences of losing are unimportant unless we wager our desserts. In war, motives are many and complex. A small motive may produce a large effect."

Father is pleased and sends me back to the dojo.

~~~~~

It is Spring Stormtime again. I am ten years old. All doors of Fortress open to my hand. My guards have grown careless, and it is easy to escape them. I think I do not need them, since I am qualified with an energy pistol and saber, both of which I wear.

I believe I can protect myself against anything until I meet a boy my age in the caverns. He stands out among the crowd of Res Publica and thralls who are sheltering in the caverns. He wears the same weapons I do, but he seems much more confident than I feel.

"Who are you?" I ask. My vambrace senses the adrenalin in my blood and releases endorphins to calm me. Just when I need the mental boost, the vambrace calms me. Stupid vambrace! As if it hears my thought, the vambrace injects another jolt of drugs.

"My name is Barri, blood of House Hynafol."

"My name is Garreth, blood of House Bleddyn. Why are you armed?"

"You are in the caverns during stormtime, and you do not know why we are armed?" Barri says. His voice holds both curiosity and barely concealed contempt. He knows something I don't.

For a moment, I am afraid. Then I remember my father's lessons about trust and loyalty. I think Barri sees this in my eyes.

"I know who you are, Garreth," he says. "I am not your enemy."

"Are you my friend?" I ask.

He looks at his sandaled feet and wiggles his toes as if he just now realizes they are part of him. He looks up. "Garreth, I cannot say. My Gens swore to your father, and our houses are allied. I was not born when the oath was made and I was not asked to swear. I am not in this alliance."

"Is this the way it must be?" I whisper. I look at Barri and see my guards approaching. I try not to show any emotion. "Can I ever expect friendship except—"

"Garreth, I will someday swear to you. Now, I must go. Your guards might not appreciate my weapons." He turns and disappears into the crowd.

~~~~~

Stormtime still rages when Telor summons me from breakfast. "A wolf in the breeding pens gave birth to a litter and the cubs have been weaned. You will feed them every morning before your own breakfast. In this way, you will learn responsibility."

The cubs are cute, and eager for their food. When I fill their trough, one licks my hand. When I pick him up, he licks my face.

Telor is aghast. "Garreth! They are wild creatures."

I put down the cub. I see his collar embossed with the letter, Γ – in the old language, *gamma*.

~~~~~

Despite my new duties, there is no letup in training. After I feed the wolf cubs and gulp my breakfast, Father summons me. "What is the Soldiers Oath?" he asks.

The question surprises me, but I am quick to answer with the short form. "Honor, valor, loyalty."

"And what does *honor* mean?"

"Integrity? … Virtue? … Honesty? … Fairness?" I stop. Each of these words holds part of the answer. Alone, none is correct. I turn my face away and look through the windows at the greensward that marks an ancient dueling ground and the home of modern festivals. Beyond the grass, trees bend in the storm wind. Farther away, lightning flashes from cloud to cloud. I turn back to Father and admit, "Father, I do not know."

I am afraid until Father speaks. "Honor is the most difficult word of the oath to grasp. Think on its meaning. Speak to your older siblings. Except Llywelyn. He will not want to talk to you. Ask the cousins who are your guards. Ask your other mates."

I look up. "How will I know the right answer?"

"You will know when you find it."

That is definitely not helpful.

~~~~~

Early the next day, before the heat builds storm clouds, Sani takes my mates and me into the garden. Where the garden walls protect the plants, flowers bloom – jonquils, yellow bells, and flowering cherries, red bud, apples, and dogwood. We sit in the sunlight while Sani sits in the shade of a huge tree and tells about talking animals.

The Wolf and the Pterodactyl

A wolf was feeding on an animal he killed when a small bone stuck firmly in his throat. He felt terrible pain and tried to convince everyone he met to remove the bone. None of the other animals would put a paw into the wolf's throat.

At last, he met a pterodactyl. "I would give anything," the  wolf coughed, trying to speak around the bone in his throat, "if you would take it out." The pterodactyl agreed to try, and told the wolf to lie on his side and open his jaws as wide as he could. The pterodactyl put his long beak into the wolf's throat. He loosened the bone until at last it came out.

"Why would the 'tero help the wolf?" I ask. "They are both carnivores. They compete for food."

"Ah," Sani says. "What is the food of the wolf?"

"The four-legs. Wolves hunt deer and antelope and our cattle. Once Telor took me on a two-person floater to watch when a pack took down a mastodon."

"And the pterodactyl? What is his food?"

"Rabbits, voles… oh. They don't compete. Except maybe when food becomes scarce," I say.

"A good thought, Garreth. But perhaps there's another reason. Perhaps the pterodactyl saw the wolf as a fellow creature in need, and remembered a lesson from his childhood, *Live and work for the benefit of all.*"

"The pterodactyl was foolish to put his head in the wolf's mouth. And the wolf was foolish to allow the 'tero's sharp beak in his throat," Elfyn says.

"What else could the wolf have done?" Sani asks.

No one has an answer

~~~~~

As long as I can remember, I dream I can fly. The dreams come from watching my guards piloting floaters. The floaters are like the toboggans we ride across the winter snow, but have radar, satellite navigation, forward-looking cameras, infrared sensors, and antigravity drive. Military floaters have rocket grenade launchers, too. I am especially happy when Telor says I might fly one, even though it's not a military model.

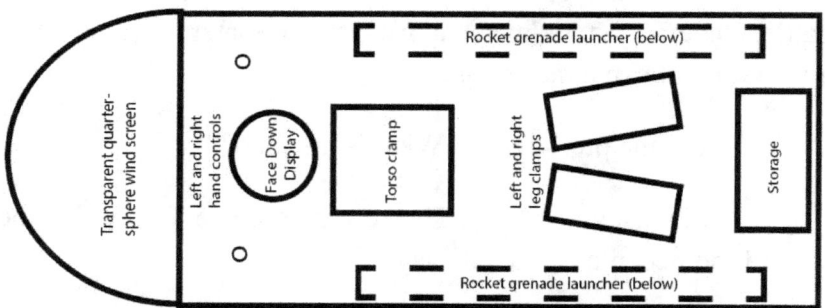

"This floater can rise about three hundred meters above the ground and travel more than one hundred kilometers per hour," he tells me. "I do not think you are yet prepared for that. Its altitude and speed are restricted to one hundred meters and fifty kilometers per hour. As you learn, I will relax these restrictions."

My pouting no longer affects Telor, so I don't try.

~~~~~

The weather has cooled with the coming of autumn. Our teachers excuse my schoolmates and me to play in the woods. Actually, our play is always a lesson because it includes games of pursuit and evasion much more complicated than hide-and-find. For this game, Lieutenant Fender holds my dagger and grace knife. I am unarmed and play the role of an escaped prisoner of war.

I protest. "This is not real." I quote an ancient directive, "Leave no companion behind; never become a captive."

Lieutenant Fender is not angry. "You are correct. However, we sacrifice reality for training. You are an unarmed, escaped prisoner of war, but your captors will be searching for you. You'd better run."

That is all the encouragement I need. I dart away, knowing I have little time to break my trail and escape.

I lead my guards and schoolmates in a chase until I can slip away. After I evade them, I climb an apple tree beside the fence of steel and energy that separates Academy from the lands of Fortress Bleddyn. The apples are ripe – red and full of sweetness. Soon, thralls will swarm the orchard and harvest the apples. I pick an apple and sit on a branch eating it, hoping to see cadets on the exercise fields. The grassy fields stretch more than a kilometer beyond the berry bushes growing near the fence.

Before I see, I am seen. A head pops from behind a bush. A voice calls, "Little boy? Are you spying on us?"

I know I am safe on my side of the fence, but I shiver. I decide to be excited instead of frightened, and reply, "I am not little; I am seven years old! And I'm not spying on you. You are spying on me!"

"Why would we spy on you?" the voice asks. The cadet stands and walks toward the fence. He holds no weapons, but wears a white padded helmet, a red shirt, and white trousers. He is barefoot.

"Why do you think I would spy on you?" I retort. "What are you doing, anyway?"

The cadet looks from side to side. Other cadets pop up from behind other shrubs. "We are practicing for a *Bo-taoshi* competition," the first one says. "We will plan new strategies. You may watch if you will give your oath not to reveal this to anyone. Who are you?"

"Thank you for letting me watch. I swear never to tell. I am Garreth Bleddyn."

"Who else would be in an apple tree in Father's orchard?" It is another of the cadets. He removes his helmet. I recognize Guffudd. I'm not sure if I should wave, but he waves and smiles, so I wave back.

I'm glad Guffudd didn't ask if my guards knew where I was. That would have been totally embarrassing.

I watch Guffudd's element and a second element erect a pole held upright only by cadets. Those two elements defend the pole, keeping it upright, while two other elements try to pull down the pole. One of Guffudd's mates is on top of the pole holding the long spike driven into it. I know he's the monkey and that his position is the most important. His job is to balance the pole, watch the attackers, and call commands.

I've been watching for a quarter hour when my guards and mates arrive. One holds my sandals; another, my trousers and tunic. Guffudd sees the guards and waves to me, then returns to the melee of cadets surrounding the pole. I pick apples and toss them to my guards and mates before jumping from the tree.

~~~~~

I need time away from my mates and the others who always surround me. On a mid-winter morning, long before Telor wakes, I escape my guards and take my floater on a flight to the north. I know Telor put locators in my boots and sandals, so I take a pair of sandals discarded by one of my mates. The weather has been clement, although patches of snow still cover the ground. I keep my path low over the forest to avoid radar that would trigger the transponder and give me away. A transparent shield deflects wind over the bow of the floater. The sun is warm on my back, but the air is cold. I turn on the heater. It will drain my batteries faster, so I watch the power meter closely.

I do not plan on pterodactyls.

They are reptilian flyers larger than a floater. My books say they avoid our farms and grazing lands, but live in wild forests and mountains. The books are wrong. Three 'teros catch me unaware and dive at my floater. The proximity alarm warns me. I look up in time to discover the threat and tilt the floater into a slip to quickly drop my altitude.

Too quickly. I am flying through trees and struggle to guide the floater through branches while burning off speed. The 'teros with their long wingspans do not like the forest and fly away. I slow and then ground the floater beside a huge tree. I release the latches and step away from the floater to catch my breath. No 'teros. Nothing but me and trees and ground covered with moss and drifts of leaves.

And a wolf who steps silently from behind a tree.

I know about wolves. I am, after all, a Son of Wolf. I know I cannot reach my floater and escape before the wolf attacks me.

I bend my knees and draw my dagger, preparing to fight for my life. I will have only one chance to kill the wolf – when he leaps to attack me. But he does not leap – he pads toward me. He is lean but not puny. His gray coat blends with the shadows under the trees. He stares at me. The only color is a bright red tongue lolling from his mouth and red, glowing eyes. He looks much fiercer than the shield of my house and he is not afraid of me.

Why doesn't he attack? Why am I not afraid of him? It's more than the calming drugs in my vambrace, although I feel them burning through my body. Something in his eyes tells me he is not my enemy nor am I his. Regardless, I shiver when he comes close enough to sniff my feet. Then, I see the frayed collar. The wolf is from Father's breeding pens and must have escaped. He—

I giggle when the wolf springs up, puts its front paws on my chest, and licks my face. I kneel, put my arms around his neck, and hug him. "Wolf, you greeted me and you protected me."

I know he cannot understand my words, but he did protect me. Not from the 'teros, but from my fear. It is an important lesson. "An ally may protect you, but be sure he really is an ally," Telor once quoted from *The Book of Proverbs*. I don't think he meant wolves, but others of the Res Publica.

I must rescue this wolf, for if Father's hunters find him, they will declare him feral and kill him. "Will you ride with me on a floater?" I ask, not expecting an answer. As if he understands, the wolf turns and steps onto the floater. He lies beside the pilot's position, tongue hanging out. I think he is smiling, at least in his mind.

I face a dilemma. I can call for help, but then the wolf and I will be caught. I will be punished and the wolf might be destroyed.

'Oh, what a tangled web we weave, when first we practice to deceive,' an ancient line runs through my mind. It is one of Telor's apothegms. He told me these sayings are guides and not law, but they sometimes hold a kernel of truth. I decide quickly and easily. I will harness the lie and spin the tangled web I began when I slipped away this morning. If I am to escape punishment and protect the wolf, I will need the brave part of 'brave and modest.'

The wolf will come with me to Fortress Bleddyn. He will not be a pet, but a companion.

"You are *Arawan*," I say and lock myself into position on the floater.

The wolf looks at me and tilts his head. This time, I am sure he is smiling.

~~~~~

The radar transponder on my floater triggers the hanger doors. I fly into the hanger and land. I am not surprised my guards and Telor are waiting for me. Arawan stays close when I dismount.

My guards tense and their hands reach for weapons.

"Stand down," Telor orders.

My guards do not draw their weapons. They do not relax, either. Arawan stands beside me. I think he is confident I can protect him from these soldiers. I feel the calming drug from the vambrace – and then realize the feeling is coming not from my vambrace, but from the wolf.

"Brother, what have you done this time?" I see the smile behind Telor's words.

"Brother, this is Arawan, my companion-wolf," I say.

"And what will you tell Father?" Telor asks.

Arawan, Father will judge you and me. He will probably not kill me. He may kill you. He may return you to the pens. I will do all I can to protect you. It might not be enough. I hope Arawan understands. Whether or not he does, he pads beside me through the halls and into Father's den.

I kneel at Father's desk; Arawan crouches beside me.

"Gamma," Father says. Arawan draws his lips back, exposing his teeth. I feel a rumble in his body, a growl. Father must feel this, but pretends he doesn't. "We were worried when you left the pens. I am pleased to see—"

"His name is Arawan. He is my Companion-Wolf." I interrupt Father.

"The ancient language for 'unrestrained wildness'," Father says. "A good choice, Son. Now, how did he come to be here? Stand. Both of you."

I stand. Arawan stands beside me. His eyes focus unwaveringly on Father. I put my hand on the wolf's withers and draw confidence from him. I feel Arawan's strength but also a little fear.

After relating the story and being quizzed by Father until I can conceal none of the details, we stand in silence for several minutes.

"Garreth, Gamma who you have named Arawan, was third of his litter. We knew he was different. Different enough to escape from the breeding pens and to survive in the wilderness. Different enough to bond with one of my children.

"I am pleased. Arawan marks the success our breeding program has sought for millennia. However, you are responsible for him. You may keep him as your companion-wolf although I'm not sure who will be keeping whom."

Father's chuckle is silent, but I feel it.

"Thank you, Father. I accept responsibility for Arawan." *This means you must behave*, I say silently to Arawan. I know he cannot understand me, but I feel what might be a chuckle from Arawan – and another from Father.

Chapter 7 Rodric

Rodric, my Brother-plus-three, and his mates often recruit my playmates and me for their games. We pretend we are pirates of the Free Islands, or explorers in the jungles, or soldiers fighting in the ancient wars on the Southern Continent. Once, Rodric led us on a raid of Sister-minus-three Alaw's playroom to kidnap her for ransom, but she became frightened. Rodric comforted her and apologized to her guards, and Father did not punish us, even though we were sure he knew.

Just before Fall Stormtime, Rodric comes to my room to tell me he will go to live at House Dolffin. "I will be gone for three years, Brother. It will be a great adventure. But I will message you, and tell you what I'm doing, and you can message me."

I am not happy. Except for Telor, I am closest to Rodric of all my brothers. Guffudd is at Academy and Llywelyn frightens me. And he won't play with me, anyway. He's too busy with his own friends.

~~~~~

Summer Stormtime is over. Today, Father tells my mates and me another story of our family. He says it will help us learn about honor and trust.

"Garreth's brothers, Telor and Rodric, are named for the two heroes of this story," Father says.

"More than one hundred millennia ago, House Dolffin were pirates, operating among the Western Isles. They preyed on merchant ships trading with the rich cities of the western coast. Some merchant ships were ours. My ancestor decided to end the pirate threat and sent infiltration elements to House Dolffin's islands. Our plan was to attack their fortress, capture the Gens, and require him to stop the piracy.

"Not to kill the Gens, Your Grace?" Gordan asks.

"No. Although House Dolffin were pirates—"

"You said that," Ceirois interrupts, and then blushes.

"It is important," Father says. "Thank you for reminding us." His words put Ceirois at ease. "Although they were pirates, they were excellent sailors and their ships were heavily armed. Gens Bleddyn saw more advantage in an alliance than in a war that would cost many lives and ships. He also saw more advantage in a land battle than a sea battle.

"House Bleddyn sent our forces on small ships that appeared to be fishing vessels, and landed them on Songbaek Island before dawn. They took House Dolffin by surprise and with little opposition moved toward Dolffin's fortress. Dolffin was prepared for a sea battle, but was not prepared for an invasion by land.

"We were closing in on Dolffin's fortress when, in desperation, Gens Dolffin sent the House Praetorian Guard against us. Our infiltration elements concentrated on the center of their one-line formation and broke through—"

"*Chojeom*, the focal-point attack!" I say. Father's displeasure at being interrupted turns into a brief smile at my understanding.

Attack in *chojeom* formation
(overhead view)

XXXXXXXXXXXXXXXXXXXXXXXX

"Yes, the focal-point attack. During a skirmish, our soldiers seized the boy who carried the House Dolffin flag and brought him to Gens Bleddyn. He was only a boy so Gens Bleddyn dismissed the guards except his two sons."

x – defender
o – attacker

"Who are you, boy?" the ancestral Gens Bleddyn demanded.

"I carry the flag of House Dolffin," the boy answered.

"True, but you are more than that. You are of-the-blood," Bleddyn mused.

The boy understood instantly. "So, you will kill me." The boy who had been hunched over like a supplicant straightened and stood tall. "Then kill me and get it done. I am not ashamed of my life and I do not fear death.

"Although, I would like to have supper first," he said and pressed his lips together in a tight smile.

Gens Bleddyn chuckled, then broke out in laughter. Bleddyn's sons looked at their father, wondering if he were insane.

"You would like to have supper!" Bleddyn gasped. "Boy, I salute your courage."

Bleddyn's face froze. Then, he spoke. "You are more than of-the-blood. You are a son of Gens Dolffin, are you not?"

The smile faded from the boy's face.

"You don't have to speak," Bleddyn said. "I see the answer in your eyes. Come here, boy."

The boy, more wary now, stepped forward until he was within arm's reach of Bleddyn.

"What is your name?" Bleddyn asked.

"Telor son of Dolffin, an it please you."

"Telor son of Dolffin, it pleases me very much," Bleddyn said.

The boy's eyes narrowed, and he shook his head. He was clearly confused.

"Is your Gens in the fortress? Would he be receptive to truce talks?" Bleddyn asked the boy. "He must know he cannot stand against us."

"I will not betray my house or my Gens," Telor said. "You will learn no more from me."

Bleddyn stood and spoke to the boy. "Telor, son of Dolffin, go to your Gens and give him this message. 'By my blood and the blood of my son, whom I send to you, you may safely come here and safely depart at a time of your choosing.'"

Bleddyn looked at one of his sons. "Rodric, go where this boy takes you. Sojourn where he or his master directs. Come back when they allow. Do you understand? Will you obey?"

"Yes, Father," the boy Rodric said. He walked to Telor and took his hand. "Well, come on," he said to the stunned boy. "Would you like supper, first?"

Early the next morning, Rodric and Telor approached the guards at the House Bleddyn encampment. The two boys escorted a veiled woman. "Let my friend and me in," Rodric ordered. "And his mother, too."

Gens Bleddyn dismissed his guards and invited the woman and the two boys into his tent.

"Your Grace," the woman said after removing her veil, "you held my son's life in your hands, but you opened them and let him live. You gave me your son's life. I return it to you. I am Gens Dolffin. Something is about to happen. I believe it is in the best interest of my house to be a part of it. Am I correct?"

Gens Bleddyn stood and made the bow of equals. "Gens Dolffin, you are correct. It is time the Res Publica cease war amongst ourselves. It is time to make fair and honorable alliances. You see the truth in my words."

"I see the truth in your words, but I also see foreboding. What you suggest will be difficult."

"It would be less difficult if House Dolffin and House Bleddyn were united. To seal an alliance, I offer my son, Rodric, as intermediary and hostage."

Dolffin was silent for several moments. "I accept your offer and your son, but as a guest, not hostage. I ask you to invite my son Telor to be a guest in your house."

"I will do so," Gens Bleddyn replied. "And I will order my house to preserve the names *Telor* and *Rodric* in each generation. They are the true heroes." He frowned at the two boys. "They must not let this go to their heads."

The boys bowed to the two Gens and, under their eyes, swore brotherhood by the tradition of those times.

"What was the tradition of brotherhood, then?" I ask.

"Much like today except they did not exchange daggers, but each carefully sliced the palm of his right hand. They pressed their hands together while reciting their oath. It was a harsher ritual than the one we use today."

I shudder at the thought of having to cut myself that way and am glad we swear brotherhood with a dagger-prick on our arms.

Before supper, Father comes to my room to ask me the lesson of the story. "Both House Bleddyn and House Dolffin acted honorably," Father says. "Do you understand?"

"Not completely, Father. But it is the beginning of understanding."

~~~~~

"What was the lesson?" Elfyn asks after Father leaves.

"He told us that honor and trust go together, and trust must be offered before it can be asked. When Gens Bleddyn sent Rodric, he was saying he trusted Gens Dolffin. Gens Dolffin returned his trust when she came unarmed and unguarded to Bleddyn's camp."

"That's not all there is, though," Elfyn says.

"It is the beginning of understanding," I say. Elfyn makes a rude gesture, his two middle fingers tucked into his palm and held by his thumb – symbol of a declawed and emasculated wolf – but I know he is joking.

~~~~~

I usually don't look forward to stormtime, but before Fall Stormtime, Rodric, my Brother-plus-three, will come home. He was fostered to House Dolffin for three years and spent the past summer in the Western Ocean on one of Dolffin's warships. He promised to tell me about his adventures. I think about pirates from the Free Islands, and shiver with excitement.

On the day Rodric is to return, Arawan senses my excitement. He growls at Nana and bristles at the thralls who serve my breakfast. If I bring Arawan with me to greet Rodric, Father will see this, and wonder if Arawan is truly under control. I take my companion-wolf to the pens.

"No, you may not run free in the forest, but there is a large place for you to play. Please be nice to the others, even though they are not smart or strong like you." I sense Arawan's snarky laugh and then excitement when he approaches another wolf playing in the run.

Before I can reach the battlements where Rodric's shuttle will land, Father calls my siblings, our surrogates and me to his den. He stands behind his desk. His face is firm, but I sense pain behind it. "Rodric is dead. An accident aboard a warship. He was high in the rigging furling a sail when he fell. House Dolffin has cremated his body. The Remembrance will be in the Great Hall tomorrow."

Father sits and then lifts a document from his desk. It is his way of dismissing us.

I try to reach Telor, but the crowd gets in my way. I find him in the library.

"Telor? Something's wrong. Father did not say everything. He was more angry than sad. Why?"

"You know Father's moods better than I do, Garreth. You may have found a mystery. But not all mysteries are meant to be solved."

Telor turns to his book. Like Father, it is his way of dismissing me.

Arawan sleeps at the foot of my bed. Tonight, he feels my sorrow and seeks to comfort me. I see images he pulls from my mind – Rodric leading his companions and mine in play. I see images he pulls from my imagination – Rodrick and me aboard a

116

warship, swords in hand standing back-to-back fighting off pirates. I push a *thank you* to Arawan and then fall asleep.

~~~~~

Late morning the next day, Telor finds me in the dojo. I am flush from the kata and think Telor will join us, but he hurries me away. "Garreth, to your room. Bathe, put on a uniform. Nana will pack for you. Macca will care for Arawan. Do not delay."

In minutes we are on Father's shuttle. I feel the hum of the engines and the brief vibration when we pass the speed of sound. "What's happening? Where are we going?"

Telor and I are alone in Father's compartment. We both know not to sit in Father's chair and are on a bench across from it.

"We go to Fortress Dolffin," Telor says. "You are right. There is a mystery surrounding Rodric's death, and we are to solve it." He tells me it is important no one in House Dolffin, especially the Gens, thinks House Bleddyn suspects them in Rodric's death.

"Why do you bring me?" I ask.

"You are inquisitive and intelligent, but not always discreet. If you pursue this, you may expose things that should not be seen."

For a moment I am angry and frown, but I know Telor is right. Sometimes I speak before I think.

"Second," Telor says, "the ancient friendship between House Bleddyn and House Dolffin must remain unbroken. Bringing a child—"

Telor sees me open my mouth to object, then says, "I'm sorry, Garreth. You are not a child. Bringing a brother, a symbol of family and house, will help maintain amity."

"You said I was impetuous."

"Actually, I said you were not always discreet."

"My elder brothers and sisters were fostered when they were my age. Is that why I will not be fostered?"

Telor stares at the wall behind Father's desk for a long time. There is nothing to look at except the gray metal of the shuttle. "Garreth, I do not know. Father does not always tell me the why and wherefore of his decisions."

Telor waited too long before answering. Does he not know or is he lying?

"Garreth, when I do not answer you right away, you think I am lying. I see it in your frown. I think before I answer. That is part of what it means not to be impetuous. Now, let's explore the rest of the shuttle. Maybe the pilot will let you take the controls."

I guess being impetuous means I'm easily distracted, because the thought of piloting the shuttle pushes all my questions from my mind.

~~~~~

After an hour of keeping the shuttle on its pre-determined flight path, I grow bored and lie down on a bench seat. Telor shakes me awake. I don't want to admit I fell asleep, but my yawn gives me away.

"Come, it's nearly noon, we outpaced the sun. Brush your hair. You look like the Wild Man of the Mountains."

The shuttle lands on the mesa where Fortress Dolffin stands. The ramparts are lower than Fortress Bleddyn, but the walls of the mesa fall steeply to the sea on one side and to forest on the others. The sun teases my eyes with moving sparkles on the waves. I have never seen the sea or the sky so blue.

Two boys meet us. Gawain is the elder, an Academy graduate. His brother, Marwin, is Rodric's age. They wear utility jumpsuits in green and black jungle camouflage. Their belts hold energy pistols, daggers, and grace knives. Slug rifles ride over their shoulders. Their companion-guards stand behind them, dressed and armed the same.

Gawain welcomes us in his mother's name and reveals the mystery. "Rodric was murdered. A line in the ship's rigging had been weakened. Our scouts tracked the sailor we suspect to be Rodric's killer. He is on a floater over the swamp northeast of Port Dolffin. We believe he heads for the free city of Ocsiwn."

"Shall we pursue him? Or will your soldiers?" Telor asks.

"I was on the ship. I saw Rodric fall; I saw him die," Marwin says. He fights to hide his emotions, but I hear his breath catch and see his face writhe. I see anger and hatred – and loss.

119

"It is a matter of honor to find this person, to interrogate him, and to execute him," Gawain says what his brother cannot say. "My mother believes the four of us must take the lead. We have two troop shuttles loaded with floaters. Our mates will follow, but at a distance. We will leave at once if you agree."

Telor draws me aside. "Father does not expect you to face danger."

"How do you know what Father expects?" I demand. "He didn't tell me I was a token child to be left behind. Besides, if you are alone with them and I am alone here, and if House Dolffin is responsible for Rodric's death, we would both be in danger. Together, we can protect each other."

Telor nods. He steps away and speaks to Gawain. "We have jumpsuits and weapons in our shuttle. Give us a moment to change."

After we change from uniforms to more practical jumpsuits, Telor pulls two slug rifles from a rack. He hands me one. I put four magazines into my utility harness, check the chamber to be sure there isn't a slug in place, and then slide another magazine into the slot at the bottom of the receiver.

Telor takes a single energy pistol from another rack. "You are not yet qualified with the energy pistol. Do you understand?"

I understand. I also remember when Father said I would not always have modern weapons. Telor does not expect me to be in the vaward and I do not let him see my reshot and bolas. I wonder why there are jungle cammies in my size if I were supposed to be left behind.

To reach the mainland, we must cross 300 kilometers of ocean. We could do it on floaters, but I'm glad we don't have to. We fly in a shuttle to Port Dolffin and unload military floaters. I lie prone with my face in a padded hole. The floater's display is at the bottom of the hole. This one combines a forward-looking camera with radar, a navigation system, and a targeting system for rocket grenades. I shiver when I see my floater has four rocket grenades and I control them. Rocket grenades are way better than an energy pistol. Does Telor know?

The military floater is much more powerful than the one Telor taught me to fly. Gawain and Telor lift off first, so they do not see me zoom to more than a hundred meters altitude. Marwin knows I nearly lost control of the floater and tries to make me not feel bad. He zooms up and moves next to me. "We'll take high CAP," he radios. Combat Air Patrol, I think, and shiver again.

Marwin and I follow Telor and Gawain. After passing over farms and hills surrounding Port Dolffin, we reach swamp and jungle extending hundreds of kilometers eastward. Just before twilight, the Dolffin War Room sends warning of a storm approaching from the sea. We are over a swamp, but must land the floaters. Gawain spots a hummock with cypress trees and leads us to it. When we jump off the floaters to stretch our legs, we discover the hummock is not solid. We sink to our knees in muck and then struggle to climb back onto our floaters and move to a different hummock.

"I do not want to spend the night in wet boots and clothes," Gawain grumbles. I'm glad an older boy says it first. I don't want Telor to hear me complain and be sorry he brought me.

121

Marwin closes his communicator. "The storm will pass in an hour. The rain bands will miss us, and our mates are on the way with clean jumpsuits. Who is ready for tea?"

From the storage box on the back of his floater, Marwin takes a naphtha stove no bigger than his fists, pumps it to pressure, and heats water for tea. Supper is field rations of pressed meat, grain, and fruit – pemmican. It is the first time I have eaten this food. It is wonderful. I am truly a soldier, now.

While we are eating, Marwin and Gawain's mates arrive with dry jumpsuits, more rations including a pastry dessert, and fresh batteries for the floaters. Telor gathers deadfall wood and builds a fire. I take comfort from Marwin's stories of battles against pirates. They are the stories Rodric would have told me.

~~~~~

A floater's cradle is not meant for sleeping. We sleep on light, insulating blankets spread on the ground. The night is warm and we need no shelter. I'm surprised the next morning when Telor wakes me. I have slept through the night.

While we eat breakfast of hard bread and tea, Marwin's thumbs fly over the tiny keyboard of his communicator. He learns from scouts the most recent location of our target and feeds it to our navigation computers. The sun breaks the horizon when we leave the hummock and fly northeastward at top speed.

The swamp gives way to rainforest jungle. Trees form a canopy that hides the ground except where an occasional river meanders toward the sea. Telor is first to spot the man's floater on radar. "There he is … five degrees right of our course, about

200 kilometers ahead. He's slow – conserving his batteries. We will catch him in less than two hours."

Telor's estimate is correct. By noon we reach the suspected killer. The man does not see us until Gawain flies past him and swings across his bow, trying to force the man to turn toward Marwin. Instead, the man dives into the jungle. I am closest and follow too quickly to feel fear.

I unlatch the clamps of the pilot's cradle and roll my body from side to side while pushing the control stick left and right. The floater responds, turning nearly on its sides. Only the centrifugal force of the turns keeps me from falling out as I follow the man between the trees.

The man is a capable floater pilot, but he is old – way older than Telor. I am young and my reflexes and courage overwhelm him. He releases his clamps. When his floater tips too far to the side, he falls to the ground and his floater crashes into a tree. He pushes himself up and runs along a riverbank. I am only a few meters behind him. I lock the controls in neutral and lift my head and chest with one arm while spinning my bolas with the other. I release the bolas to wrap around his legs. He falls. Telor's floater passes me and drops. Telor grabs the back of the man's jumpsuit before he becomes lunch for a Sarcopterygian.

When we return to Fortress Dolffin, Telor and Gawain interrogate the man. Telor does not let me watch. "There are things you are too young to see." I hear anger and acid in his voice and know not to pout or complain.

Two hours later, the four of us meet Gens Dolffin in the War Room. She makes a video call to Fortress Bleddyn. Gawain and Marwin stand with the Gens, their mother. Telor and I stand beside them. Father is the only person at the other end. Gawain speaks for us.

"The man was a mercenary who believed he had been hired by a woman from unaligned House Astin. We cannot corroborate that. The person who hired him may have misled the man. His knowledge of the person is insufficient to locate her."

I do not have to ask if the man is dead.

~~~~~

After supper, Gawain and Marwin lead us to the Great Hall. They, Telor, and I are the only ones present. Our voices echo from the stone walls and vaulted ceiling. Marwin touches a button on his communicator and the lights go out except for a single candle on a table in the center of the otherwise empty room. Two daggers whose hilts bear the leaping dolphin of House Dolffin lie beside the candle. Gawain speaks.

"Telor and Garreth, you lost a brother. By custom, we declared brotherhood with Rodric the day he arrived. Therefore, we too, lost a brother. Your father sent you to us. We shared a quest. Together, we exacted justice. Will you both accept our offer of brotherhood?"

Telor does not hesitate, but agrees. I am uncertain at first, but follow his lead. Gawain lifts a dagger from the table. He bloods it on his arm and hands it to Marwin who also bloods the dagger.

"By the teachings of Geraint, by the courage of Camalos, and by my blood and the blood of my brother, I swear brotherhood with you, Telor and Garreth." After Gawain speaks he offers his twice-blooded dagger to Telor.

Telor accepts the dagger. He bloods his arm and then mine. "By the honor of Camalos and my blood and the blood of my brother, I swear brotherhood with you, Gawain and Marwin." Telor takes his dagger from his waist, bloods his arm and mine, then offers the dagger to Gawain.

Marwin bloods the second dagger on his arm and on Gawain's and recites the words before handing the dagger to me. It is my turn. I accept the dagger and then draw the dagger my father gave me and blood it on my arm. I turn to Telor. He holds out his arm. I see his pride in me. I echo the words of the oath and offer my dagger to Marwin. We have spoken the ancient words and exchanged daggers. Immediately after the ceremony, Telor and I board Father's shuttle for the trip home.

"I don't understand," I say after the shuttle door closes. "I gave away a dagger Father gave me in blood. I exchanged it for a dagger from another house, a dagger I also received in blood. I swore blood oath to Gawain and Marwin. But it's all mixed up."

Telor chuckles. "Father will be pleased with the exchange, and he will give you a new dagger with his blood." He gestures to the House Dolffin dagger at my waist, "We will display this one in our Great Hall. You will wear it on ceremonial occasions. You will probably not collect many like it, but each one will be important to you and to House Bleddyn. Our ancestor and Gens Dolffin's ancestor created an alliance millennia ago. It is renewed in every generation by the blood oaths of brotherhood. You and I are now part of that."

"But shouldn't it be Llywelyn?" I ask.

"Llywelyn would not be interested. He enjoys fighting more than friendship. Do not say that to anyone, especially Llywelyn."

CHAPTER 8 VILLAINY AND VENDETTA

Officially, Winter Stormtime is over, but the weather does not always respond to official pronouncements. Storms keep many of my playmates from returning to Fortress. On this day, weather on Mesa is clement, and Sani and I spend the afternoon alone in the glade. The air is cold, but the trees block the wind and the sun is bright enough to warm us. The afternoon wears on, shadows grow, and it becomes colder. Sani leads me inside. We take the rabbits I killed to the kitchen and Sani tells me to go to my schoolroom and study the old texts.

I take the handle to open the door of my schoolroom and then pause. There is a smell. Naphtha, like the fuel of Marwin's stove. *That's wrong!* I push hard to hold the door closed, but flames shoot under the door and scorch my sandals and toes. My guards pull me away. I hear one calling for a medico and another calling Father.

Father arrives before the medico and is first to open the door. His face holds more anger than I have ever seen, more than when he told me Rodric was dead. My schoolroom – books, maps, wooden soldiers, computers – is destroyed. Neither my toes nor my sandals are badly burned although the medico puts ointment on my toes and bandages them.

Telor arrives. He speaks briefly to Father then to me. "Garreth, you will take Rodric's schoolroom."

There is no time to visit Rodric's schoolroom before Father summons me to his den. I kneel and stare at the floor waiting for him to speak. The cold of the flagstones reaches my knees through the wool of my jumpsuit.

"Come here, Son," Father says. His voice is strangely soft. I step toward him. He stands and pulls me into a hug. That is unusual and I am afraid.

"Garreth, Sani is dead. He was teacher and mentor to you and Telor and Guffudd and Rodric before you. We will miss him."

Father puts his hands on my shoulders and extends his arms, pushing me away while holding me tightly. He looks into my eyes. "I know you are sad, Garreth. You are permitted to cry."

"No, Father. Sani taught me much, including how to be strong. I will not dishonor his teaching by crying. How did he die? When will we burn his body on the battlements and hold the Remembrance?"

"His body has already been burned, and I am waiting for Telor to tell me the means of Sani's death. Speak to no one of this. I will summon you."

~~~~~

I sit on the floor of my new schoolroom, reluctant to touch the things that were Rodric's. Arawan lies at my side. I see him running through the forest, chasing rabbits, looking over his shoulder and pausing occasionally so I can catch up. He is trying to comfort me with images that comfort him, images of hunting and of blood. I bury my face in the fur of his back and hug him.

Hours later, Nana enters. "Garreth? Good, you are here." I expect Telor and wonder why Nana has come. Before I can ask, the annunciator chimes. Father's voice summons all members of the house to assemble. Nana takes my hand and leads me to the Great Hall where Father tells us he executed Llywelyn for treason to house and family. When I understand what he says, anger grows in my heart. I shrug off Nana's hand and run back to my new schoolroom.

Telor enters minutes after I arrive. "I know you are angry."

"Yes, Brother." My mind races. Brief memories of Llywelyn, scraps of things I heard, things I didn't know I knew, come to me, and whirl around. They grasp one another like combatants in *Jaryeondo*, form a kata, and settle.

I say what Telor does not say. "I am angry because Llywelyn murdered Sani and tried to murder me. I am angry because Llywelyn arranged Rodric's murder. I am angry because Father executed Llywelyn. Even though he wasn't a good person, he was my brother. He was family."

"Everything you say is correct and you are right to be angry," Telor says. "Please, think about what Father said and what he did not say. And think about why he did not say everything."

Telor's words confuse me, but his voice calms me. I sit at a table full of toy soldiers and war machines. I push a few soldiers into a new position, stare at them, and take a deep breath. "Father did not describe Llywelyn's crimes because the deed without the details is horrible enough. But that is not all. Something links Rodric's death and the attack on me. Something Father will not say. What is it?"

"The fewer people who know a secret, the longer it may be kept," Telor says. "Not today, but you will learn the secret. I promise. Until then, you must not speak of this with anyone."

By saying the reason is secret, Telor admits there is a secret, one he will not tell me. I'm not happy with his answer, but I believe Telor is saying all he may. "I will obey, Brother."

~~~~~

Secrets and death yield more death as one memory triggers another. Pictures, sounds, words form in my sleeping mind. My life pod moves slowly in the empty spaces between the stars while I dream.

I am preparing for bed when ululating sirens sound. The televisors talk of enemy fighters and floaters attacking Fortress. They order non-combatants to the caverns. I reach for a uniform when Nana rushes into my room. "Come, we go to the caverns."

"No, Nana. I go to the War Room. Father will want me."

"Garreth, I forget how much you have grown. Put on your uniform and go to the War Room. Don't get in the way. Arawan? Come with me." Arawan whines. He is uncomfortable being without me and unaccustomed to taking orders from Nana. I send reassurance, and he obeys.

Yellow strobes outshine the other lights in the corridors. People pass, going toward the caverns. I hug the wall and push my way to the War Room. Father turns when I enter. He gestures. "Sit here. Watch the screen. Tell me what you see."

For a moment, I stand, barely breathing. We are under massive attack and Father asks me to help?

130

I sit in Father's chair and examine the screen. It shows a view of Mesa and the surrounds from above. Red arrows ... red dots ... red boxes ... move toward Fortress from west, south, east. Then, arrows pop up in the north.

I recognize the symbols from my war games. But this is not the playroom computer. The tension in the voices of the controllers tells me it is not a game or a simulation, but war.

The more I see, the better I understand. I watch red arrows disappear. Destroyed or damaged so badly they crash. I see blue icons disappear and know they mark where our warriors die.

Red shuttles in the south approach the forest. Radar loses them. Are they flying among the trees? Not likely. They landed. "Father ... the adversary landed soldiers to the south."

Father knows the sensors cannot display this, but hears the confidence in my voice and speaks to Telor, who takes the Senior Controller's position and issues orders. "Infantry Group Seven, Floater Flights Four and Five, move to the forest south of Mesa. You will encounter floaters and ground forces. Coordinates follow."

Perhaps the attackers did not plan well. Perhaps they did not believe House Bleddyn's commitment to the defense of Mesa and of Council House and Academy. Perhaps they did not think we would use those defenses against them. Whatever the case, they are wrong. Father orders the defenses of Mesa unlocked. Telor fires two volleys of anti-aircraft missiles, which nearly annihilate the airborne attackers.

With the advantage of height, our infantry picks off the enemy from the south trying to climb Mesa. The adversary's order to retreat is too late. I look at the clock. It is not yet noon. The battle is over and I haven't had breakfast.

I follow Father from the War Room to his den where breakfast is waiting. It is strange to sit with Father and Telor at the Privy Council table with tea, porridge, fruit, and sweet rolls. I am very happy to be in their company. I think I will burst from my uniform when Father says, "You were right when you said they landed soldiers to the south. How did you know?"

"It is what I would have done, Father. It is what Elfyn did in our war games after last stormtime."

"Did you win?"

"Yes, Father. But it was close."

After breakfast, I return to the War Room and watch on a screen while Telor interrogates a captive. Telor learns House Tarren was behind the attack. Disgraced by her capture, the prisoner redeems her honor by killing herself after the interrogation. I don't watch, but I know it happened. I wonder if I would be able to do that if I were captured.

~~~~~

The next day, I ask Telor what keeps Tarren's vendetta against our house alive. "The war with the Adversary," he says. "The Adversary destroyed some of our starships, and probably some of Tarren's, too. However, Tarren thinks our house is benefitting too greatly from this war."

I remember Father talking about causes of war and excuses for war. "The Adversary's attacks on our ships were the proximate cause of the war – the sparks that lit the fire. But what

132

are the underlying causes?" I demand. Telor brings me to Father's den for an answer.

Father lectures me about blood. "Blood is important," Father says. "Blood kinship, blood oaths, and bloodlines."

"My mates and I learned the Adversary is not of-the-blood. But that is not why we are at war."

Father grimaces at my persistence. "We know the Adversary is responsible for our genetic heritage. We know the Adversary seeded this planet with cells that one day burst with their DNA and began our evolution. They created us and then abandoned us to struggle during the great ice ages that changed our evolutionary history."

I think of Soosong. "A bastard is a child whose father does not recognize him or her and who has no house. You say by abandoning us, the Adversary declares us bastards. But are they truly our fathers?"

Telor explains how we know the Adversary are our ancestors. Our starships found other planets with DNA too similar to be coincidence – too similar to be the result of amino acids drifting through space despite our understanding of chemical determinism and panspermia. "At some point, our DNA diverged from other primate lines on World. The thralls and we are descendants of primates who adopted hemocyanin. We evolved and became sentient."

Father completes the explanation. "A House Bleddyn ship found a planet with several tribes of beings who resemble the saber-tooth cats of our world, although they walk erect. Their hands have both opposable thumbs and retractable claws. They make tools and weapons; they have a language. They are sentient but they are not-of-the-blood. Their DNA matches ours to more than 93%. We are close kin to these cats. Someday, we will revisit the planet of these great cats. We will look for other planets on which we have kin. Meanwhile, I do what I must do to ensure the survival and primacy of House Bleddyn."

There is more. I think Father is hiding something. Father knows I have more questions, but he dismisses me.

I sleep little that night. Questions and arguments swirl, unsettling my mind. Father told me the ultimate reason for this war is that the Adversary abandoned us. But we became the dominant species on World. We use selective breeding to create new species, like my horse Rhiannon, to serve us. Even though we are in vendetta with enemies, we have conquered space and time with our FTL comms and starship drive.

Father says we are bastards because the Adversary seeded World and then abandoned us. Is this true, or only an excuse? Is Father distorting the truth? I'm afraid to say, 'lying,' even to myself. Why does Father want this war? He is using it to make House Bleddyn strong, but are there other reasons? It is early morning before the questions and arguments in my mind settle. I roll over, punch my pillow, and fall asleep.

~~~~~

Telor finds me at breakfast. I tell him what I decided last night. "It's like The War of Conquest. The difference between the reason for war and the excuse for war."

"A good answer," Telor says. "But it is only the beginning of understanding. House Bleddyn will not destroy seeded planets.

134

Gens Tarren is not so careful. He lands soldiers on planets where primates have evolved, and exterminates them. He destroys planets if his people don't like the path evolution is taking. We have evidence he uses nuclear fission weapons to do this. Council has rejected our evidence. Tarren says his ships will continue to do these things. Father considers that justification under the Rules of Vendetta to attack Tarren starships. Vendetta has expanded from World to the stars."

~~~~~

Thralls and soldiers clear fields and forests of the wreckage from Gens Tarren's attack. Father holds a Remembrance for our soldiers who died. Training continues. I go to my bedroom after class to change for the dojo. I put on the pants of my dobok and pick up the jacket when Nana enters. "Telor says to wear a utility jumpsuit and sandals. I am to pack for a ten-day trip. The shuttle departs in half an hour. We must hurry."

I put aside my dobok and my surprise. Nana hands me a duffle and I race to the hanger where the soldiers of the Mountain Company are loading shuttles with shovels and rakes. Telor beckons me.

"What is happening?" I ask. "Nana said ten days. Gardening tools?"

Before Telor can answer, I hear the rumble of linked treads on concrete – the sound of a battle tank. I turn to see only a bright yellow earthmover, with a scoop in the back and a blade in the front. "We're going to build a road? May I drive the earthmover? Will we be in wilderness? Will we camp—"

"Slow down, Brother. You will help House Marredudd replant the forest that burned last year. Did you forget Father offered this? Yes, you will bivouac, and you may drive the earthmover – after someone trains you. You will be gone at least a month."

A soldier wearing the insignia of the Mountain Company hustles me into a shuttle packed with soldiers. Two slide over to give me room on the bench seat between them. No one speaks during the flight; most sleep.

The shuttle lands on a hilltop from which I see acres and acres of devastation. Blackened, ragged stumps of what once were great trees poke from the grass. A space is ready for us – debris removed and the ground leveled. The soldiers erect tents, hang loud speakers and lights on poles, and set up a Field War Room. My first tasks are to collect all the shovels and put them in a rack, help unload cartons of rations, and dig privies.

I listen to the soldiers while I work.

"We'll be here for a month, maybe longer."

"At least it's not winter. Marredudd's as cold as a witch's ti—"

"It's warmer than the Southern Continent, which is where I'll send you if you don't get to work." This comes from a sergeant. She is beside us, digging, not just giving orders. I think she is not serious in her threat, but the soldiers do work a little harder.

Loud speakers call assembly for mid-day meal. I stand on line with the soldiers for pemmican bars. At another line, we fill our canteens with water. Some soldiers want to give up their places in line for me. They turn, see me, hesitate, and then turn away. Telor must have told them not to treat me as a scion of Bleddyn. I am happy and proud he did. Now, all I must do is prove to these soldiers, the toughest of House Bleddyn's Home Guard, I am worthy of this treatment and perhaps, their respect.

I sit on the ground among the soldiers. One calls me, 'My Lord' when I sit near him. I thank him for his greeting, but say, "Just Garreth, if you please, Master Sergeant." Of course, I know who he is. He's the Commander of the Mountain Company.

He laughs, and then says, "In that case, Just Garreth, I am Just Rhingyll." Then he says, to no one in particular, "There's a lot of green sprouting out there."

I look over the burned land. I see the green Rhingyll spoke of. "Seedlings," I say. "The fire was hot enough to allow the seeds to germinate. Since we didn't bring any baby trees, I guess we will dig those up and replant them in rows and columns."

"A very good guess," a voice comes from behind me. "May I join you and Master Sergeant Rhingyll?"

A woman in a jumpsuit with the House Marredudd crest and captain's flashes explains the details of the task. "After the fire, we seeded the entire area with grass to hold the dirt from eroding in wind and rain. Some seeds from the trees sprouted where they fell. Some washed downhill and then sprouted. You can see the clusters. You will need the earthmover to clear stumps.

"Master Sergeant, I understand you have charge of Garreth."

I am not sure what she means, but I soon find out. When the loud speakers signal the end of meal period, Rhingyll stands and calls me to follow him. "We must clear stumps before we can plant, but we must dig up seedlings before pulling stumps. You will need a spade and one of those canvas bags. You have gloves?"

I nod and decide no matter what he said before, the correct response is, "Yes, Master Sergeant." Rhingyll is pleased.

I am happy when in the heat of afternoon the soldiers swap their boots for sandals and strip to loincloths and, for the women, an elastic band over their breasts. I spend the afternoon digging up seedlings, carefully preserving their roots, and putting them in the canvas bag. It is hot and dirty work, but I watch the soldiers carefully and make sure my bag is as full as any of theirs.

An hour before sunset, the loud speakers signal the end of the workday. Rhingyll leads the command element, which now includes me, to the showers. I have swum and showered naked with boys and girls – playmates my age – but I am nervous among adults. The showers are pipes from a water tender. We stand on a slab of pierced-steel planking – the PSP used to build temporary roads – to keep our feet off the dirt. Only my desire to be treated as a soldier, to feel grown up, to make my new mates accept me, gives me the courage to remove my loincloth.

Naked except for sandals, I follow Rhingyll to the command element's tent. We hang our wet clothes, little as they are, on a rope and remove our sandals before entering.

A corporal who attached himself to me points to my duffle, a cot, and a sleeping bag. "Your gear is there. Evening meal will be soon. Loincloth or jumpsuit is sufficient. You did not drink enough water this afternoon. Drink everything in your canteen, now."

I feel a flash of anger at his criticism, but the vambrace controls my anger. "Yes, thank you, Corporal. Please call me Garreth."

The corporal hesitates, but he heard Rhingyll call me Garreth. "Thank you, Garreth. I am Cos, and you may use my name but I am a corporal. Master Sergeant Rhingyll ordered me to integrate you into the element. Sometimes I will give orders. Sometimes we will speak formally; sometimes we will be less formal. You are responsible for knowing when those times are."

"I understand, Corporal. This is a formal time. Am I right?"

"You are right. Now, informal time. Do you snore? I ask because my cot is next to yours."

"No, I do not snore." I try very hard to sound indignant. Then I say, "Do you snore? I ask because my cot is next to yours."

"Yes, he snores," a voice from the center of the tent calls.

"I do not snore!" Cos says.

The element tosses friendly insults at one another while drying and dressing. Another challenge for me – to be included in the teasing.

Supper is a real meal, served in a mess tent with trestle tables. Today's supper is a meat stew with vegetables and fresh bread. Dessert is apricot pudding. Apricots are a luxury and an important source of the copper in our blood. I realize despite their rugged reputation, someone takes very good care of the Mountain Company.

The next day, I learn to drive the earthmover. I guide it with levers to advance or retard power to the treads. Three more levers set the height and angles of the blade. The trick is to use those levers to scrape dirt or debris while moving forward. The scoop in the back is used to uproot stumps. The operator's seat swivels to face the blade or the scoop. The scoop is used only when stopped, which is good, because the scoop has six levers. I learn until mid-day meal and then join the element to dig up more seedlings.

The third day, I operate the earthmover by myself to smooth a large rectangle near the camp. I realize about halfway through I am creating a footy pitch.

The fourth day I plant seedlings, all day. Soldiers bring ration bars and water for mid-day meal, and we take our supper after dark. It is a hard day, but I keep up with the soldiers. They no longer hesitate to speak to me, to tease me about being no taller than a seedling, or to stand in line in front of me for rations and water. We are not yet mates, but we are moving in that direction.

The next day, and every fifth day afterwards, is a rest day, although no one really rests, but engages in games and sports, wagering little things on the outcome. At home, my playmates and I wager our desserts. The soldiers make different wagers. I am good at footy, shorter than most of the soldiers and faster than all of them. My element wins the game. They laugh with the losers, who wagered the singing of a bawdy song. I try not to blush when I hear the song, but I'm sure some of my new mates see that I do.

Corporal Cos makes sure I recharge my vambrace every fifth day, but I don't think it works. My thoughts are clear and I easily become distracted. I want to question this, but there are so many things that demand my attention, so much work to do, and I am too tired each evening to question anything.

On the twentieth day, something makes me sure the vambrace is not working. I struggle to focus on the game of footy we're playing against one of Marredudd's elements. I am near the goal, waiting for one of my team to kick the ball to me, when a Marredudd soldier steals the ball. I'm sure he catches my eye before he kicks the ball into my stomach, too high for me to intercept and I may not touch it with my hands. The ball falls to the ground. I cannot contain my anger. I control the ball and set up for a kick that will strike his face.

No! I tell myself. I visualize the positions of players and see one of my team is open. I step across the ball, kick it with my heel, and then spin. My teammate returns the ball and I kick it into the goal. Top that, Marredudd dope! I'm shaking from the reaction and use the mandatory time-out after my goal to control my feelings. When I calm myself, I understand my vambrace isn't giving me the right drugs, or not enough of them.

Without the drugs, I must control myself.

~~~~~

Our job is complete at the end of the sixth ten-day. There are still acres of forest to be replanted, but Marredudd's Home Guard started the task before we arrived and will complete it in another ten-day. We break down the camp and fill cargo shuttles with tents, pipes and PSP, cots, sleeping bags, shovels, and other equipment.

We do not return home, but go to Fortress Marredudd, where quarters are opened, showers have hot water, and thralls clean our clothes. "Uniforms for evening meal," Cos announces. "The Gens invites us to a banquet."

Rhingyll comes to our quarters to inspect my uniform. "You must be proper. You and I will sit at Gens Marredudd's table."

"No, Master Sergeant!" I am angry. I slow my thoughts and soften my voice. I am getting better at that. "I will sit with my mates. I am a soldier, not a game piece."

Rhingyll's face hardens. His eyes narrow and his lips tighten. After a few moments, he relaxes. "I will explain to Gens Marredudd. She will understand. Honor, valor, loyalty, including loyalty to your newest companions. Do not drink too much beer. Your body cannot handle as much as an adult."

After the banquet, we return to our quarters where my element salutes me and then teases me while deciding on a nickname. I hear "Cute Butt" and others even more ribald offered several times. They settle on *Ghost Runner*, for my ability to slip between members of the opposing team at footy. Corporal Cos gives me a canteen and says it took him an entire month to get me to drink enough water. At his urging, I drink it all. Beer. Oh well, they have proven themselves to be friends and I will be safe among them.

I'm no longer in control of myself when Master Sergeant Rhingyll joins the party to give me a patch for my uniform – the insignia of the Mountain Company, which he attaches just below the house crest. "My Lord," Master Sergeant Rhingyll says, "Your Father affirmed this. You are now a member of the Mountain Company."

Corporal Cos adds, "You are required by both honor and tradition to wear this patch whenever you are in uniform."

Despite the beer, I manage to stand at attention. "You honor me, and I accept your honor. However, I must know more of our history and traditions. May Corporal Cos join my companion-guards, at least for a time, to be my teacher?"

I see in their eyes and minds the approval of both men.

Father and Telor are waiting when the shuttle returns to Fortress. Master Sergeant Rhingyll is first off; I am behind him. Corporal Cos follows me. I see Telor's eyes widen when he sees the patch of the Mountain Company on my jumpsuit. Master Sergeant Rhingyll salutes Father. "Missions accomplished, sir." I understand. There was much more to the mission than planting trees.

～～～～

I am still making Arawan a part of my life and making my guards and mates comfortable with him when I learn Father is planning an attack on House Tarren using the Mountain Company. It is my company and I resolve to take part.

Months ago, House Tarren mounted a massive attack on Fortress Bleddyn – an attack we won decisively. Tarren's forces included houses not in vendetta with House Bleddyn, a breach of protocol. Father brings this to the Council, but his motion to censure Tarren fails. Therefore, Father invokes the rules of vendetta. Telor identifies a target, a fortress overlooking the Pass of Perdition. Father agrees we should capture the fortress and cede it to House Dwyer, whose territory is closer to the pass than Tarren's. He invites Master Sergeant Rhingyll and Telor to the library where they create a plan.

When Corporal Cos tells me about the plan, I demand to participate. Father is neither surprised, nor reluctant to permit this, but reminds me I must provide for Arawan while I am away. I know Brother-minus-six Macca will be happy to have Arawan all to himself while I am gone.

~~~~~

Long before we had Anti-Gravity shuttles, ground transport through the pass was critical to both trade and to an invading army. Cos explains the fortress was built to defend against medieval weapons, not AG floaters and shuttles. The curtain wall is four meters thick and fifty meters high. Narrow crenels allow archers to fire on attackers. Machicolations – overhanging holes from which defenders can fire arrows or dump boiling oil – stud the wall.

Rhingyll plans to attack from below. The water supply of the fortress is an underground river. Years ago, a turbine was suspended in the river to provide electricity. Wearing underwater breathing apparatus, we enter a sinkhole high in the mountain and allow the river to carry us to the fortress. For safety, the Command Element and I, led by Corporal Cos, are roped together. The current is swift, but each of us holds onto protrusions in the rocky channel, communicating by radios built into our masks to ensure the current does not sweep us past the fortress to the waterfall below. The Second Element follows us.

It's like rock climbing, but upside down. After several difficult hours, we reach the sub-basement of the fortress and climb to the top of the cistern. The room is empty except for us. We discard our breathing equipment and take our weapons from waterproof pouches.

Tarren's commander does not expect this attack. Before dawn, we rise from the lower levels of the fortress and catch his troops unaware. Those we do not surprise climb the spiral staircases. We hold the defenders on the stairs until the Third Element, held in reserve, fast-ropes from shuttles to the battlements and attacks from above.

Besides my reshot and bolas, which are with me always, I am armed with an energy pistol. It has only five shots, but I carry extra charge blocks. I sling a slug rifle over my shoulder.

I find the pistol more useful than any other weapon and disable or kill seven of Tarren's troops before I reach the battlements and face a soldier barely older than me. I hear the *click* when he presses the trigger of his energy pistol, but I already know it is exhausted.

"Please, I surrender," he says.

My element moves on. I see they are not in difficulty, so I may deal with this encounter.

"You tried to fire your pistol. If it had been charged, you would have killed me. You are an enemy. Why should I not kill you this instant?"

145

"I knew the pistol was exhausted. I used it to fire imaginary bolts at your soldiers. I knew it would not kill you. I know I am dead, but I don't want to be dead. Please..." The boy drops the pistol to the ground, unslings his rifle and lays it carefully at his feet.

"Your rifle still holds a charge," I say.

"Yes," he says. "But I could not fire at you. Your eyes – they cut through me."

"I have a saber for cutting things. My eyes look for targets." This does not reassure him.

I face a dilemma. I cannot abandon my companions' fight but I cannot leave an enemy in our rear. Something Telor said finds its way to my confused thoughts. "Pretend to be confident, even if you are not. This is part of valor." Another aphorism, this one from my father says, "Trust must be offered before it can be earned." I think for a moment.

"You are a prisoner of war. However, I cannot at this moment make you captive. If you will give your parole, I will not kill you. What is your name?"

It takes the boy only a moment to accept. "I am Alexi. I give you my parole and hope you will live to claim it."

He says no more about his mates or the defenses of the castle. I believe him to be honorable and accept his parole. However, I remove the charge block from his energy rifle.

When the battle is over, I return to find my parolee tending wounded from both sides. I am not needed to help, so I watch him work. He is busy with bandages and intravenous fluids. When the initial triage is complete, soldiers take him away. Master Sergeant Rhingyll calls Father with news we have taken the fortress and I am unharmed.

I become angry when Master Sergeant Rhingyll orders Alexi taken in captive's bonds to my father. When I object, Rhingyll reminds me I am not Garreth, scion of Bleddyn. "Private Garreth, he gave you his parole and acted honorably thereafter," he says. "He will not be mistreated."

I realize I can not expect more. "Yes, Master Sergeant."

~~~~~

Father summons me to his den where Telor, Alexi, and Master Sergeant Rhingyll are waiting. Alexi's eyes widen when he sees Arawan, but he does not flinch, even when the wolf sniffs his feet. I feel the wolf's approval of Alexi. Now, I must seek Father's approval.

"Telor tells me you accepted this soldier's parole."

"As you taught me, Father, '… well treated or crushed.' There was no call to crush him."

Father agrees. "You interpret Karmet's words correctly." He asks Rhingyll to escort Alexi from the room and then asks me, "What would you have me do?"

"Father, you and Telor are good judges of character. I know Telor has examined him and reported to you. Do you believe he would honor an oath of loyalty to House Bleddyn?"

Father and Telor expect the question, because both answer easily. After some discussion – mostly Father and Telor listening to me talking – Father summons Alexi and Master Sergeant Rhingyll.

"Master Sergeant, my son Garreth has a question for you." In this way, Father establishes I am for the moment not Private Garreth.

Rhingyll faces me. "Yes, My Lord."

"Master Sergeant, Alexi gave me his parole. He honored the trust I extended. He applied his knowledge and skill to bind and treat my wounded brothers and sisters of the Mountain Company. I believe he is worthy of trust and his oath is valid. Will you accept him as a recruit-private in the Mountain Company, test him, and determine if Father should adopt him into House Bleddyn?"

I detect a smile when Rhingyll asks, "Would you be a part of this?"

"As you command, Master Sergeant." My words confirm I am still a Private in the Mountain Company. Rhingyll and I have taken one another's measure and created a new understanding.

~~~~~

During the next six months, Master Sergeant Rhingyll summons Corporal Cos and me to join the Mountain Company in exercises – physical and mental. We march over rugged terrain with heavy packs. We swim in icy rivers and conduct war games of laser tag and paintball with other elements of the Home Guard and with allies. Alexi is always in our element, and Rhingyll debriefs Corporal Cos and me afterwards.

The critical test comes when we bivouac in the mountains southwest of House Eryr. Everyone is exhausted after a full day of drills among the rocks. We establish a camp near a freshet from which we fill our canteens and the cooks draw water for supper. At dusk, we hear a screech that echoes from the hills. It is followed by another.

"Bobcat," someone says.

"Bobcats – more than one," someone else adds.

 At over 70 kg of solid muscle, with teeth as long and sharp as those of the saber-tooth cats, the *Pseudaelurus* is a formidable foe. Alexi draws the short straw for the midnight watch. Corporal Cos whispers to me. His message is simple. It will be my decision to arm Alexi or to join him on watch. I take my energy pistol and two charge blocks from my utility harness and hand them to Alexi. "You will need these."

"My Lord, I cannot—"

"Recruit Private Alexi, I am not your lord. I am Private Garreth. We are both in the Mountain Company to test our mettle and our honor. Six months ago, I held your life in my hands.

Tonight, if this clowder of bobcats attacks us, you will hold my life and our companions' lives in your hands. Are you prepared?"

Alexi does not hesitate. "Yes, Private Garreth. I am prepared."

Alexi does not need the pistol and returns it the next morning. When we reach Fortress, Master Sergeant Rhingyll orders the quartermaster to issue Alexi weapons – including energy weapons – and equipment appropriate to a combat medic in the Mountain Company.

~~~~~

My teachers keep us busy and tired with exercises in the dojo, games in the forest, and lessons in the schoolroom. Winter Stormtime approaches and the weather turns gloomy. Low clouds obscure the sun. Leaves of the hardwoods turn from green to red and gold, then to brown, then fall, leaving trees dark and barren. The gloom slips into Fortress and our minds.

Telor tries to make his lessons exciting. "Today, you will learn more about the Adversary and his schedule for seeding worlds." We perk up, but only a little.

Ceirois interrupts. "One of our ships found a planet that had its final seeding, a planet where they found primates grown from the DNA capsules."

1. Cyanobacteria
2. Fungus, simple sea life
3. Simple vegetation, insects
4. Birds, reptiles, complex plant life, amphibians
5. Mammals

"Why did they seed and then abandon that planet?" Telor asks. This is what he wants us to understand.

"Something is wrong with the planet," Ceirois says. "The seeds didn't grow. Or they grew the wrong way – stunted."

Elfyn, who is usually quiet, understands. "No! They forgot, or they lost the planets. They lost their starcharts."

"Why?" Telor asks.

"Vendetta," Elfyn says. "Like the Res Publica, they are locked in vendetta. They compete with one another to seed planets. They engage in war among the stars. During war, they lose knowledge of the seeded planets."

"Council believes this," Telor says. "This is why we colonize planets we think the Adversary abandoned, even though they hold the seeds of those who might become our rivals."

I pay little attention to the rest of Telor's lesson, thinking about the war among the stars, the war between the Adversary and us, the wars among the Adversary, and the war between House Bleddyn and House Tarren.

CHAPTER 9: ESCAPE FROM FORTRESS

The weather after Spring Stormtime will be calm and warm for my escape. This will be the third time I escaped to explore the outside world. Once, Father tracked me by a locator in a sandal; the next time, by a locator implanted in my thigh. I remove the locator from my sandal and cut the one from my thigh. It is painful, but a warrior must learn pain and its lessons. The bloody locator is on my bed. It will be a clear message to Father when I am found missing. I hide the wolf-head dagger Father gave me and take a plain one from the armory.

It is easy to escape from Fortress. Doors open to my hand. The postern gate in the walls is not key-locked against being opened outward. A flaw in our security, for a traitor could open it from inside and admit enemies. I will tell Father. Perhaps it will lessen my punishment when I am caught, for I know I will be caught – and punished. It is midnight when I run across the greensward and enter the forest. I take a moment to breathe the night air. Then, I adjust the bandage on my thigh and run downhill along a game trail. The luminescence of the plants and the warmth of animals guide me.

The first dangerous animal I encounter is a small cat. It weighs about fifteen kilograms, unlike its larger, saber-tooth cousins, which live on the savannah and can weigh up to four hundred kilograms. However, its species is vicious. This one is on a branch overhanging the game trail, waiting for prey. I know it is there before I see it and draw my energy pistol in time to shoot it as it leaps from the branch. The cat provides not only my first touch of danger but also my breakfast. The energy of the pistol cooked it, and I only have to remove the skin and clean out the insides.

I do not stop to do this, but continue walking, leaving a trail of cat parts. After breakfast, I find a stream to wash the cat's blood from my body and clothes. I wade down the stream to foil the scent hounds, the trained wolves Father will send after me. I left Arawan in the pens and wonder if he will cooperate with Father's search teams. Soon, the stream crosses a road leading westward. I'm looking for a town I've only heard of – Cytgord.

~~~~~

Four days pass before the forest opens to a town. This must be Cytgord. I quiver with nervousness. I decide it is not fear, but anticipation and present myself to the guards.

"Name?" they ask. If I say Garreth of House Bleddyn, I would have to prove my identity. And they would call Father.

"Hogarth," I say. By not offering a House, I admit I am a bastard.

One sees my energy pistol. "Well armed for a bastard. Do you accept the peace bond?"

"What is that, sir?"

He pulls two strands of yarn from a pile. They are bright red. "I will wrap these around your dagger and your pistol. The bonds show you are here with peaceful intent and will not use your weapons. If you do not accept the peace bond, you will not

154

be allowed into Cytgord. If you accept the peace bond and then draw a weapon, you will be anathema and may be executed by any member of the guard."

None of his weapons – sword, dagger, energy pistol, and slug rifle – have peace bonds. I wonder if a weapon drawn in self-defense would mark me for execution. Given the sternness of the guard, I decide it would.

"I understand and I accept the terms."

Minutes later, I am walking down a wide, cobblestone street. The street is busy, but not crowded. Gray stone buildings, two and three stories with businesses on the ground floor, line the street. A crowd draws my attention. In the center of town, a message board lists openings for mercenaries. The crowd around the board shifts and ripples like water over rocks in a mountain stream. I do not resist the ebb and flow, which bring me to the board where a man is reading aloud the announcements. I realize most of the people in the crowd cannot read.

A girl stands beside me and pretends to pay attention to the reader. When he pauses, I walk away. She follows and speaks with confidence. "You're new."

"How do you know?"

"Your peace bonds. The color is bright. The ends are not ragged. Look at mine. I've been here for two months and four auctions. See how faded they are? Why are you here?"

"Why are you here?" I counter.

"I want to find a position that will bring me honor and maybe adoption into a house. You?"

"What kind of position?" I ask.

She believes her goals and mine are the same, so she answers. "We are too young to be hired as mercenaries, even to be recorded in the Guild Hall. You're too young to be an assassin unless you're hiding more than you are revealing. We might find a position as a soldier-in-training. Some young boys and girls are selected to expand the gene pool of a small house or sept. You were paying more attention to the message board than to the reader. Can you read and write?"

"Yes."

"You're lucky. You might be hired as a scribe. If you're really good, you might become a tutor for an important child of a house. You're also attractive and pleasant to look at. You might be hired as a bed warmer."

"Bed warmer?" I ask.

"Surely you …" the girl says and looks closely at my face. "No, you don't know. Where were you brought up you don't know about bed warmers?"

The girl answers her own question. "House Bleddyn. It's the closest house where attractive people – thralls and Res Publica – are not tasked to warm the bed and sometimes more for a high house member. You had a position with House Bleddyn, but you left. Why?"

The girl is curious but not hostile, so I answer. "I never left the fortress. I want to learn things I can't learn hiding behind the walls, so I ran away. Please do not betray me."

"What is your name?" the girl asks. "Tell me true and I will not betray you."

I believe her and do not hesitate, even though I have been missing long enough for news to reach Cytgord. "Garreth," I say. "Garreth Bleddyn."

"By Karmet, you are he. I am Brân. Unlike you, I am a real bastard. There must be a dozen mercenaries looking for you." Her eyes dart into the crowd that fills the street. Then, she grabs me and puts her arms around me.

"Put your arms around me and kiss me," she says.

"What?"

"I promised not to betray you. If you don't kiss me, you will betray yourself."

I feel the truth in what she says, put my arms around her, and kiss her. Afterwards, my cheek presses into hers; my lips touch an ear. I whisper. "Why?"

"Because Garreth Bleddyn would not do this. He would have nothing to do with a bastard. There were four mercenaries looking at us and trying to match your face with the images they received."

Brân invites me to stay in her room. "It is too late in the day to get your own room," she says. "Besides, it will add to your disguise. Searchers will look for a single boy."

Brân's room is on the second floor of a bar. There is one bed. A pitcher of water and a bowl for washing sit on a shelf. A small window overlooks an alley between buildings. Toilet facilities are down the hall, shared by a dozen rooms. Brân insists I remove my clothes and clean myself. "The bed is narrow," she says. "I don't need a smelly body part poking me."

She sees I am excited by our closeness, and demands I wear a protective sheath. "If I were to become pregnant by you? Both the child in my womb and I would be destroyed."

"Why? Why would this happen?"

"You are blood of the highest house," she whispers. "Your house holds power by mixing blood with women of high status. You would not be allowed to impregnate a bastard girl of no status, to bring unknown blood into your house."

I laugh. "My seed was collected, separated into many vials, and frozen. When the time is right, it will be combined with the eggs of women selected by my father. By then, I hope to be on a starship, at translight speed. I may never see my children. My father would not prohibit any relationship I found pleasant. He would not prohibit my friendship with anyone who did not pose a threat to me. No child I sired would be killed."

Brân's face freezes into a frightening picture. "Perhaps not by your house," she says. "Your faith in them is strong, as it should be. Your child would not be killed by your house, but by your enemies. You may have children you will never know. I will not bear a child who would be killed. We both are cursed."

She blows out the candle.

~~~~~

"It has been five days since you arrived," Brân says. "When is the last time you charged your vambrace?"

I count the days. Two days before I left Fortress, four days of walking, five days here. "Eleven days ago. I am without drugs for two days, perhaps three. I feel … I feel liberated!"

I see her concern. "Brân, please do not be afraid. This is not the first time I have been without the drugs in my vambrace. I am struggling to learn how to cope without them."

"But you are not coping. This morning, you chased a cockroach from our breakfast table. I'm afraid for you. If you melt down in public, you will be exposed and killed. There are chemists who will recharge your vambrace without asking questions."

"If I present my vambrace to a chemist, my father will know where I am. I thought you were my friend. Will you trust me or not?" I demand.

"If you have a seizure because you are without drugs you will be caught. It would be much worse than your Father's anger. I will help you find a chemist for your own safety."

I accept her argument, but beg for one more drug-free day. "I am only beginning to understand how to control my anger, how to focus." She agrees, reluctantly.

I wake the next morning with a headache and a knot on my head. Brân is already angry. "You had an episode last night. You were yelling and smashing your fist onto the table. If it happened in public, you would have been jailed. I stopped you the only way I could. How is your head?"

I know why she knocked me unconscious. I feel her concern and her loyalty. I forgive the insult and follow her to an apothecary.

"He will crush the pills thrall children take, dissolve them in salt water, and inject it into the vambrace," Brân says. She holds my arm while we walk through the crowds of Cytgord.

We reach the chemist's shop through an alley and up a narrow stairway. Cooking smells mingle with the sharp odors of ethanol, iodine, and others I cannot identify. Brân explains our errand. The chemist presses a buzzer to my vambrace, reads its screen, and quotes a price. I place coins on the counter. He injects the drugs into the ports one at a time using a syringe after he cleans the ports and the tip of the syringe with ethanol.

In only moments the drugs calm me. I feel myself drifting, losing the sharpness that came when the drugs ran out. This is why I hate the drugs and the vambrace.

We walk from the chemist's shop toward a café. It is the place where we are most comfortable.

"If I do not learn what the vambrace's drugs do to me, I will never learn to control myself without the drugs." I raise an eyebrow at Brân's sneer.

"You were not in control."

"I know. If you had not been there, I would have probably ended up in the custody of the guard, or worse. I owe you my life and my freedom." She shrugs.

Is this not important to her, or does she not know how important it is?

When we reach the café, Brân selects a table not in the dark recesses or on the bright patio, but in between the two. We order a meal. While we wait, we talk. Brân seems to relax. She does not see Father enter. He wears mufti. It is the first time I have seen him out of uniform. He sits at our table as our meals arrive. Brân tenses and would have drawn her dagger and broken the peace bond except I hold her hand below the table.

"Please bring another of those," Father says to the waiter.

"It has been a long time since we shared a meal at a public café, Garreth," Father says.

"It has been never, Father."

"Hmm. Perhaps it was Guffudd," he says. "I will correct that. Will you introduce your friend?"

I keep my voice low. Father is risking a lot to be in public without his guards. "Father, I present my friend, Brân," I say in the ancient language. When I say 'friend,' I use the form of the word meaning 'trusted companion.' It is only one step removed from 'sworn in blood.' Brân knows this and is uncomfortable, but I believe she will accept the next step in friendship.

"Brân, I greet you in the name of my ancestors, and thank you for rescuing my son."

"Rescuing, sir?" Bran has overcome her nervousness, and speaks boldly though quietly.

"Not all the mercenaries here are friendly to him, or me. There were several whose goal was his capture and sale to my enemies. When you concealed him from casual observation, you also concealed him from them. Quick thinking on your part. Ah! My food is here. Why have you two not begun? It will not be good cold."

Father fills our meal with small talk. He asks me about my journey through the forest and suggests our lunch is better than the cat I killed.

"Actually, Father, that was the first time I killed and ate my prey. It was a special taste I will never experience again."

Father looks at me. "Another thing I missed in your life; something I can not correct. I am sorry."

He asks Brân about her life and her goals without seeming to pry. At the end of the meal, Father stands. Half the people in the café stand at the same time. Some move to the entrance; others follow us. Brân would have hung back except Father takes her arm companionably and leads her to an unmarked shuttle that lands in the street.

"Brân, you saved my son's life. Surely that is worth more than lunch at a mercenary café. Please, join us at Fortress Bleddyn for supper."

"I'm worth both a lunch and a supper?" I say. Father has something more in mind, and I tease him to relieve Brân's anxiety.

162

"Oh, perhaps a bit more. Once you complete your punishment for running away." Brân is thoroughly confused and I know if I say anything else Father will tie my words into knots.

~~~~~

The trip from Cytgord is mercifully short, because Brân's nervousness has moved to her belly, and she is in danger of becoming airsick. I feel her relief when she steps from the shuttle onto the solid ground of the landing pad. Then, I feel her awe when she sees Fortress Bleddyn.

"It's huge…" Her voice is soft.

"Mostly empty, now. Family, servants, and the Home Guard. Fortress is full only during stormtime when kith and kin and thralls seek shelter. Then, it's really full. Come, I'll take you to a room where you can rest and clean up. A thrall will bring you something to wear to supper."

I see her reluctance. "Father will expect formality at supper. It will be a uniform, and you may wear dagger and grace knife. The soldier," I point, "will take your energy pistol for safekeeping. It is a sign of Father's trust that you kept it on the shuttle."

When the chime sounds to assemble for dinner, I escort Brân from her room. She wears a house uniform, but the shield is not the Wolf of Bleddyn, but an intricate design of interwoven circles. I do not know what it means, if anything. Seven siblings and their surrogates, plus five relatives who are tutors and eight more who are not, plus all the children's playmates plus Father makes a huge family table. Brân's nervousness returns. I insist she sit between Nana and me. Telor introduces himself. He holds

Brân's hand a little longer than necessary, which comforts her. Nana, a gracious hostess, speaks gently to Brân.

After all are seated, Father stands. "Tonight, we are joined by Garreth's friend, Brân, whom he met during his recent visit to Cytgord. Brân, be thou welcome." He sits without further ceremony.

"That's all the formality," I say. Around us, people eat and chatter. "That and everyone being in uniform or nice clothes. You should see the kids' lunches … jumpsuits, doboks, warm-ups, loincloths, the little ones naked, whatever." By now, Brân is relaxed enough to enjoy the meal and the conversation.

After supper, Father takes Brân and me into his den, and offers what Brân hopes for – a chance to train as a soldier, to enter service to House Bleddyn or an ally, to bear a legitimate child, and perhaps adoption into a House. "There are no guarantees. Your friendship with my son opened a door. What happens next is up to you."

"I understand, Your Grace," Brân says. "I will try to live up to your expectations – and Garreth's."

I escort Brân back to her room. She chuckles. "Pretty good for a bastard." Then, she sobers. "I will not be close to you again for a long time, if ever. I do not think I want to kiss you again, but I will never forget our first kiss or our nights together."

An empty feeling in the pit of my stomach nearly keeps me from answering, but I understand she has to break away. "You said the kiss was to save me, and it did. I hope you find what you seek."

I change from uniform to sleep pants, lie in my bed, and order the lights to dim. Instantly I see images of Arawan against the darkness. I'm not sure if I am asleep or in a waking dream. I feel guilt, because I have not yet visited him since my return. Arawan's feeling of satisfaction and release overwhelms my feeling of guilt. He is mating! I feel what he feels. My mind recoils for a moment. Then, I feel Arawan's snarky laughter, and his image of Brân. He knows! The wolf's thoughts wakened a question. What did I unleash? The question keeps me awake until the comfort and safety of my own bedroom lull me to sleep.

The next morning, I go to Brân's room to escort her to breakfast, but learn she departed earlier by shuttle.

~~~~~

I do not forget Brân. Before noon, I bring Arawan to Father's den. He is standing by a window looking at the clouds. "Welcome, Garreth. How is microbiology?"

"It is going well, Father. Telor provided samples from cadavers of both the Res Publica and thralls. We compared their cells and DNA and found us to be more alike than we are different. I know others have done this, but what I do is more for learning than proving what we already know."

Before Father can ask another question, I ask him mine. "Where is Brân? Why can I not see her?"

Father almost smiles. "Brân is attending a special school where she has the freedom to create her own future. You, however, must do that for which you were born."

165

"Father, I wish to see this school."

Father knows I will ask because he answers easily. "Tomorrow," he says. "Sleep well tonight."

~~~~~

Father wakes me in the earliest hour of morning. "Put on your uniform," he says. "We depart immediately."

Wearing a uniform and carrying my boots I run to follow Father. His shuttle waits on the battlements. After takeoff, a soldier serves breakfast of pemmican and hot tea. I watch the repeater instruments in Father's compartment and know we are traveling toward the Western Isles. At four thousand kilometers per hour, we outrace the sun. It is sunrise when we land.

A woman I recognize meets us and bows to Father. His bow to her is as formal as hers – the bow of equals. "Gens Dolffin, you know my most curious son, Garreth," he says. I add several degrees to my bow.

She knows of the brotherhood ceremony Telor and I underwent with her sons after we captured Rodric's assassin. "Your son – brother by blood to my sons – is most polite and most welcome." She turns to me. "How may we address your curiosity, youngling?"

I tell her I met someone who befriended me. "Father says she is in school, here."

"Brân, of course. She may not see you; therefore, you may not see her. I assure you, what you see will be a true picture of what she experiences."

166

Our guide wears the uniform of House Bleddyn with a secondary patch of House Dolffin. She is Captain Tywyll, the Commandant of Cadets. "These are boys and girls who could not enter Academy because they have no family or no family strong enough to sponsor them. They are as intelligent, healthy, and qualified as anyone admitted to Academy. Houses Bleddyn and Dolffin rescue them and give them this opportunity."

We watch teams playing footy and *Bo-taoshi* on sports pitches. We see training in the schoolroom, in simulators, and in real fighters, floaters, and shuttles darting around the island. Fighters engage in mock battles over the ocean, diving low enough to be washed by spindrift and to create rooster-tails of water behind them.

"Upon graduation, they will become crewmembers of Dolffin's or Bleddyn's fleet on the sea or in space, guards at Cytgord, part of our Home Guards, or will supervise the operation of farms, mines, and industries."

After the tour, Gens Dolffin leads me to a room lined with televisor screens. She presses a button and one screen brightens. I see eighteen youngsters, boys and girls, all a few years older than me, in a forest, sitting around a fire.

"We recorded this on uninhabited Chindo Island over a period of one month. It is edited, but remains true to life." She presses another button, and the sound comes on. The youngsters are talking about – boat building? Some said they'd never seen the sea, and none had ever been on a boat, much less built one.

"Has anyone ever built anything?" one asks.

167

"My father's a wainwright," a girl says. "A wagon-maker," she explains to raised eyebrows and puzzled looks. "I've helped build wagons. They're used on farms and to bring things to market towns."

"My family are coopers," a boy says.

"Barrel makers," a redheaded boy fills in for him. "The two of you can work with wood. What other skills are there? Anyone?"

One by one, the others responds to the redhead's prodding. One lives in pine forests. His family bleeds trees for their sap and makes pitch to seal barrels. Another's family operates a flax mill, pounding flax to make cloth.

"We'll need sails, but flax is pretty scarce and hard to work with," someone says.

"But I know how to sew strong seams," the boy answers.

Twelve of the youngsters offer skills to the mix. The other six look at one another. One grins. "I guess we are the strong backs and hands who will work under others' leadership. You," she points to the redhead, "You will be our leader."

"Not I," he says. "Our leader must know much more about wagons and barrel-building, about cloth and seams, about pitch, and about other skills than I. You must select a different leader."

There is a long silence. The flax-maker's son breaks it. "Maybe we don't need a leader. We will work at different tasks, but we know what we want. A boat. One to bring us safely to Songbaek Island."

The televisor screen goes black. Gens Dolffin speaks. "We took them to Chindo and gave them tools, seeds, and some food, but no instructions. They could build a boat to bring them to an inhabited island. They could build homes and plant crops. They could burn the tools in a signal and hope to be rescued. They could sit and hope we would come back for them." She restarts the recording.

The flax-maker's son is correct. They do not need a leader. They work easily together. Problems are settled among them. Leadership changes when tasks change. Conflicts are resolved by discussion around a fire each night. The eighteen become a team. In a month, they build a boat. They have neither flax nor any cloth and propel the boat by oars. Pitch caulks both the boat and the barrels of fresh water it carries. Without cloth for sails, the flax-maker's son becomes a hewer of wood to keep the fires burning to thicken sap into pitch.

The recording ends and Gens Dolffin turns off the televisor. "What do you make of it?" she asks.

I recite something Sani once told me. "If you want a boat, do not command your people to build one, but lead them to the sea."

On the shuttle returning home, I speak to Father. "The school, it is one way you make House Bleddyn strong."

"It is the beginning of understanding. You are learning."

169

CHAPTER 10 TELEPATHY TRAINING

After Llewellyn's death, Telor has been named Father's chancellor. His duties keep him busy, and the time he saves for me becomes more important. Fall Stormtime is barely over when he leads me to the hanger and points to a pair of military floaters. "Let's hunt saber-tooth cats."

These giant cats raid our auroch herds, and Father placed a bounty on them. I frown. "That's not very honorable. Military floaters have rocket grenades."

"Look again," Telor says.

I look more closely, and see the rocket grenades were removed and a slug rifle clipped beside the pilot's cradle.

Before we depart toward the north, Telor reminds me of our pursuit of Rodric's assassin and asks me – for at least the hundredth time – not to unlock the cradle.

We pass farm fields and fly toward grazing land. Telor treats this as a teaching moment, and radios to me. "The cats have sexual dimorphism. That means—"

"I know. It means the sexes are different – in more ways than one."

"Funny little brother. The males are noticeably larger than the females. You'll need to see two together at first. But you'll learn. We kill only the males."

"Why?"

"Our goal is to protect our herds, not to make the cats extinct. They help keep the wild herds of four-legs strong by killing and eating the weak and the old. Follow me, and look ahead. There … a pair … the male is stalking the aurochs on the west edge of the field. The female … she looks pregnant. See how low her abdomen hangs. She's staying back. We will land, and you will take the first shot."

Telor points to the waves in the tall grass that show the direction of the wind. We land with the wind blowing from the cat toward us so the cat won't smell us. I lie on the ground, braced on my elbows, and aim at a spot behind his front shoulder. His heart is somewhere near there. I squeeze the trigger and feel the rifle recoil against my shoulder. Unconsciously, I blink and then look across the rifle's sights. "He's gone! He's not there. What happened?"

"He's lying in the grass, likely dead. His mate fled into the woods. The shot startled the aurochs, but they're too stupid to run away."

172

Telor lifts his floater a few feet off the ground. I follow to where I last saw the cat. He is there. Not moving. Red blood surrounds his body and leaks from the wound and from his mouth. A good shot. A quick kill.

Telor dips his hand in the cat's blood and smears it on my forehead. This is part of the ceremony I missed when I killed the cat on my way to Cytgord. I will wear this blood for five days, an ancient tradition.

"We can't leave him here," I whisper. "He was a noble creature. Not of-the-blood, but noble."

Telor presses a button on his communicator. "I've sent a locator signal. Thralls will arrive soon. They will make use of the meat and the hide."

Four days later, a thrall from the kitchen staff brings me the cat's claws and huge, curved teeth. "They were cleaned and drilled, My Lord. You may make a necklace of them to remind you of the nobility of the creature you defeated."

A trophy. A reminder I killed a huge beast. He is not like us. His blood is red. He doesn't think like we do. He had a mate and was the father of her kits. But he could have harmed my family. Does that mean it is honorable to kill him?

~~~~~

I string the teeth and claws on a thin, strong length of leather. I knot the leather between each piece. Before I finish, Telor opens my door. "Garreth, there is something I must tell you."

We are alone in the room. Telor seals the door. I stand and face him. I am afraid but Arawan lies quietly on the foot of my bed. I feel his calm and my fear fades but does not go away.

"Garreth, you must never fear me."

"I was afraid, but only because you were afraid. How did you know I was afraid? How did I know you were afraid?"

"I sense your feelings because I am a demon, although we say 'telepath.' So is Father; so are you."

Telor sees me struggling with the word. "Certainly you can suss the meaning."

My eyes narrow. "To suffer at a distance?" Then my eyes widen. "No. To talk at a distance. Of course. Demons are telepaths. Is this why you made me learn the Old Language?" I am only a little in earnest; more so, angry. "Why didn't you tell me?"

Memories flash through my mind. The games of hide-and-find when it was too easy to discover a player who held a token. The times I knew what people were going to say before they said it. Glimpses of feelings from others. The times I let my vambrace run low on drugs, especially when Brân was afraid for me. She must have guessed I was a demon; but she did not betray me. The images and feelings that seem to flow from Arawan. I look at the wolf and hear his silent, snarky laughter.

"Why does it work only some of the time? It's the drugs, isn't it? You've been lying to me! Why are we alive and Glint is dead?" I am angry, but the vambrace doesn't fill me with the anger-blocker. I stay angry, but not so angry I want to hurt Telor.

"You are angry," Telor says. "But you're not going to hit me, are you?"

His voice calms me. "No," I say.

"You are right. I lied to you. I hated it, but I lied to save your life."

"Telepaths are killed," I whisper. "Glint was executed because too many people saw he was a demon. You and Father and I, we are protected."

"Yes. The melatonin in your vambrace wasn't to put you to sleep or to calm you. Melatonin suppresses telepathy. For the past three months, your doses of melatonin and the calming drug—"

"The blocker. The anger-blocker," I interrupt.

"Yes. The anger-blocker and the melatonin were gradually reduced. Now, you and I and Guffudd, will—"

"Guffudd, too?" I interrupt, again.

"Yes, Guffudd, too. Tomorrow, the three of us will take a shuttle on a secret mission. We will go to a safe place on the islands and teach you about telepathy and how to control it. Then, the melatonin will be restarted—"

"Restarted? Why?" I demand.

"Restarted because Father orders it, because you must not accidentally give away that you are a telepath, lest you be killed. Restarted because you are young and impetuous and you need to learn so many things."

"Why was Glint not protected?"

"Glint was discovered in public before he could be protected. No one knew until the day," Telor says. I know he means the day Glint died.

~~~~~

Guffudd pilots the shuttle. Telor, Arawan, and I are the only passengers. Guffudd invites me to take the copilot's seat. Even that isn't enough to break my near-trance. The shuttle lands in a clearing. I step out, and see a building made of logs, a thrall's home, in the middle of the forest. I know I am safe because Telor and Guffudd allow Arawan and me to run ahead of them.

"What is this place?" I ask when they catch up.

"It was Grandfather's hunting lodge," Guffudd replies. "Now, it is Father's place of quiet and contemplation."

I am surprised Father needs such a place. I wonder how often he visits it, and why I've never heard of it.

I split wood for the stove. In between strokes of the ax I ask, "Where are the thralls to do this? Why are they not here to serve us?"

"We will not always have others to serve us," Telor replies.

"Sometimes, we must take care of ourselves," Guffudd adds. "Besides, it is tradition."

"Tradition. An excuse to make younger brothers do unpleasant tasks—"

Guffudd interrupts. "Garreth, you must clean the solar-electric panels, or we will have no light tonight." I wipe the sweat from my face with my sleeve and follow him to another part of the clearing.

By suppertime, I am hungry and exhausted. I hauled water to fill a cistern, chopped wood to fill a woodpile, and prepared supper. All this, while my brothers relax.

The coming darkness brings anxiety. "Are we safe?" I ask after supper.

Telor points to a chair, one of three set at a small table in front of the fireplace. "Sit. We are safe here. For all of us to stay safe, you must obey, and in obedience, learn."

The next morning, Telor prepares our breakfast and Guffudd cleans. I am no longer their servant, although Telor explains I will have chores including food preparation and cleanup. I spend most of the time listening to Telor and Guffudd explain telepathy.

"First, you experience the feelings parts of telepathy. Then images. Later you will hear thoughts and can project your thoughts to other telepaths."

"Not everyone has the same abilities. Some can only feel what others close to them are feeling. We call them empaths – they can sense others' emotions. Some can hear the surface thoughts of telepaths farther away. Some can communicate over long distances with others like themselves and can draw thoughts from others' minds. Some people think a strong telepath could control them. It is not true. However, that is why people fear demons."

My mind buzzes with thoughts – my own, but also Telor's. They come together like pieces of a puzzle. I speak with absolute confidence. "Llywelyn killed Rodric because he was a telepath. He tried to kill me because I am a telepath. He killed Sani to cover his crime. Llywelyn knew. And Father executed Llywelyn because Father knew why Llywelyn did those things. Because Llywelyn was not a telepath, he could not become Gens."

I surprise Telor. The flood of thoughts from his mind shuts off abruptly. "You are picking up my thoughts, which is good. But you must learn how to block – and how not to pry."

"Telor, both you and Father are telepaths. You and he must know everything the other—"

"No," Telor says. "Father and I agreed, long ago, we would never *read* one another. If Father and I were linked, we would act as one, and perhaps overlook something important. We have kept our promise—"

"But you both *read* me, whatever that means."

"Yes, Garreth. You are still a child. Sometimes the only way to protect you is to use my telepathy to keep a watch on you. But only when you are about to get into trouble. Even Father does not read you unless he senses something important in your mind."

The storm, the lightning, that's how he knew, I think. Then I wonder if he knew about the nights I spent with Brân, but Guffudd doesn't give me time to ask. He continues my lesson. "We believe you will be able to pull into your mind the thoughts of others."

"The things I feel from Arawan – is that empathy?"

This surprises both Telor and Guffudd. Telor question me closely, and then says, "I have never heard of telepathy between a human and an animal. I don't know if what you sense is your talent or Arawan's."

My legs are shaking, but they still support me. My mind flies from idea to idea trying to absorb what Telor and Guffudd say.

"When you learn to control your thoughts and to block unwanted thoughts from others," Telor says, "the melatonin will be reduced, then eliminated."

That night, I dream. My dream is of Arawan, running free in the forest. I see him escape saber-tooth cats and kill rabbits and other small game. The dream shifts, and I am walking down a game trail, on the way to Cytgord. I see the cat leap from the tree and die by my energy pistol. It is my first kill. Arawan's howl of triumph wakes me and I realize he is dreaming with me.

At breakfast, Guffudd complains Arawan's howl wakened him. "He was dreaming of the hunt," I say, and share a silent, snarky laugh with my companion-wolf.

~~~~~

Guffudd allows me to pilot the shuttle back to Fortress. When we arrive, Nana and Telor overwhelm me with preparations to enter Academy. I still have thirty days, but they don't let me put off any task. The hardest is parting with Arawan. The Academy will not permit me to bring a companion-wolf, even though I am a Son of Wolf. Macca, who is now five years old, solves the problem. He rushes into my room.

"Brother? May I take care of Arawan while you are at Academy? I promise to feed him and play with him and take him out to poop even on the wettest days and dry his paws when we come in and …" The boy runs out of breath.

Macca does not ask me to give Arawan to him – which is something I could not do in any case – but only to allow him to care for the wolf. I believe the boy understands the difference, and will honor his commitment. For nearly two years, Macca played with Arawan and cared for him when I left Fortress for missions and training with the Mountain Company. I see Macca's wistful looks when we visit the breeding pens after a new litter is born. Now, the only obstacle is Father.

I lead Macca and Arawan to Father's den. We boys kneel; Arawan crouches. Father commands us to stand. "You wish to ask something monumental," he says.

"Father, I do not want to return Arawan to the pens or the forest; Macca offers to care for him. May he?"

"Have you asked Arawan?" Father uses the wolf's name for the first time.

"Father, that's silly!" Macca says. Arawan turns his head and licks the boy's face.

180

"It appears Arawan agrees," Father says. He speaks to the wolf. "You will have to behave."

I sense Arawan's laughter, and realize Macca and Father do, too, and understand the empathy, the images, the shared laughter are the wolf's talent, not mine.

~~~~~

Just before Winter Stormtime, we are summoned to celebrate the elevation of Telor's son, Selwyn. Family and thralls fill the Great Hall. Telor is on the dais with Father, so I stand with Guffudd. Guffudd tells me Selwyn is the son of Gwenallt, who used to be Soosong. She was a visitor at stormtime and taught me *Jaryeondo* kata and gymnastics. Then, she disappeared. "She is no longer on World, but is a crewmember on one of our starships."

~~~~~

Every day, Winter Stormtime gets stronger. Wind whistles through the crenels of the battlements and down the chimneys. Dampers above fireplaces are closed. The sails of wind turbines are furled and electricity is limited. Fortress is cold, but our blood was made for cold.

Sister-plus-six Aelwen graduated from Academy and celebrates with a dozen of her element mates. I will be thirteen years old in four days, and will enter Academy the day after Stormtime. There is one task incomplete and I expect Father's summons. The cold of the stone floor penetrates my uniform and stiffens my knees. He tells me to stand and leads me to a chair in an alcove where ice covers the windows and only a nacreous glow penetrates the room.

"Did you find an answer to my question?"

181

He wants to know if I learned the meaning of honor. "No, Father, I do not know what honor is, but have the beginning of understanding."

He sees my hesitation and prompts me. "What have you learned?"

"Honor means doing the right thing because it is the right thing to do, not because one fears punishment or hopes for reward, and not because it is custom or written in law." I look at Father for a reaction, but his face is immobile and I feel nothing from him.

"Honor is also adhering to a code of conduct, but not all codes are honorable," I say. "That was the most difficult notion to understand. Many Gens Tarren who tried to destroy House Bleddyn were honorable by that rule, but their code was not honorable."

Father interrupts my thoughts. "Did not all the Gens Tarrens follow the First Constant Factor, the Moral Law causing the people to be in complete accord with their ruler, so they will follow him regardless of their lives?"

"I thought on that, Father, and decided the ruler's task is not to lead the people in the wrong direction, which Tarren did."

"Go on."

"The Gens of any house, like every leader, must have wisdom, sincerity, benevolence, courage, strictness – and honor. I cannot know the mind of Gens Tarren, but I think he was more about strictness than the other virtues."

"You think you have defined honor?" Father asks.

"No, Father. Honor is far too complex. I think I will learn more and my understanding will change. I think you knew that when you first asked me.

"A good answer, Son."

≈≈≈≈≈

Tomorrow I will enter Academy. The drugs in my vambrace – the anger-blocker, the ones that keep me focused, and the melatonin to block telepathy – will gradually be reduced. I must learn to control my emotions and telepathy. I will face danger. My guards will no longer protect me. I know of attacks on Bethan, Delwyn, and Daffyd. I lived through the death of Rodric. I saw my brother-cousin, Glint, taken away to be executed. What dangers will I face? How will I answer them? Will I be able to serve with honor, valor, and loyalty – and modesty?

That night I remove the Wolf of Bleddyn and the patch of the Mountain Company from the uniform I will wear the next day. I know it will make no difference whether or not I wear a patch. I will never be only a cadet. I will always be a Son of Wolf and a target for our enemies.

The day after Winter Stormtime I enroll in First Form at Academy. Telor says he barely had time to pee the first three months, then he laughs. When I tell him I don't think it's funny, he laughs again, and says, "It's what Father told me my first day."

Academy is west of Fortress Bleddyn atop the mesa that also holds Council House. Although older brothers and sisters attended Academy, I have never been

Academy Calendar	
Day	Event
1	Year Begins
7	Winter Stormtime Ends
8	Academy year begins
125	Spring *Bo-Taoshi* competition
139	Recognition of First Form Cadets
140	Spring Stormtime begins
147	Spring Equinox
155	Spring Stormtime ends
287	Summer Stormtime begins
294	Summer Solstice
302	Summer Stormtime Ends
425	Fall *Bo-taoshi* competition
435	Fall Stormtime begins
442	Fall Equinox
450	Fall Stormtime Ends
581	Graduation Ceremony
583	Winter Stormtime begins
590	Winter Solstice

inside the massive buildings with quarters, classrooms, gymnasia and dojos, and armories. Starting today, I will find out what else they hide.

Over the entrance, in the old language, are the words *Cooperate and Graduate*. I wonder what they mean. All my life, I have competed with other boys and girls. Few games were cooperative. Mostly, we competed with one another, striving to win. Any cooperation was temporary, and only during a particular

185

game. I know what *cooperate* means, but I've seldom done it. What else will be new?

Telor and Nana release me to older cadets of the cadre with hard bodies and even harder eyes. Aelwen, my Sister-plus-six, is an instructor. I wonder if I will see her. She told me we may not have any unofficial contact. I'm not sure what it means. Probably that we can't talk to one another except during free time. Not, as Telor warned, will I have much free time.

A cadre member guides me to a pod and give me to the Element Tactical Officer. He is a lieutenant in the Home Guard of House Emrys. I wonder what his name is. Another boy asks, first.

"My name is *Tac* or *Sir*," the lieutenant says. He frowns. I'm glad the other boy asked first.

My sleeping room has two double-bunk beds. There are four lockers, with space to hang uniforms and drawers for other clothing. We do not need many personal possessions and there is little room for them. We were told we might bring a dagger and a grace knife. I also bring my reshot and a bag of smooth stones. Tac is surprised when he sees them. He raises an eyebrow. "The law prohibits weapons other than daggers and grace knives," he says.

"The law is made for those who cannot think for themselves," I reply. I am careful to keep my voice low so others don't hear me challenge him. "Besides, thralls may have reshots, but not weapons. Therefore, this is not a weapon."

Tac stares at me for a moment. He is trying not to smile. At least he is not angry.

186

He says I may keep the reshot and my communicator. "You may keep your communicator because your father desires it; however, you may not use it except during free time or to signal an emergency." I realize others in my element may not have communicators. *One more thing to make me different and separate me.* I silence the alarm and shove my communicator deep in a pocket.

After directing me to store my gear, Tac takes me to the common room and tells me to sit. "Talk quietly until everyone has reported." The room is about twenty meters square. Along one wall are nine carrels, each with a computer terminal and two chairs. Tables and chairs for eighteen – the number of cadets in the element – fill the rest of the room.

I recognize two who arrived before me – Barri and Deryn. I met Barri once in the caverns under Fortress, during stormtime. I met Deryn when he bullied a smaller boy at a Harvest Festival, and Deryn and I fought. I sit at their table. Barri speaks first. He does not acknowledge our past meeting. His words are abrupt and he seems uncomfortable. "I will be Element Commander during First Form. Deryn is my second. What weapons are you rated expert in?"

Barri quizzes me, and then others when they arrive. Besides weapons, he wants to know where we are from, and if we can pilot a floater or a shuttle. His manner is neither friendly nor unfriendly, and I think he will be a good commander. I pay close attention to his interactions with the others and I memorize their names.

One name I do not need to memorize is Bräu. He is the heir-designate of House Tarren. Telor told me Bräu would be in my element. "Be wary of him. He will be your companion-student, but do not trust him."

After all eighteen cadets arrive, Tac herds us into an auditorium with other First Forms. A man with Field Marshall's flashes on his shoulders enters and speaks without introduction or preamble.

"You will experience the Four Pillars of Discipline. Physical Discipline, meaning strength of limb, fleetness of foot, and proficiency in weapons of all kinds. Academic Discipline, through the study of history, strategy, and tactics. Mental Discipline, including focus, single-mindedness, self-control, courage, and self-confidence. Moral Discipline includes honor, valor, and loyalty – and obedience to authority."

I am glad Father and Telor taught me so much. Telor made me understand physical and mental discipline in *Jaryeondo*. Father demanded I understand honor. I know my understanding is shallow and wonder what new things I will learn.

The Field Marshall steps aside. Another figure, this one wearing a ceremonial robe, takes center stage.

"Most of you are under oath to your house and your Gens. The oath you will take now is subordinate to those older oaths. Nothing in this oath will violate those oaths."

I listen to the words he recites and accept the conditions of the oath – to act with honor, to be loyal to my element, to maintain amity with other students, and to obey my superiors at Academy. I wonder why he said only most of us were already under oath. Who would not be, and why? The only answer is that

188

some of my classmates are bastards, without family or house. I think of Brân and wonder if she found her place in our world.

~~~~~

It is the third day when I find opportunity to speak privately to Deryn. I am reluctant to force him to acknowledge our first meeting, when he bullied a smaller boy, and I killed him with a strike to his solar plexus and stopped his breathing. I started his breathing and saved his life. Deryn does not want to speak of it, either. We establish a comfortable, but not close relationship. It is fitting. As Barri's deputy, Deryn is in a command position. I am a scion of House Bleddyn, yet I am his subordinate. A complex change in our relationship.

During free time, I call Telor. "We swore an oath of amity with other cadets, yet you told stories of vendetta among cadets. What is the truth?

Telor looks at me from the screen and blinks several times. I learned this means he is thinking, not preparing to lie.

"Your oath of amity is important, but you did not take it in blood. In the past, even the recent past, cadets have claimed an oath not taken in blood is invalid. They used that excuse to declare vendetta with other cadets and to challenge others to duels. The Council prohibits vendetta and duels at Academy, but if no one is killed or seriously injured, the faculty will say nothing. Another reason for you to be careful."

~~~~~

I watch my mates during our testing in physical and academic disciplines. Barri excels at physical discipline although I am not far behind. Betsan scores high in strategy and tactics.

Cledwyn scores high in physical, but low in academic. I see in him a depth of knowledge the tests do not find. Bräu struggles to reach a mediocre but passing score in each area, and I remember what Telor and Father told me about hidden mutations created by inbreeding in the Tarren line.

I am second or third in every test and think I can overtake those who score higher. As if he knows this, Telor sends a message on the next night.

<<Too much self-confidence may lead to hubris – false pride.
Build on your strengths without pulling down others.
You do not need to beat everyone at everything.>>

~~~~~

Our earliest classes are history – the history of the Res Publica, our conquest of the thralls on the Southern Continent, and our war with the Adversary. My element sits in a classroom with the other three elements of our group.

"Our people, the Res Publica, are at war with those we call The Adversary. They…" My instructor's voice drones. I learned more than this from Father and Telor. My mind wants to wander, but I remember an early lesson from Telor – Doubt everything for doubt leads to questioning, and questioning leads to truth. I resolve to compare what I hear with what Father and Telor taught.

~~~~~

Ten days remain in First Quarter. Spring Stormtime is only a few days away, but the weather is clement when the four elements of First Form cadets assemble for our recognition ceremony. We face the Sixth Forms of Squadron Phoenix with considerable trepidation. They lead us to the advanced obstacle

190

course of wooden beams, steel rods, narrow culverts, mud holes, and hemp rope. It includes rocky trails up and down steep hills. The trails hold their own challenges – rope bridges and chasms. We have only run the beginners' course. The advanced course will be a significant challenge. It will be dangerous since we do not know the proper way to approach many of the obstacles. However, the older cadets demonstrate each obstacle.

After showing us how to pass over spiked walls, crawl under laser beams, squirm through tunnels and culverts, and swing across flooded ponds, the Sixths take us to the start of the course. The Squadron Commander addresses us. "No member of Squadron Phoenix fails to complete this course in less than one hour. Begin." He fires a powder pistol with a blank cartridge. We charge the course.

It is then the injunction to *Cooperate and Graduate* takes on meaning. Although we have been together barely a quarter of a year, we learned one another's strengths and weaknesses. Those with good hand-eye coordination catch the ropes and pass them to the next cadet in line. The strongest stand at the exits of the culverts to pull their mates from the holes, shaving seconds off their time. Those who can jump the farthest are first across the chasms and brace one another to catch anyone whose jump is short.

The Commander waits at the finish line. He lifts the powder pistol when the last member of my group rounds a bend in the trail. The cadet trips and falls on his face. Two cadets who already completed the course run back and grab the boy's arms. They lift him and sprint to the finish. The boy's feet barely touch the ground. I see the Squadron Commander hesitate. I know the allotted time passed, but he does not fire the pistol until these three cross the line.

"You succeeded." He points toward an opening in the forest. "That trail leads to Academy. Return to your pods. Shower. Put on clean uniforms. Report to Assembly Room 17 in one hour."

The boy who fell isn't the only one who needs support on the run back to Academy. We want to stay under the shower for the rest of the day, but we clean ourselves and dress while those faster call the time to us.

The older cadets, Second through Sixth Form, are waiting in the assembly room. They welcome us and urge us to tables covered with food and drink. Violating Academy rules, older cadets ply us with enough ethanol to sooth all aches.

~~~~~

We are constantly busy and always tired. It is easy to fall asleep and hard to wake. After recognition, the schedule eases as if the faculty knows we are thinking of spring break more than our lessons. I contact Telor, who assures me I may invite as many friends as I wish to visit Fortress, but must give him their names and receive his approval, first. "Father would not want a mole slipping into Fortress."

"None of my friends are moles, they're boys and girls – oh, you mean…"

"Yes, someone who would use their friendship with you to enter Fortress, but who means harm to you or House Bleddyn."

The notion is frightening. I just began to make friends and do not like having to look at my element-mates differently.

Telor approves Barri and Deryn, first. He must know I discovered they are more than fellow students but are my protectors, assigned by Father. I invite others. Only Betsan accepts. I feel disappointment from those whose families insist they come home. "Another time," I promise.

Even though Fortress will be full during stormtime, my guests will not be crowded. I give Barri and Deryn their own room and feel their happiness.

I remember how I felt during stormtime when my elder siblings would not play with me, so I invite my younger brothers and sisters to join some of our games. Alaw has never known an older sister. Aelwen was fifteen years older than she; Delwyn, eighteen years older. They were seldom at home when Alaw was growing up. Alaw latches onto Betsan and follows her everywhere. I am afraid Betsan will resent the attention and distraction, but Betsan seems happy to be a surrogate older-sister, and shows Alaw both games of war and girl things.

At three years old, Eurion is too young to play most of the games, but watches our acrobatics, unarmed combat, and weapons practice. At first, I wonder if my friends will think stormtime an extension of Academy. Then, I realize they do, and are happy to learn things Academy does not teach.

The first night, my bedroom door opens. I sense Arawan and am not surprised when he and Macca enter. "Arawan says we gots to sleep with you," Macca says and crawls into the bed. I feel

193

Arawan's weight on the foot of the bed when he springs into the place he claimed on his first night in Fortress, years ago.

~~~~~

My Brother- and-Sister-plus-twelve, Daffyd and Delwyn, were assigned to the Home Guard after graduation from Academy. Before stormtime is over, they announce they are assigned to starships. "Two corvettes will launch in six months to explore different parts of this arm of the galaxy."

I ask Telor why Daffyd and Delwyn are sent into space on separate ships.

"The twins are both medium grade telepaths," Telor says. "Your father hopes they may encounter telepaths of other species."

"Telepaths are important to House Bleddyn. We are one reason the house is strong."

Telor nods. "It is the beginning of understanding."

~~~~~

A late storm makes the return trip to Academy bumpy. Because my friends and I arrive early in the morning, we have extra time to prepare for inspection. Barri is thorough, but not eager to award demerits. Maybe Second Quarter will be a little easier.

I thought we would receive energy pistols and rifles, rocket grenade launchers, and other weapons, but I am disappointed. Wearing heavy padding, we practice with blades with dulled edges and points. We receive classroom instructions in advanced weapons – lessons in safety, the weapons' capabilities, and how to repair them. That is expected. But when Second Quarter continues with laser tag and paintball, I wonder when we will use real weapons. However, I learned to let others ask questions.

Nudd's name means "fog" in the old language. He said he was named for the fog that wreaths the gymnosperms on the mountains of his family's land. We learned he is always curious. "Why do we practice with laser tag and paintball when we will have energy weapons?"

Tac looks to us for an answer, Cledwyn, scion of House Caerwyn, speaks. "Someday, you may find yourself without weapons and at the mercy of someone with a stone ax."

I remember something Sani said and say, "Or just a stone."

"Besides," Deryn adds. "The more ways you know how to fight, the more likely you will win a fight."

Tac seems pleased at our answers and not angry with Nudd for asking the question.

We learn to use rawhide to attach a stone to a stick and how to knap stones to create sharp edges. Instructors show us spear points and arrowheads created by knapping, and we make them. We make a spear and atlatl, and a reshot.

~~~~~

My element faces challenges as individuals, as an element, and with the other three elements in our group. Lilith, a member of a group which competes with us, seems determined to make me fail, to make me angry, or to injure me. Lilith is from House Cythrual, allied with House Tarren.

The day is warm; Summer Stormtime approaches. We are engaged in a game of *Bo-taoshi*. It is the game Guffudd's element practiced while I watched from an apple tree.

Betsan is the monkey and stands proudly atop the pole, grasping the spike. She signals readiness. A referee's whistle sounds and the game begins. I am among the defenders surrounding the pole. The attackers elect a *chojeom*, or focal-point attack. Like an arrow, a phalanx of cadets rushes toward us. Lilith is in the vaward. Her eyes focus on me.

Lilith throws herself downward to slam into my legs. With her speed and the force of those behind her, she could easily break my legs. In an instant, I turn so the force of her blow does not hyperextend my knees. The attack fails to break our defenses.

After a Tac's whistle ends the game, and he awards the win to our group, I offer my hand to Lilith. She sees my hand and snarls. "Never, spawn of Bleddyn. You cheated."

A Tac hears her charge, and assembles us with a single blast from his whistle. He calls Lilith and me to face the Tacs. They listen to Lilith's charge and my answer. They rule neither of us acted improperly and uphold our win.

That evening, my element and I are in the common room studying or practicing war games on the computer terminals. No one is relaxing or gossiping. A chime announces someone at the door. It is Lilith. There is no reason to prevent her entry, so Cledwyn opens it to her.

Lilith speaks the ancient language. "I charge Garreth Bleddyn with deceit and call him to the field." Before I can answer, she turns and is gone.

Cledwyn closes the door. "What was that?" he asks.

"She challenged Garreth to a duel," Barri answers.

"Duels are prohibited," someone says.

"Yes," Deryn says. "But they happen. Garreth, what will you do?"

A good question. If I refuse, I will be branded a coward, despite the prohibition of duels. If I accept, I may be hurt or killed. Both Lilith and I may be expelled from Academy. However, since I am the challenged party, I may select the weapons. "Let me think on this," I say. "Deryn, will you be my second?"

I ignore Deryn's reluctance and push him to accept. He owes me, and I will collect, and, perhaps, strengthen what I hope will be a bond of friendship.

Betsan visits me after showers and before sleeptime. "There may be a way," she says. I listen to what she suggests, smile, and send Deryn to Lilith with a message.

Two days later, during a scheduled session in the dojo, Lilith and I face one another with quarterstaffs heavily padded on the ends. We stand on a narrow board supported a meter above the floor of the dojo. The exercise recapitulates an old story in which the hero encounters an outlaw on a bridge. Lilith acknowledges this to be a legal response to her challenge even though I know she hoped for something more likely to be lethal.

I should have won when I knock Lilith from the pretend bridge. However, when she regains her footing, she shouts, "Another cheat by Garreth Bleddyn. Come down here and finish the battle."

All the cadets are eager for the duel to continue. The Tacs nod. I jump from the board to the floor. Although I land on my feet, Lilith is ready for me. She swings her padded quarterstaff, but I block.

For the next several minutes, we strike and parry.

Enough of this, I think. Summoning all my strength, I spin my quarterstaff and strike her on the left side of her head. Despite the padding and helmet, I injure her and she falls, not to move. Our seconds exchange looks, and then nod. Lilith's second acknowledges my victory.

~~~~~

Summer Stormtime is forecast to be mild, and I plan games in the forest for my visitors. Bräu accepts my invitation to visit Fortress. I'm sure Bräu won't learn anything he shouldn't. He's still the last ranked in academics.

Bräu also lacks courage. He shrinks back and hides behind Barri and Deryn when he sees Arawan. The wolf runs to me, leaps up to brace his front paws on my chest, and licks my face. I hear a shriek from Bräu. I wonder if Arawan is being spontaneous, or if this is something Macca taught him. The boy giggles – if he didn't teach the wolf, he knew it would happen.

On the third night of stormtime, my communicator buzzes. The call is from the War Room. "We found your guest,

Bräu, wandering the halls. His movements seemed odd. At first, we thought he was looking for something. Then, we realized he was walking all the hallways on one level before going to the next level and doing the same thing. We accosted him. He carried a recording position locator. He was mapping the interior of Fortress. The Gens summons you to his den."

This is a betrayal. Father and Telor are waiting for me.

I speak before Father recognizes me. "I am responsible, Father."

"Stand, Garreth. No blame attaches to you."

Telor explains. "I approved Bräu's visit. Father encouraged you to treat Bräu as a mate and your Academy oath enforced that. I remember stories our grandfather told. When he was a cadet, on his first shipboard assignment, indicator lights on the controls were labeled, "Press to Test." In many cases, that was the only way he could know if the lights were working. You just "pressed to test" House Tarren. Learn from it."

Father picks up the narrative. "Bräu is on a shuttle to Fortress Caerwyn. Caerwyn will take him to Gens Pugh, who will take the boy home. We confiscated the locator, and the extra memory sticks in his duffle."

"What will we tell Gens Tarren? What will I tell the others?" I ask.

"We will tell Tarren nothing. The boy may tell his own story; however, I doubt he has the courage to tell the truth. When Tarren sees the locator is missing, he will draw the correct conclusion. You will tell your guests Bräu asked to return home, which is true. Make no other explanation."

The weather is fair for the next several days. We play a paintball battle game, which includes my younger siblings. Macca demands I allow Arawan to play, and Betsan agrees, privately, to look after Alaw. I don't want Selwyn to feel left out, so I invite him to be my companion-soldier in the game. Adding Barri and Deryn, gives us four teams of two. We disperse into the forest.

Patches of undergrowth – shrubs and young trees – provide concealment. Selwyn and I lie on our stomachs behind a meter-tall patch of laurel bushes whose candy-striped flowers attract butterflies.

A timing signal from our communicators begins the game. Immediately, I sense Arawan's excitement and see the image he sends Macca – a direct line to my position. *You're supposed to behave!* I send. The wolf's snarky laughter echoes in my mind before I hear Macca crashing through the underbrush. The boy needs to learn how to move in the forest. I wonder if Arawan can teach him.

Arawan locates me from my thoughts. I use the blocking skills Telor and Guffudd taught me and pull Selwyn through the brush on our bellies, whispering for him to move slowly and showing him how to pass through the undergrowth without noise and without leaving a trace. We can't disguise our scent. If Arawan encounters our trail, he will surely lead Macca to us.

Alaw and Betsan save us by painting Macca and Arawan before the wolf finds our scent. Barri and Deryn, however, find us; then, Betsan and Alaw win the game by sneaking up on the two boys. Alaw is delighted when she and Betsan are awarded the win – and the losers' desserts, which Alaw's surrogate insists be spread over three days.

Macca, Alaw, and Selwyn are too young for the training range of the Mountain Company, but the holographic simulators dazzle my friends and by the end of stormtime, we are energized and ready to face the final quarter of our first year.

~~~~~

As the end of the year approaches, Telor tells me nine mates will remain in the element for Second Form. Of them, Barri, Deryn, Betsan, Cledwyn, and Nudd accept invitations to Fortress Bleddyn for Winter Stormtime.

Sister-minus-three Alaw has grown a lot in the past months, but greets Betsan enthusiastically, and drags her to her dojo to show how much she learned since Betsan's last visit.

The evening before I return to Academy, Father summons me. We talk about honor and leadership and I tell him what I've learned from Barri and Deryn.

"What about your Tac?"

"Tac is more a watcher than a leader. He is always present; he monitors our progress. But he never interferes, except to talk to Barri. Tac expects Barri to correct us, and to steer the course of the element. It is one way of being a leader.

"There is more than one kind of leadership," I say. "But which one is best? Which one should I use?"

201

"You will have more time at Academy to answer that. New members and a new Tac will join your element for Second Form."

CHAPTER 12 SECRETS REVEALED

My second-form element includes nine familiar faces. New members include Gwaethafwyr – who we call Gwen – and Lowri, who is a bastard. I wonder who sponsored her and if she might be a mole, whose task is to harm me, perhaps kill me.

Cledwyn will command. He selects Nudd as his deputy, which surprises many. I think of Nudd's constant questioning and believe Cledwyn made a wise decision.

~~~~~

I turn when I hear footsteps behind me. Barri and Deryn stand close together. "May we be your roommates?" Deryn asks.

Barri sees something in my face because he hesitates. "Are you unhappy?"

"My father placed you and Deryn in my element."

Adrenaline triggers Barri and Deryn's fight-or-flight reflex and pulls blood from their faces to their muscles. Their faces darken until their vambraces react, then lighten as the drugs take effect.

"I know you are my guards and swore your life to me. Does that make me unhappy? I am not unhappy you are in my element, for you are good and stalwart companions."

"Then why are you unhappy, because I know you are," Barri asks.

How does he know? Is he a telepath? I wonder, but only for a moment. His eyes are on my face; I decide he is only reacting to my body language.

"No. I am not angry with you, for I know you are following oath and orders." The two boys stand, silent.

"I am unhappy you promised to give your lives for me. Please sit." I gesture. They sit on the bottom bunk. I feel them draw comfort from one another. I also feel their puzzlement.

"I hoped when I came to Academy I would blend in, be just another cadet, treated like everyone else. That didn't happen. From the beginning, faculty and cadets treated me differently. Before the first Spring Stormtime, I knew who you were. If I asked my father, he would remove you. Of course, he would replace you with others."

Their faces freeze until I reassure them. "I will not do that." I look at the bunk where I put my duffle. If I were to take a different bunk...

"I know you two share one spirit. I will take the other bunk."

They could not be more afraid. I sense their thoughts as they remember the room I gave them at Fortress.

"You knew?" Deryn whispers. "Is that why we always shared a room when we visited?"

"Yes."

The boys look at one another, then at me. Barri speaks. "Garreth, we swore to your father; will you accept our oaths to you?"

"You offered your oath years ago, in the caverns below Fortress," I reply.

"You remember?"

"I do." I think of the customs and laws Father and Telor taught me. But Father often says custom and law are for people who cannot think for themselves. "Even without our Gens permission, I would swear brotherhood with you. Will you accept?"

The ceremony is simple. Barri and Deryn are surprised when I ask for their daggers and use them and mine to seal our oaths with blood. "It is customary to exchange daggers, but I have only one. And, we must keep this oath secret. But we made it in blood and it will be recorded in House Bleddyn archives." And won't Father be surprised.

~~~~~

Cledwyn, our new commander, assembles us in the common room. "Listen up, boys and girls. We all wear vambraces, and we know they control the hormones of puberty. So, we're boys and girls. But we are boys and girls in an adult situation, a place where mistakes can cost not only our place at Academy and in our houses but also our lives and the lives of our mates."

I watch my element-mates absorb his words. We all know he speaks truth, but no one before has said it so clearly.

"In the next few days, we will set goals for this year. The faculty says they evaluate us on the Four Pillars of Discipline – physical, academic, mental, and moral. They grade our performance in games and classes. The flaw in the system is that they cannot measure mental or moral discipline, so they depend on what they can measure. However, our mental focus and our moral compass must guide us. Think about this, and create at least one specific, measurable, achievable goal related to the faculty's measurements, which we can accomplish during the year."

Some goals, like, "Create a new strategy for *Bo-taoshi*," meet his criteria. Others lack specifics. However, he writes them all in big letters and posts them in the common room.

Second Form is not as difficult or stressful as First. We do face greater pressure to perform on the sports field and in academics. The sport of choice for the faculty is *Bo-taoshi*, and every ten days, regardless of weather, we assemble with our group for practice or competition. Some of our practices bring us close to Father's apple orchard, and I look for my younger brothers in the apple trees, but I do not see them.

~~~~~

Low, dark clouds spit snowflakes onto the firing range, but our blood sings in the cold. There is an energy pistol and two charge blocks at each position. This is the first time we have used energy weapons at Academy, although the classes in safety and maintenance almost qualified us to build one from scratch.

Our targets are silhouettes of human figures – no different from those we fired on using slug rifles. That's what we think until the first time we hit a target. If the strike hits a death zone, the target explodes in a very satisfying burst of flame and smoke and another target pops up instantly – not at the same place, but usually farther downrange. After the instructions about stance and target picture, we all get passing scores.

When we exhaust our charge blocks, Tac orders Arwel to collect the pistols. While Arwel is doing this, an element of Sixth Form cadets arrives and takes positions. Arwel reports to the armory to turn in the pistols and charge blocks. The inventory is one pistol short. Arwel runs back to the range. The Sixth Form element has begun their training and rebuffs Arwel's questions. Arwel is arrested.

"It's so unfair!" Catrin growls.

"What can we do?" Gwen asks. "One of those Sixth Form Cadets probably took the missing pistol."

"Yes, but how do we prove it? The only way to rescue Arwel is to find the missing pistol." We think and plot, but we can't come up with a plan.

Arwel is a member of allied House Caerwyn. He is also a mate. My responsibility is clear and my decision is easy. It is also easy to leave my element's pod after midnight. The entrance to the Sixth Form barracks is code-locked, but a cadet with a weak bladder is awake. I push past the melatonin and pull the code from his mind. It is more difficult to find the cadet who took the pistol. The vambrace reacts to my nervousness and injects more drugs. I fight to keep my telepathy working. I find the cadet with the pistol in the third element I scan. My question, now, is what to do with the information.

I call Telor. Despite the early hour, he listens to my explanation and offers a solution. "You overheard one of the cadet's mates warning him about the theft and possession of the pistol. This was in the mess hall, one place where all cadets mingle. It is plausible, and once the pistol is found, there will be no reason to question you."

The next morning, during breakfast I wander through the mess hall. Trays are filled with high protein breakfasts – fish, eggs, auroch meat. I try to look purposeful, while being aimless. I find two boys whose minds are not on their meals.

Before first class, I approach Tac. "Sir, the missing pistol is in the hands of a cadet in Sixth Form, Element 32. I overheard one of his mates warn him about concealing the pistol."

Tac takes me to the Squadron Tac. His office is starkly luxurious. His desk, the chairs, and a table have sharp corners and flat, polished wooden surfaces to reflect the light. Behind the desk, certificates and weapons decorate the wall. The room is designed to intimidate. Tac questions me closely. "Sir, I overheard a conversation in the mess hall. I can identify the two cadets face-to-face if necessary, although my father prefers I not be named."

The Squadron Tac understands and settles my concern. "There are too many who would consider reporting a fellow cadet's misconduct to be dishonorable. They would be wrong." He triggers his communicator, and orders a search of the entire pod of Element 32. The pistol is discovered by noon. The cadet is arrested within minutes, and my role is hidden.

They release Arwel a day later. He will serve punishment for not counting the pistols, but will not be expelled.

I think of the pterodactyl who put his beak down a wolf's throat and risked himself to help a fellow creature. This time, it is a Son of Wolf who risks. Telor warned me against using my telepathy, but he and Father understand.

~~~~~

It is unusual for shuttles to fly during stormtime, especially Winter Stormtime, but before I can talk to Father, Telor invites my mates and me to fly with him to the spaceport on Namhae. Actually, the invitation is a command. "It may be a bumpy ride, but it will be safe," he assures us.

Bumpy? Definitely. But we land safely at the shipyards of Namhae and sit impatiently while tugs lock onto Telor's shuttle and tow it into a hanger.

Uncle Madox introduces a young thrall. "This is Emlyn. One of our soldiers in Cytgord discovered her when she got past the electronic locks of his shuttle, hacked the computer, and was about to steal the shuttle."

The young woman's skin could hardly get any more pale, but I see her blush as blood rushes to her face. Her blood is the same as ours, I remember. We are both of-the-blood.

Uncle Madox must have known he was embarrassing her. "She has been an important member of the team designing new life pods. She will tell you more about them."

209

When Emlyn speaks, enthusiasm overcomes embarrassment. Emlyn designed new guidance software for the life pods and programmed the autopilot to seek a standard star, find the largest planet, and reach a libration point. "Ships of the Res Publica searching for life pods will know to look at those places."

"Life pods don't have stardrive," Deryn says.

"When a tachyon signal is received from a destroyed ship, a search will begin at the source of the signal, and then on a line leading to the nearest standard star, finally, at libration points," Betsan says. "It makes sense."

"The searches, they might take thousands of millennia. The computers controlling the pod would be subject to quantum fluctuations. They would decay and no longer be reliable," Barri objects.

"The computers use ternary logic," Emlyn responds. I feel she is happy with the question and her ability to answer it. "They will *wake up* every century, compare three memories, and – if there is a difference – accept the two most in agreement. It's not foolproof, but it is better than random chance."

"That is brilliant," Betsan says. "But where will they find power?"

Emlyn blushes at Betsan's praise, but is not too embarrassed to answer. "The life pods have a small ion impulse engine. Just enough to give them some speed toward their target and then maneuver into Libration Points $\lambda 4$ or $\lambda 5$, which are the most stable. The radioactive decay of a block of Element 90 with a half-life of seven million millennia provides heat to a thermo-electric power supply for the ion engine, the computer, and the cold-sleep wake cycle once the pod finds itself in a suitable environment." She didn't need to tell us if someone were to force open a life pod, it would explode, killing the occupant and anyone around it. It is a practical response to the ancient command: 'Leave no companion behind; never become a captive.'

A life pod holds only one person. The opening is a hole, about one and a half meters in diameter, at one end. There is a bar across the top. Emlyn demonstrates entry by grabbing the bar, curling her knees to her chest, swinging her feet into the opening, and then sliding into the pod. She sticks out her head. "This pod is not powered, but on a ship, when someone enters the pod and lies on the couch, the entrance will close, the pod will seal and eject, and place its passenger in cold sleep."

Emlyn invites us to climb into the pod. We resist until Telor insists. "Academy doesn't teach the proper way to enter the pod nor how to inspect or program a pod. Someday, knowing these things may make the difference between death and life for you. Climb in." His eyes are hooded by his eyebrows and there is no humor in his voice.

Emlyn demonstrates the trapeze-like entry again, and then explains the external control panel. "There is an automatic program that can be overridden if you are close enough to a known star and have time to enter its coordinates. Otherwise, the pod will search for a standard star."

"If an Adversary ship was close enough to critically damage one of our ships, wouldn't they be able to see the ion trail left by the pod?" Barri asks.

Again, Emlyn seems excited to answer the question. "Yes! Unless overridden at the control panel, the pod will drift for a thousand days and then ignite the ion drive."

The bumpy ride from Namhae to Fortress is no less unsettling than the news that awaits us. Our Element Mate, Bräu, is dead. The message from Fortress Tarren is brief; rumors are rife, especially when we learn Bräu's Regent declared himself Gens Tarren. Bräu was not a popular person, however, my mates and I hold a brief Remembrance. I wonder if Bräu were killed because he had been sent home for being exposed as a spy.

~~~~~

After the Remembrance, I deal with another of my problems. Barri and Deryn are nervous when I insist they follow me to Father's den. I kneel; they nearly prostrate themselves. Father knows I have brought to him something froward, but I do not sense anger.

"Father, I know you placed Barri and Deryn in my element to be my guards. I know they swore to defend me with their lives. We have sworn brotherhood in blood, but not exchanged daggers."

Father's words relieve the boys' fears. "Barri of House Hynafol, Brother of my son, stand. Deryn of House Dolffin, Brother of my son, stand."

Barri and Deryn are no longer afraid. I am. After all, I am still kneeling.

"Garreth, Son, stand." He removes two house daggers from atop his desk. I hadn't seen them until now. Father knew. He knew all along.

"Barri, Deryn, you swore brotherhood with my son; will you repeat your oath and accept these daggers?" he asks.

Barri looks at Deryn. Something passes between them. Deryn nods, and Barri speaks. "I swear brotherhood with you, Garreth Bleddyn." Deryn echoes the oath.

I take the daggers from Father, and blood them on my arm and speak the words of the oath. I give the daggers to Barri and Deryn. "You may not wear these until after graduation. We must keep this secret, for it could destroy our element."

Barri and Deryn understand. So does Father. I think he is pleased.

~~~~~

Before Second Form ends, Telor tells me who will be in my element for Third Form. By then, the elements have stabilized. Barring a training accident or other cause of death, or interference by some powerful Gens, the eighteen cadets will be together until graduation. I know Father ensures Barri and Deryn are assigned to my element but I wonder why Lowri remains. She is a bastard who joined the element in Second Form. Someone important has sponsored her at Academy or she would not be here.

All my current and new element-mates except Andreas of Tarren, who replaced Bräu, visit Fortress Bleddyn during Spring Stormtime. Most are happy, but I feel Lowri's reluctance. Although she is a bastard, sworn to no house, she knows she will be a member of my element for the rest of our time at Academy. It is important she feel welcome and included. Alaw, my Sister-minus-three, does that. Alaw is very happy to have another older sister to play with, and her unconditional acceptance eases Lowri's concerns.

Selwyn is in trouble with his father. The boy thinks Uncle Garreth can get him paroled. I think about the ways Father punished me and agree with Telor that cleaning the wolf breeding pens during stormtime would be a suitable punishment. We do not tell Selwyn the thrall supervisor will teach him about the breeding program and his reward may be a companion-wolf cub.

~~~~~

Third Form Symbol

Winter Stormtime is mild and the sun shines brightly on my friends and me when we step from the shuttle onto the ancient flagstones and walk through the main sally port of Academy. In a tradition as old as the flagstones, we each touch the Third Form symbol on the door of our pod. The three vertical arrows instill both pride and a little anxiety. We will face greater challenges. Andreas of House Tarren has been a member for less than a year, but will be our commander. Before stormtime is over, he messages this and appoints Bryn his deputy. I watch Andreas and Bryn closely. Andreas is firm while Bryn is soft. In less than ten days I realize they are playing roles. When I describe this to Telor, laughter crackles over the communicator. "Andreas is playing you and your mates like a fiddle. His harshness triggers fear of failing. He makes himself your bulwark against outside forces. But he also makes himself unapproachable and his deputy a sympathetic ear – the one to whom you can take your fears.

"Give them a chance and tell me at Summer Stormtime what you think about this style of leadership."

~~~~~

When I return home for my fifteenth Summer Stormtime, Telor asks me what I think about Andreas's leadership.

"Andreas's leadership will work only in the short-term. It is already breaking down. His deputy is the real leader, and Andreas is isolated and ignored."

"Why?"

"Because we are not stupid. Everyone realizes it is an act."

Telor leads me to the breeding pens, where Selwyn has forgiven me for assigning him to clean the pens and is the proud companion of one of Arawan's pups.

~~~~~

The highlight of the Fall Quarter is the annual *Bo-taoshi* competition. My element and the three other elements in the group gather to plan our strategy. Usually, the defenders form concentric circles around the pole and fight off attackers. The attackers try to drag defenders away until the attackers can reach the pole and topple it. The battle almost always becomes a melee attack and defense. The day before we are scheduled to compete, Tac lectures the element on strategy and tactics.

Tac acts more and more like he is the Cadet Commander. This is wrong, and it weakens Andreas further.

After Tac dismisses us, Lowri pulls me aside. "Your sister won both attack and defense two years running. What was her secret? What can we learn from her? Tac was wrong to tell us what to do."

"The most important lesson I learned is that we are not her element. The second lesson is that the only difference between teams is spirit and will."

Despite Lowri's superb performance as monkey, we place barely above the 50% mark in the competition. In front of the element, Tac reprimands Bryn but not Andreas. I am not surprised. Andreas is of House Tarren and Tac is afraid of Gens Tarren.

The element becomes more and more dysfunctional. Friends snap at one another; Andreas awards demerits for the least infraction – unusual in Third Form. We all are looking forward to Winter Stormtime and Fourth Form.

~~~~~

Our shuttle ride to Fortress is bumpy and the weather foreshadows Winter Stormtime's promise. I show my mates to quarters. Barri and Deryn share a room; so do Gwen and Betsan. I know Barri and Deryn are more than mates, and sense Gwen and Betsan may be, too. While they unpack, I look for Telor.

Telor is waiting in the anteroom and takes me to the medico who removes my vambrace. The drugs that dull my mind, stimulate my body, and hide my telepathy have been reduced to nearly nothing; now I will no longer be protected at all. With the removal of the vambrace, I am also officially an adult, with adult duties and responsibilities. I am also a demon – a telepath.

Without the vambrace, I will no longer have help from the melatonin. I will have to rely on blocking techniques Telor taught.

Only minutes later, Father summons Telor and me to the War Room. Forecasts for Winter Stormtime are grim. Stormtime is two days away, but our people and allies already report storm damage, power outages, and deaths. Our War Room mobilizes to coordinate relief efforts. I sit at a terminal and distribute messages from our outposts and our allies. Telor sits at the console beside mine, monitoring messages intercepted from our adversaries and those not allied with us.

He touches my arm. "What are you hearing?"

"Message from the Power Station on Sehwa Island. The central tide generator broke from its mooring and lies on the bottom of the ocean. The secondary is operating, but provides only 30% of the power needed."

Before Telor can offer advice, I send a message to Sehwa Command to cut power to all but the hospital and instruct Kosong and Namhae Islands to divert 20% of their power to Sehwa. I hope the underwater cables will hold.

I receive acknowledgments from the islands as the next emergency message arrives. House Caerwyn reports a major hurricane moving east along the coast. It will dissipate before it reaches us, but allies are in its path, allies who no longer have downlinks from weather satellites. I prepare messages and relay them by starships through the FTL – Faster Than Light – system that gives us instantaneous communication with ships and colonies thousands of light-years away. It is not intended for ground-to-ground communication, but we are glad it operates without the need for satellite dishes.

Winter Stormtime dies a graceful death, and the day is sunny and calm when my mates and I return to Academy for Fourth Form. After the tension of Third Form, Andreas's approach to leadership, and a hectic stormtime, we are hoping for a calm Fourth Form.

The faculty names Ilym Element Commander. He has been quiet until now, but seems sure of himself. I do not share Ilym's self-confidence. He is quick to give orders, but slow to listen. He never asks for suggestions and seldom accepts those we offer. I decide he is insecure in his position and the pendulum has swung too far. There must be a middle ground. It must be possible to accept advice from a Tac without giving up leadership; it must be possible to direct people without giving orders at every opportunity and on every subject. Individual competition should not be at the expense of the element or the mission. But it happens. The leader must harness our energy to satisfy both individual needs and element success.

Garreth's Element 4th Form (Initial)
Garreth
Barri
Deryn
Betsan
Cledwyn
Nudd
Mawrith
Catrin
Gwen
Lowri
Arwel
Bedwyr
Brynmor
Andreas
Deri
Ilym (Commander)
Cari
Isca

219

~~~~~

My mates Barri, Deryn, Lowri, Betsan, and Arwel return to Fortress at Spring Stormtime. Barri and Deryn share a room as do Betsan and Lowri; Arwel shares my quarters. I feel sad Arawan does not bring Macca until I learn they moved into Selwyn's quarters with Arawan's pup. The first night, Arwel and I stay awake, whispering gossip about instructors and other cadets. It is after midnight when we fall asleep and seems only moments later when an alert tone on both our communicators wakes us.

Arwel shuts off his alarm and mumbles, "Must be a glitch – something from my house? Can you tell if—"

"Not a glitch. The War Room summons us both. Jumpsuit and sandals; they won't expect a uniform at this time of night."

We change from sleep pants in record time. The *slap-slap* of our sandals echoes from the stone walls of the hallways. I key the door and signal the guard to admit Arwel.

Telor has the night shift. He calls us to the command terminal. "Arwel, a tornado struck Fortress Caerwyn and destroyed most of their antennas. What survivable systems does your house have? What are the frequencies? We need to know what has happened."

Arwel understands and asks for access to a comm terminal. "I can establish connectivity with my house," he says.

I watch more and more information from House Caerwyn appear on a screen. It takes a while, but the screens show the status of House Caerwyn and our controllers direct resources to help.

Telor dismisses us when morning comes. Arwel thanks me for trusting him in the War Room. "You must have known I would see things most houses keep secret, even from allies."

"Sending aid to your house is more important than any secret in our War Room," I say.

"But there are still secrets."

"Yes, but even though there are secrets between us, may we be brothers?" I ask.

My words surprise Arwel but I see his understanding. Vendetta and blood. Links and broken links. Allies and enemies. For millennia, the Res Publica built its civilization on sand, not rock. Perhaps Father's ships with colonists from many houses, and my friendship with Arwel and others I meet at Academy can help change this. I have asked for brotherhood; Arwel agrees, and another blood ceremony will be kept secret from our element mates.

~~~~~

I want to use Fourth Form to continue my study of leadership and to decide which style best suits me. However, the year is too confusing. We lose Ilym, our first leader, before Summer Stormtime. He is crawling behind Cari and Mawrith, urging them to hurry, when a pyrotechnic triggered by a timer explodes under him. The explosion kills Ilym. Cari and Mawrith are not injured, but are washed out of Academy without appeal.

Only days later, our second leader, Bryn, is expelled for cheating on an exercise. A referee from his house gave him information. The referee disappears. We hear whispers he was summarily executed.

≈≈≈≈≈

I invite only five members of my element to the Fortress for Summer Stormtime. Barri and Deryn, Betsan and Lowri, and Arwel. After I settle my friends in their quarters, I seek Telor, who listens to my plan and takes me to see Father. I stand confidently in front of his desk.

"The two cadets who washed out were in my element since First Form. I know them well and believe they were not afraid, only uncertain. The cadet leader who died created the uncertainty."

Father listens quietly and then asks, "Where did your mates go?"

"To their houses, unjustly stripped of honor and suffering the contempt and insults of their elders and the mocking of their juniors."

"And you propose to restore their honor?"

"No, Father. Only they can do that. But I know a path they might take." I have seldom surprised my father, but I see his right eyebrow rise when I explain my plan.

When I finish, his eyebrow lowers to normal height. "You may draw on the house account. Take both Lieutenant Fender and Corporal Cos. I will inform the Academy Provost you will return late after stormtime because of house business. A good plan, Son."

I take those words with me to the War Room where a controller sets up the first call. The controller at the other end is reluctant to connect the call until I identify myself.

"Garreth, I'm surprised to hear from you." It is Mawrith.

"We have been mates and friends for more than three years. Our houses are allies. I am sorry we had no chance to speak before you were dismissed—"

"Kicked out. Literally pushed out the sally port into the wind to wait for a shuttle to take me back to Fortress Eryr in disgrace."

"Academy acted with undue haste. What will you do, now?"

Mawrith looks down at something that does not show on the vidscreen. I see his right arm move. *What is he holding?*

He looks up and speaks. "I have been rejected even as a recruit in the Home Guard. None of our ships' captains or caravan masters want me on their crew. The only thing left is the mercenary auction, but my expulsion will be on my record. No one will bid."

"I will."

"You? What? How? You mean for your house?"

"I cannot say what your assignment will be, but it will be honorable. Will you do this?"

Mawrith stares at the screen. He lifts his right arm. I see what he is holding – his unsheathed grace knife. It is a miniature of an ancient sword. He raises the knife.

"Mawrith—" Horror stops my voice.

He jabs his left arm with the knife and lifts it. I watch his blood flow down the blade. "By my blood, Garreth, I will do what you ask."

My relief must have been obvious. "Mawrith, thank you. I will be at the first auction at Cytgord after stormtime."

The call to Cari is less dramatic. After challenging several of her siblings and cousins to *Jaryeondo*, and in her words, "kicking butt," they no longer tease her. "However," she says, "I have no future here except supervising thralls in a packing house."

She accepts my offer.

I talk to Lieutenant Fender and Corporal Cos, and schedule the next step in my plan.

~~~~~

I know I will find Telor in the library. Before he can put down his book, I speak. "Father wants me to have a leadership position at Academy. The confusion in my element might open an opportunity. I do not want this."

Telor doesn't respond. He knows I have more to say. "Bryn kept himself isolated from us. The only time he spoke was to give orders. He watched us constantly and saw every failure and mistake to be a reflection on him."

"Did this work?"

"Marginally. We rank just above fifty percent, and will probably stay there. We would be in the top ten percent, perhaps higher, if everyone worked to his or her potential."

"Your element finished barely above fifty percent the past two years, but you had no washouts," Telor says. "You had three washouts and one death this year and you are at sixty-five percent. Which style of leadership is more effective?"

"That's what I do not know and why I won't accept a leadership position next form. The confusion in the element created a situation I cannot unravel. I would be inviting failure. Further, I haven't had enough time to understand what leadership means, nor how to exercise it."

"You have watched Father closely for years," Telor says.

"Father's leadership is based on his telepathy, blood, High Justice, and absolute power. I cannot lead cadets that way. The Academy mantra to *cooperate and graduate* requires leadership based on consensus. That may have a place, but takes too much time in a crisis or a battle. Trust must be created before a crisis or battle, but it takes time. It's a lot different from what Father does."

"I will tell Father," Telor says. "And make sure he understands."

~~~~~

Two days after stormtime I fly to Cytgord in Father's shuttle with Lieutenant Fender and Corporal Cos. Cytgord lies in the territory of House Bleddyn but is an open city. Father and Gens Dolffin maintain the garrison that provides security and order. We will stay overnight in their barracks. First, however, we visit the Registrar of the Auction. I stand in line, with Lt. Fender and Corporal Cos behind me. When I reach the Registrar, I present my communicator. "Please register me as a hiring agent."

The Registrar looks up, and laughs. "You? You're a cadet. Shouldn't you be in school?" He gestures toward Lieutenant Fender and Corporal Cos. "Move aside. There are real agents waiting behind you."

Fender and Cos move to stand beside me, but stay silent.

"They are not agents," I say. "They are my companion-guards."

The Registrar stares at the house crest on the adults' uniform, then sees the wolf rampant and the crest of the Mountain Company on mine. He sputters and takes my communicator. When my identification and the depth of my funds appear on his screen, he stands and bows. "My apology, Garreth of House Bleddyn. Please understand—"

"Please, complete the registration." I lower my voice and whisper. "There really are agents waiting in line."

The next morning, we enter the Hiring Hall to find several of the local garrison holding seats for us. The first candidate is a man wearing body armor, with an energy rifle and an old-fashioned powder pistol. A broadsword at least 150 centimeters long is slung over his back. The bidding starts at 1,000 coppers for a year's service and reaches 1,800.

"That's incredible," I whisper to Lieutenant Fender. She points to her communicator, which displays the auction program and the man's qualifications and experience. "Wow!"

"Please show me Mawrith and Cari," I ask. She shows me.

"Ten coppers for one year?" I say. "Pretty stingy."

"They would also receive food, shelter, clothing, weapons, and training," she says. Then, she surprises me. "You should not bid on them. If people realize House Bleddyn wants them, their value would increase."

"But, that's why we are here," I say.

"The garrison commander has agents in the audience who will bid. And collect the payment from you later." She chuckles.

About mid-morning, Corporal Cos nudges me, and shows me the computer record. "Garreth, would you bid on this one?"

A young woman stands beside the auctioneer. She wears a camouflage jumpsuit with a utility harness. Auburn hair falls in a braid down her back. We are close enough to see her green eyes. She carries a slug rifle and wears both energy pistol and saber.

"You need a girlfriend?" I whisper to Cos.

"No! Actually, yes, but Master Sergeant Rhingyll asked for her as a candidate for the Mountain Company. She's got a reputation with a saber."

"How high should I go," I ask after adding 50 coppers to the first bid of 100 coppers. I watch the amount and my name and house appear on the bid board. "And why won't my bid drive up her price?"

"People will see your bid on an experienced mercenary as a routine transaction. Your bid on two unknowns would raise suspicions."

"Oh."

My bid of 700 coppers wins the auction for the woman. Corporal Cos is pleased. I am a little nervous about Father's reaction. Other than a few coins to buy treats at Harvest Festival and now, bread, cheese, and ale at the Cadet Café, I have never been concerned about money.

The garrison agents hire both Mawrith and Cari at 25 coppers. We leave to meet them.

"You should introduce yourself to your girlfriend," I whisper to Corporal Cos, and send the certificate of hiring to his communicator. He bares his teeth and snarls deep in his throat, but I know he's not angry.

Mawrith and Cari greet me with firm, warriors' grips. I sense their relief.

Father's shuttle brings us back to Fortress where Master Sergeant Rhingyll takes charge of the woman. I bring my friends to family quarters for showers and clean uniforms with the House Bleddyn colors and crest. "Father will conduct the ceremony later," I explain, "but you are already members of House Bleddyn. This is Selwyn, my nephew and protégé. He will bring you to supper. Oh, and he promises the wolf is tame." The wolf cub inherited more from his sire than I realized – I see a bloody rabbit, hear a familiar snarky laugh, and feel the cub's smile.

Then, I hurry to Father's den.

"Seven hundred fifty coppers," he says.

"Uh—"

"A good sum for the woman and for your friends. We will hold the ceremony in the Great Hall after supper. You, Lieutenant Fender, Master Sergeant Rhingyll, Corporal Cos, the mercenary – and your new Brother and Sister."

With those last words, Father puts his seal on my decision. I feel his approval, and it feels good.

~~~~~

The ceremony begins with the Ritual of Camalos. For the woman, her oath to Master Sergeant Rhingyll is a second step. Then, Father conducts a final ceremony, adopting Mawrith and Cari into House Bleddyn, and giving them daggers with his blood – and mine.

The next morning, I go to bring Cari and Mawrith to breakfast, but they are not in their rooms. My communicator chimes. The message is from Father.

<<Your new brother and sister arrived on Songbaek Island.>>

I understand. He enrolled them in the school where they will start their lives over with a clean reputation and a harder curriculum even than Academy. I promised Father they would excel. I hope I am right.

The rest of Father's message worries me.

<<You must return to Academy. Provost Myrmidon
is angry – at me, not you, but he will take it out on you. >>

~~~~~

When I reach Academy, I learn Bedwyr named me his
deputy. He orders me to plan an exercise.

"Paintball or laser tag? And who should I ask to be our
opponent?"

Bedwyr hesitates to make even these simple decisions.
"Laser tag. Invite another element to join us as Blue Army, and
two others from the squadron to be Green Army." Bedwyr's
speech hesitates and his voice is a drone, with little change in
pitch or volume. He doesn't want this job. He doesn't care enough
to be a leader. I am his deputy, so I must deal with this. I can take
control without being named commander. Or, I can inspire
Bedwyr to take responsibility. The first would be easier, but the
second is more honorable.

I find three elements – one Fifth Form, one Sixth, and one
First – who want to join us. With a member of each element, I
plan an exercise on the Academy training range – the sand dunes
on the east coast. Instead of the usual capture-the-flag with a
defending army and an attacking army, we agree to re-create
skirmishes among mobile infiltration elements during an ancient
war. I describe the exercise as a massive game of hide-and-find
with laser tag. The others are excited to do something different.
We agree to instruct the shuttle pilots to land both armies at
locations unknown to each other and between forty and sixty
kilometers apart. We will scout and locate, and then attack. If we

are located first, we will defend – not a flag in a fixed position, but ourselves. After agreeing to the plan, the Blue Army and the Green Army hold private meetings.

I think about *Cooperate and Graduate* and agree with the Commander of the First Form Element to split our forces. This is a new idea for him, but is consistent with House Bleddyn's independent infiltration elements during the war to conquer the thralls and later, to defend against House Tarren.

I describe the plan to Bedwyr and try to sound excited without being too proud of it. I hope to stir his interest, but Bedwyr remains gloomy and uncaring. All he says is, "You will command the element; I will observe."

When the shuttles land, our Global Positioning Sensors show us to be too close to the southern border of the training range for the Green Army to be south of us. The Green Army is likely north of us, but they could be east or west. We split. Scouts from my element and those of our ally, the First Form Element, fan out. The scouts encounter the Green Army north-east of our original positions. We are better at moving through the brush and sea grass and surprise the Green sentries. We accept their parole – and the charge blocks for their laser-tag rifles. The Green sentries do not willingly give up information about their forces, but a chance remark by one helps us.

"They set up sentries but did not send out scouts. One sentry said he would 'miss lunch.' Maybe they set up a base camp," I tell the other element commander, and suggest we form two parallel lines of cadets, running south-north to approach the camp from both east and west.

"It's a split *hagik-jin* – crane-wing formation – but it gives them two escape routes," the First Form element commander says. We agree to pinch closed the ends of the lines during the attack. The plan gives us an easy victory. Taking lessons from my house's infiltration elements and what I learned from the Mountain Company, our cadets sneak through the brush and sea grass, duck-walking, crawling, or walking on their knees depending on the height of the cover. They encounter Green Army sentries close to the base, but we neutralize them before mounting a coordinated attack.

When one of my mates secures the hands of the Green Army Commander, the commander complains, "We needed more time to get ready."

He had as much time as we did. The thought forms in my mind but doesn't escape my lips. At the unsanctioned after-exercise gathering at the Cadet Café, the Green commander agrees he moved too slowly, and calls us, in his words, "Very sneaky warriors." It is a compliment, and we do not take offense. Besides, he and his mates are buying the ale.

Bedwyr wants to award the win to me, but I refuse. "Two elements, including one First Form, worked together even though we shared command. No single person was responsible for the win." Bedwyr is not happy, but I think I planted a seed in his mind.

~~~~~

My next chance to work on Bedwyr's attitude comes at our fourth-quarter *Bo-taoshi* competition. I drop hints about tactics, but he does not respond. Finally, when I know he is alone in his room, I break protocol and enter. He is sitting at his desk with an open book but his thoughts are elsewhere. I give him no time to react before I speak. "Bedwyr, this element needs a commander who is a leader. You have not led. Ilym pushed, and that got him killed. Bryn cheated, and that got him expelled and a Tac executed. You have done nothing but delegate – and not just your authority. You tried to delegate responsibility. No one can delegate responsibility, and I will not accept yours. You must accept your responsibility and you must lead."

This shocks him and he starts talking. "It won't matter. Everyone in Academy knows we lost four cadets – one killed and three expelled. There's a cloud hanging over us – and me. If they really wanted someone to pull the element up, they would have named you commander, but your father made sure you won't be tainted. I will never—"

"Cach!" I interrupt. The vulgarity in the ancient language – the word for excrement – shocks Bedwyr. Not because I never use that kind of language, but this time I yell it in his face while pressing my fists together in challenge. His mouth snaps shut and his eyes widen. I sense his fear and relax my arms.

"I'm sorry," I say. "I was angry, but I shouldn't have been. The reason I'm not Element Commander is Provost Myrmidon doesn't like me or my father, and Gens Tarren supports the Provost. My father does not want to challenge Gens Tarren over this – yet."

I look into Bedwyr's eyes. "Please do not tell anyone I said that."

Bedwyr understands I shared a confidence with him and offered my trust. "I was afraid of you," he says. "I have always been afraid. I hoped Academy would teach me to conquer my fear."

I reply with one of Telor's lessons. "As far as fear and courage go, you come out of Academy the way you came in. The only thing is, you are smarter and have more tools to deal with them."

Bedwyr seems unconvinced, but there is something more important I need to say. "When I am commander, I want it for an entire year. I asked my eldest brother to convince Father not to make me commander for half a year after Summer Stormtime."

"I will still be disgraced," Bedwyr says.

"Not if we work together, but you must both command and lead."

Fourth Form cadets do not have a curfew, but we must wake in time for roll-call formation, breakfast, and our first class. Both Bedwyr and I are groggy after spending much of the night making plans, but we are confident in those plans.

~~~~~

It takes several practice drills before Bedwyr performs his new role. Our mates who are accustomed to me acting for Bedwyr are reluctant to accept Bedwyr's command. I think the most reluctant will be Barri, Deryn, and Arwel – those sworn to me – but it is Nudd. I find him in the common room at a computer terminal, sit beside him uninvited, and speak quietly.

"Nudd, you owe loyalty and obedience to Bedwyr. You don't show him either."

"I can't respect him; he failed as a commander and leader."

My words wake Nudd from his boredom. "I said 'loyalty and obedience,' not respect. Master Sergeant Rhingyll, the commander of our Mountain Division, tells each new soldier, 'I demand your loyalty; I will earn your respect.'

"Those words echo a lesson my brother, Telor, told me. Respect is a two-edged sword. The sword is not whole unless each edge is sharp. The sword is sharpened upon a grinding stone. Respect must flow between two people. They are the two edges of the sword. Respect must be earned. That is the grinding stone. But, respect must be offered before it can be earned. That is where the analogy of the sword breaks down.

"Bedwyr is in a position of authority; he has certain responsibilities. By our Academy oath, we owe him obedience and loyalty. Will you agree, and will you give him time to earn our respect and our trust?"

"I knew you understood," Nudd says. "You should be our commander. You —"

"I will be, someday," I interrupt. "But my understanding is still shallow. Will you also give me time to learn?"

Nudd sits quietly while the computer times out and the screen goes blank. Then he agrees.

~~~~~

Bedwyr becomes more engaged, and our element gains momentum and spirit. We score in the top twenty-five percent in

Bo-taoshi and the top ten percent in academics. Just before Winter Stormtime, Nudd comes to me.

"You were right," he says. "And Bedwyr earned our respect. I hope we will be together next year, and that you will command."

"My father is still reluctant to challenge Gens Tarren over this. Other things, including Tarren's attacks on our territories and allies are more important."

~~~~~

I invite all my element-mates to Fortress Bleddyn for Winter Stormtime. Andreas is the only one who does not accept. After Bräu's expulsion from Fortress for spying and his death, no scion of Tarren wants anything to do with House Bleddyn. Seventeen members of the element gather around a table in my small dining room, but we are not eating. We are planning a battle. Bedwyr takes charge with the others' support. The battle is a recasting of a famous battle between the Pirates of the Free Islands and the combined fleets of Dolffin and Bleddyn. Our opponents are an element spending stormtime at Fortress Dolffin. They will be the pirates. Our computers will be linked; both teams will see the same holographic images. Bedwyr draws ideas from each of us.

Telor enters and interrupts our planning. "I received word from Academy. Gwaethafwyr – Gwen – will be Element Commander during Fifth Form." That is all; he turns and leaves.

Most of our mates are excited and happy for Gwen. I am happy because Father did not force me unprepared into leadership. Bedwyr is happy he is able to turn over to Gwen an

236

element that is not failing, but has moved to a higher ranking. He's also relieved. He still doesn't like command.

Garreth's Element 5th Form
Garreth
Barri
Deryn
Betsan
Cledwyn
Nudd
Maddy
Catrin
Gwen (Commander)
Lowri
Arwel
Bedwyr
Halee
Andreas
Deri (Deputy)
Gavin
Fionn
Isca

Gwen is stunned. She looks at me and I sense her puzzlement and a touch of fear. I respond. "Gwen, you showed us your mettle – your strength and enthusiasm – from the first *Bo-taoshi* match after you joined us in Second Form. You will be a fine commander." I walk to a cabinet and remove a tray of demitasse glasses and a bottle of Father's *dŵr y bywyd*. I pour it and speak. "This is 'the water of life.' It is proper to salute our new commander with it, for she will have great influence over our lives in the coming year."

I raise my glass in salute, but before I can speak, Gwen lifts hers. "When one is saluted, it is customary to respond. Garreth offered his salute whilst pouring, although he may not know it. Here is my response, and I ask you to drink to it. *Gan fy gwaed a'm mywyd ond dim ond gyda'ch cryfder y gwnawn hyn* – by my blood and my life but only with your strength will we do this."

Although somewhat startled by the twist in protocol, our response is unanimous and spirited. "*Gan fy gwaed* – by my blood."

After offering Gwen the arm-clasps of warriors, we resume planning. Now, we are under Gwen's command. I sense Bedwyr's relief and wink at him.

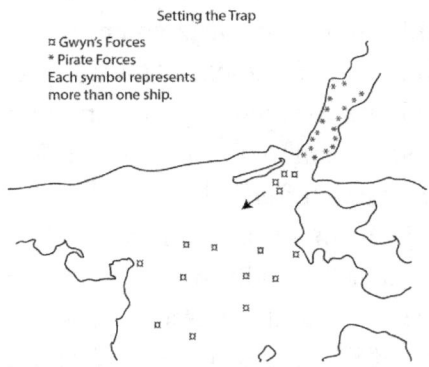

Setting the Trap
¤ Gwyn's Forces
* Pirate Forces
Each symbol represents
more than one ship.

"We are outnumbered 74 to 54. Our ships are smaller, but more maneuverable. I want to draw the enemy into a trap in the open sea." Gwen's plans are clear.

"We will lose the advantage of maneuverability," Gavan says. He is a new member who replaced Ilym only this past year.

"No, the channel is too narrow to maneuver, even for our ships. Besides, if we are in open waters, the enemy sailors from sinking ships will drown before they can swim to shore," Maddy says.

Planning continues into the night. The next day, we link computers with those at House Dolffin, and start the battle.

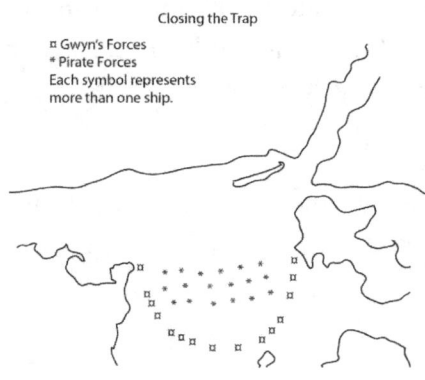

Closing the Trap
¤ Gwyn's Forces
* Pirate Forces
Each symbol represents
more than one ship.

At first light, Gwen sends seven ships into the channel where the pirates are anchored. The rest of our forces are spread randomly south of the channel in a large bay and show fishing nets. When the pirates spot our seven ships, our captains order

238

their ships to sail southward. The pirate fleet sees an easy victory and follows.

The instant the pirates enter the open bay Gwen orders our fleet into *hagik-jin*. The wind is at our backs, and our ships drop their nets, complete the maneuver and bombard the pirates with cannon and fire-arrows. The pirates in the rear turn and flee into the channel; however, our forces sink 37 pirate ships and capture 12.

~~~~~

I found one of Karmet's aphorisms buried in *The Book of Proverbs:* "As extraordinary claims require extraordinary evidence, so does great reward require great risk." Gwen takes this to heart. Even though she isn't officially our commander until the first day of Fifth Form, we accept her leadership from the moment Telor announces her appointment. She takes us into more risky situations in the computer game. We win, but were not sure of victory until midway into the battle. If the wind shifted, we would have lost. I wonder if she will lead us this way when we return to Academy.

My first chance to study Gwen's leadership is during training for the Spring *Bo-taoshi* competition. Four elements of Group VI of Squadron Phoenix seek a private place to practice strategy and tactics. Gwen's notion of risk – and her confidence – sway the other element commanders. They cede leadership of the group to her. I am impressed with her boldness, but wonder if it is enough to bring us victory.

Her strategy for attack is both strong and lively. We will attack in *chojeom*, or focal-point formation. However, unlike most attacks, ours will not break into a melee attack, but continue to strike the enemy in a single place. She convinces not only our element but three others not to break up, but to maintain the attack. We succeed, toppling our opponent's pole and pulling down his monkey in record time.

Her strategy for defense is nothing more than linking arms and not giving in to the attackers. It risks no more than any simple defense and is no more successful than most. We lose all defensive matches, but by spirit and strength keep our pole erect long enough, and win enough attacks, to score in the top 25%.

The leadership lesson I learn from Gwen is that a bold and risky strategy must be backed by more than bravery and foolhardiness.

~~~~~

Early in fifth form, we train in fighters. The fighters have both anti-gravity pods and reaction engines powered by high energy-density liquid fuels created from methane scavenged from our sewers, animal waste, and composting. They also have only one option for peeing. Before we pilot a fighter, we learn that option. Although it works, it is not pleasant. The urine collector for boys is a cucumber-shaped funnel connected to a hose valved into a planet's atmosphere or into space. Actually, it is fun to pee over Gens Tarren's lands, but I am careful no one sees me do that. There are different style funnels for men and women, and the boys always ask for the largest size.

All this is worth the effort when we take command of a fighter with no restrictions on the controls. We chase one another thousands of meters in the sky and into cislunar space. Our weapons are low-power lasers, although we train to use more powerful masers and torpedoes.

Our enthusiasm for flight training carries over to other things. We excel in academics and rank in the upper twenty-five percent in athletics. We are a happy group when we are dismissed for Winter Stormtime. Five of my mates join me in the shuttle to Fortress. I sit with Alwen, Sister-plus-six. She is an instructor, but I am in none of her classes. This is the first time we have spoken since last stormtime.

"Father will be angry if you do not ask for leadership in your last Form," she says.

"I did," I tell her. Although she is my sister, I am nervous. She took her element to School Championship twice, a record not broken since.

"Telor told me you didn't feel you were ready, last year," Aelwen says. "Father was more sharp in his comments." She doesn't ask me why I did not ask for leadership.

"I wasn't ready," I say. "I didn't know how to be a leader. Now, I think I do." I explain the different styles of my previous cadet leaders and their weaknesses.

"What did you learn?" she asks.

"There is no single correct kind of leadership," I say. "Leadership must respond to the individual, to the situation, and to the element. Teaching a junior cadet who makes an honest mistake is better than expelling a cadet. Punishing a cadet by giving him or her a dirty job to complete is better than expelling the cadet. Daffyd told me about helping Aurin of Ellis dig a cesspit, and how it was a key to their bonding."

241

"And you are prepared to do this? To judge your people and respond in the way they need?"

"Yes." I say.

"And where did you learn this? Not from your leaders the past few years."

I grin. "No, Sister. From you. And from Bethan."

"From me?" She seems genuinely puzzled.

"You must know by now that spies from other elements recorded all your training for *Bo-taoshi*," I say.

"I know it, now. Didn't know it until the day before the final exercise. Barely had time to change our strategy. We did win though."

"I found the recordings and studied them. They were quite good, and the audio picked up everything you said. Actually, I learned several new words Father would not approve."

Sister chuckles. She and I sit in companionable silence for the rest of the journey home.

~~~~~

Wind whistles down the chimney and sleet beats against the windows when I report to Father's den.

"I asked Aelwen if you applied for leadership next year. She would not answer, only shrugged and said I would have to ask you." My father is more angry than curious. I think he assumes the worst.

"Yes, Father. I asked for leadership of my element."

Father is silent for several minutes. I know he is thinking, incorporating the knowledge I applied for leadership into his plans. He is always planning. Years ago, he completed genetic modification. He could live for twenty millennia or more if he is not assassinated like his father was.

"Garreth! Are you listening?" Father snaps.

I pull myself from my wandering thoughts. "Yes, Father."

"Find Telor and bring him." Father turns to the computer screen, dismissing me.

~~~~~

I find Telor in the library. It is his favorite place where he reads and studies.

"Telor, Father summons us," I say.

Telor looks up from his book. "Garreth, I am glad you are home," he says. He puts a marker in the book and stands. He takes my hand. "Come," he says. "Take me to our father."

The physical contact amplifies Telor's thoughts. He is my first eldest brother. When I was growing up, my other older siblings were often busy with their friends and had little time for me. But Telor was there, always.

~~~~~

"Father, Telor and I are here," I say, even though Father knows we entered the room. I kneel. Telor is Chancellor and does not kneel.

Father is silent, thinking. Then, "I ensured Garreth will lead his element next Form."

Father was busy communicating with our allies while I sought Telor.

"Garreth will face new dangers. Leadership will put him more firmly in the sights of our enemies. My other children at Academy face their own difficulties. They cannot protect him except in a dire emergency."

"I understand, Father," Telor says. "Corporal Cos and Lieutenant Fender will join the Academy faculty as Garreth's defenders."

Father nods. It is the only way he ever shows approval. Both Telor and I understand. We also understand he dismissed us.

Telor leads me away. "You know there are things Father and I kept from you. Now is the time to tell you some of them. Not everything, not yet. In the next few days, I will tell you what is most important."

Telor tells me about the aftermath of my elevation, the assassination of Gens Tarren, and that my Aunt Gwenallt, who was once Soosong, was the assassin.

"Does Selwyn know?" I ask. My concern is for Selwyn. Although he is Telor's son, he is my protégé and nephew, and child of Soosong, once my mentor but now my aunt. Some

244

relatives think he is not of-the-blood of House Bleddyn. I know Father elevated Selwyn in the presence of the house and named him, so I do not understand why some speak against him.

"Selwyn is only ten years old," Telor says. "I will tell him his heritage soon. If something happens to me and I am unable to tell him, you will do this."

~~~~~

The next morning, Aelwen and Telor summon me to the library. I sit between them in a corner, surrounded by shelves of books and facing a window that overlooks a raging storm. Trees bend in the wind. The only sound from the storm is the hiss of pellets of ice striking the windows.

Telor's words pull me from the storm. "The cadets in your Fifth Form, including Andreas, will be in your Sixth Form." I expect that, although I know Telor, Aelwen, and father have been busy ensuring loyal friends will surround me.

"We know all of them," Telor explains. "Not all are sworn to you or House Bleddyn."

Barri and Deryn are sworn to me. They are always in my element. Betsan and I have long been together, too. If she agrees, she will be my Second. I smile when I see Arwel's name. Arwel is the only one still wearing a vambrace. I think his drugs are not quite balanced. He is obsessive about too many things, and always a little jittery. However, he is a good person and a good companion – and a Brother-in-blood. Isca is the quiet one, but he thinks deeply and never speaks until he has something important to say.

I am no longer surprised to see the bastard Lowri's name. We have been mates most of our time at Academy and she is often a visitor to Fortress. She is a skilled pilot and fearless warrior. Maddy, Halee, Gavan, and Fionn have been part of the element for only a year or so. I will need to learn more about them.

Garreth's Element
6th Form

Garreth (Commander)
Barri
Deryn
Betsan (Second)
Cledwyn
Nudd
Maddy
Catrin
Gwen
Lowri
Arwel
Bedwyr
Halee
Andreas
Deri
Gavin
Fionn
Isca

"What are the chances they can all visit Fortress before stormtime is over?" I ask.

Telor is happy to accept the challenge of flying through the storms, and I issue invitations to those who are not already here.

CHAPTER 14 LEADERSHIP AND CONSENSUS

A leader doesn't look
for consensus;
a leader builds
consensus.
— Geraint
The Book of Proverbs

Stormtime still rages and my guests are bragging to one another about the excitement of their shuttle rides through storms when I call a meeting. Most think we will play a battle simulation, but I have other plans. "My father ensured you were assigned to this element and that I would be commander. We have had five years to learn that *command* and *leadership* are not the same, although they are closely linked. I intend to be more a leader than a commander, and this is how I plan to lead. The Academy tells us to *cooperate and graduate*. We first saw how this worked during our recognition ceremony when we were First Form Cadets. When there is time to plan, we will act through consensus. In the heat of battle, leadership demands instant obedience.

I see eyes widen when I say Father arranged my position and their assignment to my element. Everyone knows powerful Gens can do this, but no one speaks of it openly.

"Garreth, we all knew this, but you surprised us when you said it," Barri says. "I am glad you told us." The others nod agreement. I hide my relief. If I had not brought it into the open, they would wonder and question, but remain silent. It would be an open wound to weaken the element.

I am not surprised when Nudd speaks. "You remind us Academy tells us to *cooperate and graduate*. But the faculty judges us as individuals to determine our ranking at graduation which affects our placement thereafter – in our house or the Mercenary Guild or elsewhere." He did not ask the question I saw in his mind, *What's in this for us as individuals?* I was glad he wasn't thinking, *What's in this for me?*

"A good question, Nudd. You won the place of Element Inquisitor. Not, however, to torture your mates, but to question everything anyone offers – including me. Watch and learn, but share what you learn. To answer your question, my father has a saying based on our house's long history as sailors – 'A rising tide lifts all boats.' I believe the higher the element is ranked, the higher ranked each of us will be. And that is my goal."

I admire Nudd for his ability to frame and ask the right question, so I am happy he agrees. He relaxes in his chair and lifts a mug of tea. He looks at the others and sees their understanding.

"Strength will come from connections, camaraderie, and confidence in ourselves and each other. Success will come from strength," I say.

The door opens. Nana leads thralls bearing trays. The lunch they set is infinitely more important than my speech. While we eat, the food knits us together as friends and mates and we chatter of inconsequentials.

After lunch, I realize I said all I want to say, and I sense my mates becoming restless. "Meeting adjourned. Thank you. Lowri, would you pilot us to the café?"

I didn't need to say which café. There are several public houses on Mesa, but only one near Academy that caters openly to cadets. It is off-limits to us, but since Sixth Form has not officially begun, we may visit. Not that we never did during earlier forms.

A dozen other cadets arrive early. Instead of submitting to Academy rules and discipline, they book rooms above the café. They recognize us as mates and invite us to join their already large table. It does not take long for the publican to shoo us all to a private room. "It will be more comfortable." And a lot less noisy, and much less damage when we fight, he thinks.

One of the newest members of my element, Halee, isolates me for a moment. We stand in a dark corner of the hallway while the others pass. Halee is scion of the small and politically weak House Itan. Itan is an ally of House Bleddyn and Halee is fearless in conversation, although she pitches her voice for my ears, only. "Are there not members of more powerful houses you could recruit?"

"Yes, many. However, there are none who score higher than you in tactics. My goal is a winning element, and I find it easy to sacrifice politics for skill and courage."

I take a moment to think. "On my first day at Academy I watched Barri quiz each member about his or her skills. You have been an element mate for a year. You will be our training coordinator. Identify anyone who has deficiency in skills. Then, use that to guide our training program."

My offer startles her, but she agrees. "I will do this, but you must tell the others soon. I will not spy on my mates, even in this."

"Tomorrow at breakfast."

She agrees, and we follow the others into the private room. A discussion is underway. My mates saved a place for me at the head of the table. I feel interest on everyone's part, but no thoughts of the fight the publican feared.

"… no matter how difficult the problem or how complex the puzzle, there was always an answer," someone says.

"Or an escape," Isca says. "That is what we learned, but it is not always true."

When the others look toward him, Isca continues. "My father is a baker. Even though thralls work for us, he is always in the bakery early in the morning. Starting when I was six, he brought me with him. I learned to knead dough and mold it into shapes. That's what happened to us. We faced problems and puzzles together, without the traditional beatings, and are now a cohesive element of true and loyal friends, molded and bonded by experience. That is where we will find our success."

Our conversation draws in the other cadets who recognize our element to be special. More reality than seeming. Like moths to the flame, they congregate around us until after midnight when the publican declares the café to be closed. Lowri stays sober enough to pilot my mates and me back to Fortress.

Early the next morning, my element and I arrive at Academy and find Andreas of Tarren already there.

"Why is Lowri still in the element?" he demands. "I should not associate with persons of such low station." Andreas hisses his esses when he speaks.

"She is the school champion shuttle pilot," I reply.

"Don't expect me to work with her." Andreas snorts.

I put my face in Andreas's and lower the pitch of my voice until it is a growl in the back of my throat. "You accepted this assignment and swore loyalty when you entered Academy. Your Gens wants you in this element, or you would not be here. My Gens made me Element Commander despite your Gens. I expect you to work with every member of this element. Do you understand?"

Andreas realizes I am serious. He agrees, but I see his reluctance. I must watch him.

~~~~~

Two days after I return to Academy, Corporal Cos confronts me in a hallway. I feel his fear when he gives me a package. "Garreth, during your next exercise you may face real enemies. Keep this hidden. Do not use it unless your life or the lives of your mates are threatened."

When I am alone, I open the package. My eyes widen. An energy pistol. Academy controls these weapons, and issues them to cadets only at the training range under close supervision.

Something is wrong, and Cos believes we will be in great danger during the exercise.

That afternoon I swallow my fear and address my element.

"Before first light tomorrow, we will board a shuttle. We do not know where it will take us, except it will be an uninhabited part of the Equatorial Continent. We do not know if the terrain will be mountain, rain forest, rain-shadow desert, savannah, or swamp. We will not know where to find food and water. We will not know what animal life is dangerous until we confront it … or it confronts us. Other than what we carry, which will include slug rifles, we do not know what supplies and equipment we will have until we receive them, and we may receive nothing."

I look from one face to another. "We have been six years preparing for this. We studied the geography and the flora and fauna of World. We climbed mountains, swam rivers, trekked through jungle and across desert. We are prepared except for the unknown. When we face the unknown, it will no longer be unknown. We will know it and we will adapt. We will survive. We will do more than survive. We will thrive!"

I see confidence growing. "Each of you will think on the unknowns we may face and add what you think necessary to your standard kit."

"Garreth," Arwel says. "My brother told me in his element one person prepared for desert, one for rain forest, one for high plateau, one for the glaciers above House Eryr—"

"Yes. But we will do this my way. If they separate us, each will be at least minimally prepared to survive if we are separated.

252

When we are united – and we will be united – we will discard equipment unsuited to the situation."

~~~~~

After a flight of six hours, we land in a small clearing in the middle of a jungle. The shuttle loadmaster harries us into heat and humidity. We would have lost anything we were not wearing or carrying. The shuttle takes off before the door closes.

I am the first to board the shuttle and the last out. When I jump to the ground, I see my element in a defensive circle with weapons pointing outward, each one alert. In past exercises, our weapons were only paintball or laser-tag rifles. Today, we have swords, daggers, and slug rifles. The slug rifles suggest we will face real enemies, although Academy's explanation is that we might encounter wild animals. Will these arms be necessary? What are Academy's plans for the exercise? Will another element harass us? Will we face real slugs from others' rifles? How true is Academy's explanation? Will the energy pistol be necessary? If so, why?

I push these thoughts aside for the moment and check my compass. The sun-angle shows the time is just after dawn. We flew westward, outracing the sun. Southward, too, based on the sun's height above the horizon. I guess we are somewhere southwest of House Ellis territory. I'm not sure it helps to know that. No house claims these lands, and no house will aid us, even if they discover us.

"This is hot. I'd rather snow," Gavan says. He is of House Eryr. His home is among some of the highest mountains and glaciers on the Equatorial Continent.

Cledwyn of House Caerwyn laughs. "It's like home." He drops his pack, removes his uniform, and stands in loincloth and sandals. I envy his freedom, but stay clothed. My uniform and insignia are one source of my authority. At this moment, I need their security.

"Everyone accounted for, sir." It is Betsan, my Second. She has polled each member of the element.

"Thank you, Betsan," I say. "Cledwyn, you know the jungle, take lead scout and mark a path southward. We will follow you."

We move less than 200 meters into the jungle before Betsan catches up with me. "South, Garreth? Everything I've heard says to stay close to the drop point, so—"

"That's the problem," I interrupt. "It's always 'everything I've heard.' I heard the same stories. But I'm not interested in repeating others' stories, or waiting for whatever Academy plans to happen. I will make my own story – on this exercise and for the rest of my life."

Betsan thinks she understands, but she doesn't. I am afraid, but I must not show it. Cos's gift of an energy pistol is a warning, but a warning of what? The sense of doom – is it real, or is it something I create in my mind? I look at the members of my element and feel their adrenalized excitement. I hold in my hands the lives of seventeen cadets, my friends, brothers and sisters, and companions. I shake off my fear and follow Cledwyn's marks into the jungle.

~~~~~

The whine of an energy weapon is unmistakable. The bolt comes from our left and strikes Betsan. She falls onto the drift of dead vegetation that covers the ground.

"Adversary abeam to port. Take cover, suppression fire," I order. Even though we are in a jungle, kilometers from any body of water, the nautical phrase energizes my mates. I drop and wriggle until I am shielded by a copse of ferns. The instant I reach shelter, I push the emergency recall on my communicator.

This is what Cos feared. We were attacked with an illegal weapon less than an hour after we landed. Someone knew and was waiting for us.

Over the staccato crack of my element's slug rifles I hear Betsan moaning.

"Cease fire. Deryn, see to Betsan," I call. After Betsan, Deryn is strongest in medical knowledge. I know he will need bandages. I use my dagger to cut my pants legs into strips.

Cledwyn returned when he heard the shooting. I order him to scout in the direction the shot came from. "Do not be seen or captured." Cledwyn drops his pack and rifle. Naked except for loincloth and armed only with dagger and grace knife, he disappears into the jungle.

I pull the communicator from my pocket. There is no acknowledgment of my emergency signal. I send a test signal to the nearest satellite. Nothing. The communicator is not working. I look for Betsan's. Destroyed – struck by the energy burst that scorched her legs. We are isolated. Telor once said, "There is always an escape." I wonder if he imagined a situation like this. Did Academy create this situation? No, it is a real enemy – House

255

Tarren. I remember Father saying Gens Tarren would kill one of his own if it meant he could kill a Bleddyn.

"We need to move," I say. "And we must carry Betsan." I sacrifice my tunic and the others' to make a stretcher, two sapling trees laced through the sleeves of the tunics. It is the best we can do.

We are now half naked, except Deryn, who brought an extra tunic, and Arwel, whose kit includes a complete uniform.

"Garreth," Arwel says. "You should wear this uniform. It will be a little large—"

My laugh surprises the entire element. "Thank you," I say to Arwel. "But you are the one who thought to bring an extra uniform, and it should be you who wears it. Who knows, we might need a uniformed emissary." I laugh again. "Besides, this is more than I wore when playing in the forest."

I take off my boots and attach them to my pack. I think of the time I ran away, shot and ate a predatory cat. I think of the times I ran along animal trails in the jungle, along sandy beaches, and stony mountain trails wearing nothing but a loincloth. Primal thoughts spin through my mind. I shuffle them aside, but keep them close. I think I will need them before this is over.

~~~~~

Cledwyn returns and reports. "Only one person fired on us. He then rejoined his unit. They are adults, not cadets. I counted ten, but there may be more. They have slug rifles, energy pistols, and multiple blades. None are close now."

"Mercenaries," I say. "Catrin, you are second while Betsan is injured. Assemble the element."

"We came under attack, and our attackers are near," I say when everyone is close by. "The attackers are enemies of my house. They target me. You are innocent—"

"Garreth! We know what you will say," Catrin says. "But we stand beside you. Any attack on you is an attack on us."

I understand what my element is thinking. "There is something else I must tell you," I say. I remove the energy pistol from my kit. "Allies of my house feared we might find ourselves in danger and provided this. There is only one. Its charge block holds five shots and I have no extra charges. I believe I am the best marksman in the element; therefore, I will keep it. Bari? You are second best. You will hold it if I am disabled or dead."

I face puzzled looks. "Commander, given Betsan's wounds we should call for pickup," Arwel says. "Surely—"

"I signaled for pickup. My communicator does not work. Nor does Betsan's. Mine was sabotaged to fail; Betsan's was destroyed in the attack. We are on our own. However, we will survive and we will thrive!"

Their whispered affirmations are not enthusiastic, but under the circumstances, adequate. There will be time, later, to build confidence. For now, I choose to resume the march, turning southwest, away from the enemy.

The exercise is scheduled for ten days. We barely began the first day. An enemy of unknown size and composition outguns us. We are in dense jungle, half naked, including Arwel, who re-packs his spare uniform.

Just before dusk, Cledwyn removes a blowgun from his kit, and offers to hunt for us. I know he grew up in jungle terrain, and approve. He rewards my decision when he brings back in time for supper a large four-leg. We watch Cledwyn butcher the animal.

"Most will spoil before we can eat it," he says. "And we have neither time nor concealment to smoke the meat. I hate the waste, but our lives will depend on it."

Cledwin cuts small pieces from the liver and feeds them to Betsan. The others feast on the tender loin meat. There is enough light remaining to see the blood running down our faces and chests – and the broad smiles we exchange.

"Not likely any other element will have such an experience," Betsan whispers before Deryn injects her with anti-pain medicine and she falls asleep.

Catrin sets a rota for guard duty. The first shift takes position; the rest of us try to sleep, but I cannot. My mind races. Will the enemy find us tonight? Can we avoid them? Should I seek an encounter with them? How best might we use the single energy weapon?

The next morning while breakfasting on more of the deer, I explain the decision I made. "Betsan needs care we cannot provide. We have no working communicators. The mercenaries probably do. Our objective now is to capture a communicator. We were fired upon from ambush; we are free to fire on them without warning. If they capture any of us, we will attempt rescue and fire upon the adversary without regard for the captive's life. It is far better to die than become a captive. It is far better to die than to become a bargaining chip. We will leave no one behind."

I conflated the ones who attacked my element with the Adversary of our people. It is not true, but it is necessary. I also reminded them of two rules of combat inherited from the Conquest: *Leave no companion behind; never become a captive.*

"I do not expect that to happen. They think we are unseasoned cadets, armed only with slug rifles and swords. These mercenaries are not used to operating as a team. They do not know the spirit of this element which makes us stronger than a hundred mercenaries."

"He who does not fear death will live; he who seeks to live will die. If a solitary defender stands watch at a strong gateway, he may drive terror into the hearts of an enemy numbering in the thousands." Cledwyn quotes.

Although the cheers of my element are muted, I see determination grow in their minds.

Two carry Betsan and continue toward the southwest. Others guard the rear and the fore. I send Cledwyn east to scout the enemy. At noon, we reassemble.

Cledwyn reports contact. "Two mercenaries were tracking us through the jungle. They lost contact and no longer see us. Eight others push southward. They may know something about the terrain we do not – an impassable river or a spur of a mountain perhaps – that will force us to turn toward them."

"They will set up an ambush," Catrin says.

"Then we will ambush them, first, How fast are they moving? Can we move faster?" I address the questions to Cledwyn.

"They are not burdened with a litter, but carry heavy packs. Likely food. They are killers but not hunters. We can move faster than they."

Tetrapod

The next morning, I send Cledwyn to scout while we press ahead. Before dark, Cledwyn returns with our supper – a tetrapod. "It crawled on the bank of a stream to lay eggs. It feeds on the dark-green vegetation of the marshes, and will be a good source of nutrients."

We depend on dark, leafy green vegetation for the copper essential to our blood. The herbivores that feed on such vegetation are a better source because the copper accumulates in their meat.

The tetrapod is not as easy to chew as was our first supper, but Cledwyn is right about the eggs, which he cuts from the creature's belly and feeds to Betsan.

~~~~~

"What are you doing?" Nudd asks after supper.

My fingers are flashing to braid small vines and tie them to pouches cut from an undershirt. The three pouches each hold a smooth rock plucked from a stream.

"He's making a bolas," Deryn says. He has seen me use a bolas, and understands.

260

"It will be good only for one use," I say, "but it is silent."

After four more days' march, Cledwyn returns at dusk to tell us our adversary reached a wide, rushing river. "It flows from the east. Even without an injured companion on a stretcher, we could not safely cross the river. There is a clearing thirty meters short of the river. The mercenaries camp there."

"They will set an ambush near the river," Catrin suggests.

I listen to my soldiers' reports and ideas, and then announce, "In two days, the moon will rise an hour after sunset. It will give enough light. We will attack at first light."

By moonlight, we push through the jungle. Before sunrise, we take positions around the mercenary camp. Lowri, Barri, and I take rope and climb into trees. The mercenaries are too confident. The guards never think to look up. It is a weakness shared by many.

At first light, before the mercenaries stir, we attack. I fire the energy pistol four times, carefully and precisely into the midst of the encampment, then fire the last bolt as I swing from the tree. The fifth energy bolt is the signal for the others to attack. Lowri sits in the crook of a branch, fires her slug rifle several times, then swings down. She lands on her feet, unslings her rifle, and fires, picking her targets carefully. At the same instant, Barri fires a full magazine on automatic then fast-ropes from his perch. His sword flashes and a mercenary loses his head. Nudd pops up behind a bush. His bolas wraps around a mercenary's neck, strangling the man. Nudd unships his rifle and fires. Others of my element fire their slug rifles from concealment. Six mercs are killed; four, wounded. They destroy their long-range communicator before we capture them.

"When they do not report, someone will come looking for them. We must flee," Deryn says. I know he wants to protect me.

"No," I say, emboldened by victory. "Our objective is to escape with Betsan. When others come, we will kill or capture them and take their communicators – and their transportation."

And whoever comes looking will lead me to whoever sent these assassins. My thoughts are dark.

Cledwyn does not want to wear the bloody clothes of a dead enemy but I ask him to put on one of the merc's armor and lie on the ground as if wounded. Catrin is not reluctant, and grins when she takes armor from a dead mercenary. "Convenient," she says, hefting the armor. "She was my size. May I keep it?"

"Catrin, I owe you the best armor my house can make," I say. "You may keep this, or that which I give you."

Catrin grins. "I accept your offer of new armor. But I will keep this one. It belongs in my house's trophy room."

Gwen is first to spot the shuttle approaching. She whistles a signal. Those pretending to be dead stop wiggling and whispering. The shuttle crew – a pilot and loadmaster – expect no resistance. Catrin pulls the loadmaster from the ramp and subdues him while Deryn and Barri drag the pilot from the cockpit. The rest of us enter the shuttle.

If we are to escape detection, we must fly through the treetops. Lowri is the best pilot and takes control of the shuttle.

Barri demands to sit in the copilot seat. He uses the butt of his rifle to wreck the radar transponder. "Could have done this without destroying equipment, but I didn't have enough time." He grins. I reply with a thumbs-up.

The rest of us sit in the aft compartment with our captives. I kneel beside Betsan who is on a stretcher clamped to the floor. "We will go directly to House Bleddyn's hospital on Sehwa Island."

Unseen by the others, Betsan takes my hand. She whispers, "Garreth Bleddyn, you saved me. I swear my life to you."

I see the truth in her pledge. I am surprised, but I am also happy. I feel a rush of adrenalin when I speak and know it comes from within me. It is different from the adrenalin my vambrace injected. This hormone does not interfere with my thinking. I realize the vambrace was not only to control us, but to teach us control.

"Betsan of House Griffin, I accept your oath and swear to you."

Lowri hugs the treetops and keeps the shuttle below radar. When we reach House Caerwyn territory, I use the shuttle's comm to call my house's War Room. An hour later, we are met by Father and three armed shuttles and a score of fighters that escort us to Sehwa.

~~~~~

Father recalls Corporal Cos from Academy for unspecified house business. The business is a forensic examination of the exercise area. We keep secret from Academy that we left the exercise and are at Sehwa Hospital. The enemy who hired the mercenaries knows something is untoward, but they aren't talking.

Three days later, soldiers and the forensics team return from the exercise area. Corporal Cos, Telor, and Father join me at Sehwa.

"The team swept the camp and interrogated the survivors you brought. The evidence is strong, but not conclusive, that Gens Tarren ordered the attack on Garreth and his element."

"Andreas of Tarren is a member of my element," I say. "This is not the first time Gens Tarren disregards the life of one of his own."

~~~~~

Five days later, Betsan is released from hospital and we return to Fortress. The damage to her legs will require tending and frequent dressing, but she is stubbornly ambulatory. The look on Father's face – surprise and approval – when I tell him I accepted Betsan's oath and wished to swear brotherhood with her was worth all I had gone through.

Like my oath with Barri, Deryn, and Arwel, Betsan and I must keep our oath secret until after graduation. Those three and Betsan are the only ones present besides Father, Telor, and me. Although Betsan must continue to wear the dagger of her house, she and I both blood it. She accepts, to keep hidden, a dagger with the head of the Wolf of Bleddyn.

Afterwards, I find Telor, alone. "Brother, did I do the right thing attacking the mercenaries and risking the lives of those in my command? Am I suited for leadership when I have such doubts?"

Telor closes his book. "Any time you are a leader, you will question and challenge yourself. However, you must not allow questions to stop you from acting. Do not question the decisions you make in the heat of battle. If you live, they were the right decisions. If the decisions are wrong, you are dead and it doesn't matter."

"The words of Karmet," I say. Telor nods and opens his book, dismissing me.

~~~~~

Father allows us three more days to recover and recuperate following what he calls our adventure and then flies us in his own shuttle to Academy. We are now eight days late returning from the exercise. The shuttle's arrival draws Provost Myrmidon and the senior staff to the pad.

We step from the shuttle in full armor, made by the thrall-smiths of my house. We carry slug rifles and the energy weapons we seized from the mercenaries. Nudd's captured grenade launcher startles our welcoming committee. I insist he disarm it, but enjoy watching Myrmidon and his sycophants cringe when they see it. Father's guards take our more dangerous trophies to be kept until graduation.

We are disappointed no other cadets greet us, not even those in our squadron, but realize Provost Myrmidon does not want them to know about our adventure. Too late, I think. Last night, every cadet in my element told the story to others in his or her house, and they relayed the story to Academy. Father wants it known cadets from many houses were attacked, and joined one another to defeat our enemy.

That night, everyone in the squadron visits. The common room is full of cadets wanting to know more about our adventure, and some wanting to know if Academy planned it.

I want to know that, too. Since Bleddyn and Tarren are in declared vendetta, it could have been a legitimate attack on me, but Tarren targeted cadets from many other houses – including his own. I would like to expose Tarren's perfidy, but Father and Telor order me not to. All I can say is it was an exciting exercise, but given Betsan's injury, Academy will probably not plan any more like it.

~~~~~

The accidental death of Provost Myrmidon in a fall and the appointment of a retired Field Marshall of House Lagon as Provost are not considered remarkable. Only Father, Telor, and I understand. Myrmidon revealed our landing point to the mercenaries, but he failed Tarren for the last time.

~~~~~

After our jungle adventure, we face the demands of the final six months of Academy. Now, *Bo-taoshi* competition consumes our attention and effort.

When we return from Summer Stormtime, I gather my element and the three other elements of our group. We are in the meadow near the apple tree from which I watched Guffudd's element practice a dozen years ago. Selwyn is in trouble as often

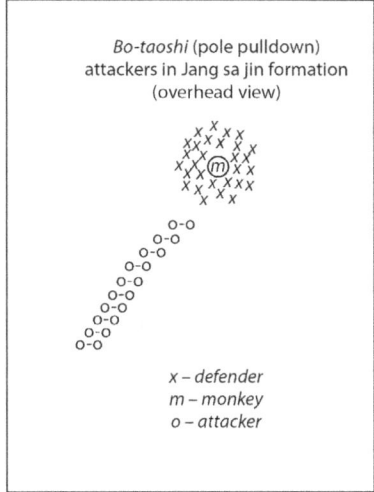

Bo-taoshi (pole pulldown)
attackers in Jang sa jin formation
(overhead view)

x – defender
m – monkey
o – attacker

as I was at his age and I wonder if he is watching, but do not see him.

"We will attack first," I say. "Two days later, we will defend." The commanders of the other three elements agree to accept my leadership. I wonder why. Have I really shown leadership? Are they bowing down or sucking up to the scion of a Greater House? Do they think I was responsible for our success against the mercenaries in the jungle?

"We will practice the tactics of offense and defense that were most successful in the past. We will be prepared to change our tactics in a flash when our enemy sees what we are doing. We will practice in secret one tactic never tried before."

"We will not lock arms in a circle, but in pairs. In past matches, when the circle is broken, defeat is quick to follow. We will both defend and attack in teams of two. In attack, we will be bullets from a slug rifle, one pair after another in *jang sa jin* – the long snake formation. In defense, the pairs will move into places where the circle is in jeopardy."

Our attack strategy is successful and our two-person attack teams are formidable. The first teams break the defenders' circle and the next ones completely scatter them. Other teams reach the pole and push it. Their monkey compensates, but we throw him to the ground when the final teams grab the monkey's leg and pull him off the pole. We win the first round. In the second round, we will defend.

"Lowri will be monkey," I say. At first, Lowri is reluctant to accept the assignment. She wonders if I am trying to expose her as a bastard; she wonders why I would select her.

"Lowri is not only light but also quick," I say. "She proved her mettle as shuttle pilot escaping unknown forces. She has the reflexes the monkey needs." I watch Lowri swell with understanding. The monkey's role requires agility of body and mind, and Lowri is best suited. "She is nimble, quick of thought, and has the stamina to hold onto the pole throughout the battle." I look around, and see no objections.

Our defense is strong, but the other side breaks between two pairs, and swarms the pole before pulling it to the ground. We do keep our pole erect the longest in the competition and earn enough points rank first.

~~~~~

The effect of defense
may be great enough
to overcome any offense.
— Karmet in *The Book of Proverbs*

My unit visits the quartermaster and collects rock-climbing gear: rope, carabineers, harnesses, cams, nuts, hexes, wall hammers, and more rope. Gwen is our best climber. She inspects each person's equipment, including mine. The next supply station issues paintball guns and magazines of paintballs. At the next station we collect gloves, helmets, boots, heavy cloth jumpsuits, sleeping bags and hammocks, and canteens. The last stop is for field rations.

A shuttle takes us to the base of a perpendicular granite cliff, about 300 meters high. We will scale the cliff and set up an observation post at the top. Gwen tells us the climb should take two days. The real exercise will start when we reach the top. I am not looking forward to sleeping in a hammock suspended from the face of the rock.

We usually climb with all eighteen cadets roped together. To speed the ascent, I order the element to climb in teams of two. Gwen and her partner, Cledwyn, lead. Both Gwen and Cledwyn are big and suited to being a climbing team. I am roped with Andreas, despite the risk of climbing with a scion of Tarren.

Six hours later, at noon, we hold perilously to the face of the cliff when high-power paintball guns fire on us from below. Who? I wonder. Is it our designated adversary, Element 447, or someone else? Whoever, it is not the plan. The exercise is not to begin until we reach the summit, but someone ambushes us. It is like the jungle exercise, except the shots are not from energy weapons. I push the thought aside to deal with reality.

"Into a crevice!" I call. Those who are not in range of my voice hear me on their communicators. "Fix pitons and secure yourself without your partner's rope. And prepare to repel boarders!"

Each team must find its own safety. My command to repel boarders compactly says we are under attack and to respond. Once again, I appeal to the nautical heritage of my house. My element understands. They swarm into various crevices in the granite.

When Andreas and I are safe inside a crevice, hanging from pitons driven into cracks in the rock, I open my communicator. "This is Garreth, count off safe or in danger. One, safe," Andreas reports.

"Two safe," I hear on the comms. Then, "Three, safe." The count continues until I speak. "Eighteen, safe."

"This is what we will do," I say. "They attacked us before they should have. That's a violation, and they'll pay. Meanwhile, we must treat this as real. Does everyone understand?"

"Cheaters," is the only response.

"We need reconnaissance," I say. "Who is in a good position?"

"This is Lowri, fourteen. I have a good observation point."

"Garreth, why do you listen to her?" Andreas whispers. "She's a bastard. I don't know why she's even allowed—"

"Wait!" I snap at him before ordering Lowri to move into position and report.

I turn to Andreas. "She answered without hesitation. She is willing to risk herself for the element. At the moment, her status is the same as ours – frightened cadet hanging in a crevice and under fire." I laugh, mostly from tension. "Whether she has honor depends not on her birth but on what she does as a member of this element."

Despite the danger, the tension, and the need to plan, my mind wanders to the time I escaped Fortress and met Brân. Her birth was not an issue. It was not important. After five years as an element mate, Lowri's birth is not important, either.

Lowri un-ropes from her partner and finds a position near the opening of the crevice. The information she provides is enough to plan a counter-attack. She remains at her position, exposed throughout the battle. Our elevation gives additional power to our paintballs. Lowri's reports give greater accuracy to our aim.

Lowri's position is precarious. If she were struck by the attackers' high-power paintballs, she might fall and die. I watch Andreas closely. He is seldom exposed, yet he does not hold back when it comes time to fire from our concealment.

We paint our attackers, annihilating them. There are no casualties, although there might have been. The referees declare our victory and end the exercise. Afterwards, when I award the win to Lowri, Andreas seems sincere in congratulating her. I am glad. The most important part of my job is to create a team that can function beyond the boundaries of status and house.

~~~~~

The next time I am home, I find Telor in the library.

"The rock-climbing ... it was a trap," I say.

"Yes, it was a trap," Telor says. "It was also a test. You found an escape."

"The ascent," I say. "Academy didn't expect us to reach the top."

"That is the weakness of Academy. At Academy, you will always have an escape. You may not always find it, but there will always be one."

"And what you and Father call our adventure in the jungle? Did Academy plan an escape, then?"

"No." Telor's abrupt reply startles me. "That was outside the scope of Academy training."

"The greatest flaw in Academy's training is that we will not always have an escape when we face the Adversary," I say.

"You are correct," Telor says. "But you learn to seek an escape, even when it appears you cannot win."

CHAPTER 15 CORVETTE *CARDIS*

You will never do anything in this world
without courage. It is the greatest quality
of the mind after honor.
—Geraint in *The Book of Proverbs*

My element sneaks away to the Public House we call the
Cadet Café. It's off limits, but we're sure the faculty knows about
it and knows we visit it. We sit around a table in one of the private
rooms with yeasty bread, sharp cheese, smoked auroch meat, and
pitchers of ale when Betsan reminds us we still face a final
exercise. This one will be unlike any other. It will involve the
entire Academy corps. We will be in the rain-shadow desert east
of House Astin's volcanoes. The rumors boil down to one thing –
Academy faculty plans something new.

My mates have confidence in me. But they are wary. I
have a long way to fall if I fail and I would take them down with
me.

~~~~~

The Academy planners assign my element to be forward
scouts. We travel in an APC – an armored personnel carrier. At
night, before moonrise, we penetrate enemy territory. At dawn,
we reach an abandoned desert town when we see the dust trails of

APCs coming toward us. Bigger dust trails behind them mark the battle tanks. Command does not alert us and we cannot escape before the enemy surrounds the town and cuts us off from our allies. My plan did not survived contact with the enemy and I have no exit strategy. I failed in two things Father and Telor hammered in their lessons.

"To that building!" I point toward an adobe, two-story house surrounded by a sturdy, mud-brick wall. A parapet surrounds the flat roof where the occupants sleep in the summer. "To the roof. Put the APC against the wall, away from the house. Deryn, remove the valve stems and flatten the rear tires. Perhaps the enemy will believe we abandoned it long ago. No one is to fire on the enemy without my orders."

When we reach the roof, I take an inventory. We have nothing but paint guns, daggers and grace knives, and food and water for a few days. Without being asked, Barri lifts the ladder to the roof and puts it beside the hatch. Then, he closes the hatch.

Andreas whines. "If we're captured, we'll wash out. We'll have no chance of a military position in our house. You led us into a trap."

A trap designed by the faculty, I think, and wonder if Gens Tarren had a hand in it. Now, I must deal with Andreas before his attitude effects the others. I speak to the element. "We are cut off from our forces by an adversary. Do what you are trained to do. Just because they wear different colors than you, do not fear them."

Andreas takes no comfort in this speech, although the rest of the element operates with greater energy. The enemy is unaware we sit atop the building. We hear footsteps and voices. I open my mind to the enemy troops. A six-person team walks past the APC; one member kicks a flattened tire and laughs. The team walks through the lower level of the house and then departs.

~~~~~

The first night, I stand watch on the roof. I can see most of the town and surrounding territory. I am scanning with night-vision binoculars and relaying enemy positions to command when, "Garreth! Duck!"

I don't hear the words. Rather, an image penetrates my mind. The image is Andreas crouching. He holds a pistol pointed at me. He plans to kill me! I roll to one side, turn, raise my paintball rifle, and fire three rounds in quick succession. All strike his face. One hits Andreas in the mouth. The paint is edible and non-toxic, but that doesn't protect Andreas when he inhales it. Before I can stand, Barri appears from a shadow. He seizes the pistol. Andreas's feet rattle against the rooftop. He is dead – suffocated. Barri and I are alone on the roof.

Barri is an empath and he is frightened. I feel fear through the mental link he creates.

"Barri, give me the pistol. Faculty will interrogate us. Do not say you warned me. You did not reach the rooftop until I was standing over Andreas. There is no pistol."

I look closely at the pistol. It is familiar. It is like one an assassin used in the forest years ago. Compressed air and a poisoned dart.

"Barri, do not be afraid. By my blood, I will protect you. Go, summon Betsan."

When Barri disappears down the ladder, I shove the pistol deep into a pocket and exchange Andreas's paintball gun for mine. These long-guns are not issued by serial number. No one except Barri could say I made the switch.

Betsan arrives; Barri follows. Whatever happens, he will make himself part of it. I feel strengthened by his loyalty, even though I must test it by lying.

"An accident," I say. "Andreas thought his weapon jammed and turned it to look into the barrel. At that moment, the weapon fired. He inhaled one of the paintballs. Death was quick, but not easy. Betsan, please report this to Academy."

Minutes later, Telor's voice comes from the speaker of the communicator. Of course, he is monitoring our comms, and he probably has a satellite over the town, too. I check to see the communicator is on a secure channel. "Father will order the exercise suspended—" Telor says.

"No!" I interrupt. "This is our graduation exercise. We must complete it. We will escape and we will return with Andreas's body. We will cremate him at Academy. His mates, my element, will conduct the Remembrance."

"What do you need me to do?" Telor asks. His voice is slow, soft, and without emotion. It calms me.

"Tell Father of my resolve. Do not let him terminate the exercise. Notify Gens Tarren of Andreas's death and protect us from him."

I hear Telor chuckle. "You don't ask for something easy, Little Brother."

"I am not little!" I say and then turn to Betsan. "Please summon the rest of the element from downstairs. I will explain."

Minutes later, everyone reaches the rooftop. They see Andreas's body. They do not speak, but from loyalty hold their questions. "Andreas died when he accidentally fired paintballs into his mouth. The exercise will continue. This will not affect our grade. Andreas reminded us if we did not complete the exercise both Academy and our houses would penalize us. We will continue the exercise as a tribute to him."

I feel unclean using Andreas's death in this way and try to blame my feeling on the urgency of the moment. Later, I think about my motive. Do the ends justify the means? I want to believe I am more concerned for my mates than for myself. I am First Rank of House Bleddyn; none of the others are more than Third Rank of their houses, and Lowri is a bastard of no rank. Academy means more to them than to me. Failure in this exercise would hurt them more than me. I have Telor and Father to defend me. I am doing right by my mates, but does that justify using Andreas's death to motivate them? It is a question of honor I never considered.

Years ago, Sani asked me if it were better to be honorable and thought to be a scoundrel, or secretly to be a scoundrel and thought to be honorable. After our talks, he resolves the question by saying I had to depend on allies who thought I was honorable; therefore, it was better to be a scoundrel and be thought honorable.

I challenged Sani. "You are asking the wrong question. You created a faulty dilemma. Your argument assumes one cannot both be honorable and be seen as honorable. I do not accept that premise."

Sani praised me for understanding. Now, I use this understanding to guide my instructions to the element.

"Our objective has changed," I announce. "We must not only escape, we must escape with Andreas's body. His Gens knows Andreas is dead. It is open knowledge his house and mine are in vendetta. Will Gens Tarren try to harm you and me? Unknown, but we must consider it. That is what I know. What are your thoughts? How will we escape?"

We create our plan in whispers; everyone takes part. There is risk, but we agree it is acceptable.

We remain undiscovered the next day, but continue to observe the enemy and send their strengths and movements to command. Dusk falls. The clouds seem like a purple-gray. An hour later, the sunlight is gone. The risen moon and stars provide the only light. Cledwyn slips away, enters the APV, and returns with a body bag. Andreas's body is stiff from rigor mortis, making it easy to slide into the bag.

Nudd and I sit in a corner of the compound waiting for the moon to set. We are the ground watch whose task is to alert the others if an enemy approaches the compound. Once there was a gate, but it is long missing. We select a place from which we can see the opening, backlit by fires a long way away.

When the moon sets an hour before first light the next morning, I order our escape using the armored personnel carrier.

The wheels have inner, hard doughnuts that allow us to run on the flattened tires. We rejoin our allies with more information we collected on enemy forces. When our side defeats the enemy army, our reconnaissance is credited with the victory and we are awarded the win.

~~~~~

We cremate Andreas's body on the battlements of Academy. His Gens attends the Remembrance surrounded by his guards and watched closely by my father's. I see his feelings in his face. He cares little about either Andreas or the ceremony and is present only because tradition demands it. However, he shows sadness tinged with a bit of anger toward me. Gens Tarren is dishonorable, but wants people to think he is honorable. In my speech, I give the win to Andreas, which puzzles some of my mates. Afterwards, Betsan silences them. "We agreed to carry on because Andreas wanted it. It is honorable to give him the win." Honorable, I think. Andreas was a tool of his Gens. Giving him the win was more about politics than honor. Is honor so malleable?

~~~~~

We ride the wave of our success in the exercise for the rest of Sixth Form. There are no more major exercises to test us, although the final *Bo-taoshi* competition is brutal. Our opponents and we have reached full growth in height and weight. I am now 1.6 meters tall and weigh 70 kilograms. Many of the boys in my group are taller and outweigh me. The impact of bodies during the matches is often painful, although my element avoids injuries worse than bruises.

We rank in the top ten percent at graduation. Father wants our rank to be higher and for me to be a group commander, but I am pleased by what I accomplish in only one year. My element will never be together again. I invite everyone to join me at Fortress Bleddyn after graduation. Stormtime is forecast to be severe, but I hint there will be new and exciting things to occupy us even when restricted to Fortress.

I jump from the shuttle. Father surprises us by bringing Mawrith and Cari from the House Dolffin School. They look very sharp in House Bleddyn uniforms.

While my mates settle in quarters, Telor leads me to Father's den.

"Academy changed in the twenty-five years since Telor entered and you graduated," Father says. "There is less harassment and more training."

Telor chuckles. "Cadets are free to sneak away to one of the public houses you allow to operate on Mesa. That is a relaxation of the strict rules of the past. It creates greater bonds within and among elements. There is still a core of duty, discipline, and morale that relies on the old rules."

Father gestures us to seats in front of the fire, and reminds me of my heritage. "The Garreth for whom you are named was both brave and modest. It seems, however, you are more prudent than modest. Telor, please pour so we may salute Garreth."

The salute with *dŵr y bywyd* is anticlimactic after Father's earlier words. Brave and prudent. I vow to make those words my compass.

Father allows us a day to recover from the excesses of graduation and then summons us to his den where he seats us at the Privy Council table. He stands at the head of the table. "It is customary for Academy graduates to spend a month or two weighing various options and offers before choosing a career. Some of you were offered places in the Home Guard of your own house. Some have been selected to become crew or colonists on starships. Others will take different paths. Tonight, with the permission of their Gens, I offer Barri, Deryn, and Betsan a place on a starship of the House Bleddyn fleet. The corvette *Cardis* will launch in about nine months and escort a colony ship. Garreth, too, will be a crewmember."

Lowri has no house and no offer to join a home guard. She believes she has little choice but to place herself in the mercenary auction. Father surprises her when he gifts her with the shuttle she flew escaping from the jungle exercise. "This comes with an invitation to join the Home Guard of either House Bleddyn or House Dolffin," he says, "as a shuttle pilot."

Lowri shows she is strong when she replies. "I would swear myself to House Bleddyn."

Father nods and dismisses us to continue our celebration – this time, without ethanol.

Two days later everyone departs except Lowri, Betsan, Deryn, and Barri. We go to the Great Hall where Father accepts Lowri's commitment and adopts her into House Bleddyn. I think there are a few tears in her eyes, but she makes her oath with a strong voice. Earlier, Lieutenant Terrwyn and Master Sergeant Rhingyll argued over whose command she would join. It surprises no one when Master Sergeant Rhingyll wins.

Macca will enter Academy after Winter Stormtime. I ask him what he plans for Arawan, and learn our youngest brother, Rodric, has already adopted the wolf – or vice versa. Rodric is named for our elder brother, murdered in vendetta, years ago. Father is keeping the name alive, as his ancestor promised.

~~~~~

Some years ago, Gens Tarren attacked a planet of the Adversary and captured a starchart. It was a map of part of this spiral arm of the galaxy showing the planets the Adversary occupied. Tarren's people then destroyed the planet. We learned this when our spies infiltrated Fortress Tarren and copied the star chart and the log of the ship that captured it.

Telor explains this to me, and says Father believes the Adversary will eventually find and attack World, and Tarren is responsible.

I challenge him. "Father created this war," I say. "Even though it was for his own reasons, Tarren followed Father's lead. Why are you and Father so worried?"

Telor's answer is not reassuring. "The chart shows both we and the Adversary are exploring and settling the same kind of planets in the same spiral arm of the galaxy – planets inside the comfort zone of the star, close enough for liquid water to exist but far enough away that solar heat hasn't boiled away all the water. The likelihood we will encounter one another has increased significantly."

Telor summons Barri, Deryn, Betsan, and me to the library to tell us more about the starchart. I think it will play a large part in our future. "When we found the starchart, Father increased the rate at which we build and launch colony and exploration ships. He invited all our allies and unaligned houses to include members on our ships. We are focusing our efforts on planets we know the Adversary seeded with the basics, but which do not appear on the chart – planets we think they forgot."

I must have looked puzzled, but then I remember an old lesson. "Planets the Adversary seeded, but lost. Lost contact, forgotten, or overlooked. We assume the locations were lost because of war among the Adversary, but we really don't know, and that creates risk. It is, however, the least risky of our options at the moment."

~~~~~

Five days after Winter Stormtime, my three companions and I fly to the hospital on Sehwa Island for genetic modification. First, however, medicos harvest Betsan's eggs and the seed of Barri and Deryn. Father flies to Sehwa afterwards. "You swore to my son, Garreth. You did so without promise of reward or recognition. By my blood, your eggs and seed will be preserved and within a decade you will become parents of a child-by-blood of House Bleddyn. Like Garreth, you will likely never know your children, for you embark on a journey with no fixed end. However, your children will become members of my house."

Betsan accepts Father's pledge with equanimity. Barri and Deryn seem inconsolable. I break protocol and enter their room, where they sit on a bunk, holding one another, crying.

"Why do you cry? What made you so unhappy?"

283

Barri is first to regain control. "We are not sad, Garreth. We cry happy tears. We thought we would never have children to carry our blood. You always respected and supported us—"

"My oath," I interrupt.

"More than an oath, Garreth," Deryn says. His voice is soft. "What you did for us went beyond any oath ever sworn."

I realize by promising children of House Bleddyn to these, my sworn companions, Father protects me, even now.

~~~~~

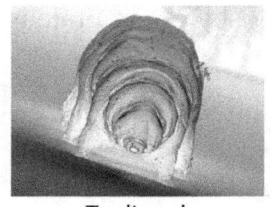

Tardigrade
(Photomicrograph)

In the first step toward near-immortality, the medicos use sub-microscopic machines patterned after RNA to splice a new gene to the ends of our DNA to keep the strands from unraveling during cell division. Other splices block parts of the master-genes, the ones that turn our bodies to senescence. The medicos enhance the body's original DNA-editing genes and add a gene to create a protein from tardigrades, the oldest known living multi-celled organism on World, to protect our cells from damage by ionizing radiation. They add two fish genes to protect our bodies from the cold of space. Next, they inject nanobots into our bloodstream. The nanobots are organic sub-microscopic machines, patterned after the cells of our immune system. They will patrol, heal, and replicate themselves.

When we return to Fortress, I ask Father how we can call ourselves "of-the-blood" when clearly, we are something different.

Father's answer is blunt. "There are many things that define us, including law and custom, family and blood. Ultimately, we are what we declare ourselves to be. Racial purity? It is a fiction misused and misapplied in history to justify pogrom, murder, and vendetta."

I bow. I understand.

At eighteen years of age, we are at the peak of our physical and mental development. Like Father, we could remain there for twenty millennia or more – unless we meet with accident or are assassinated.

~~~~~

After Spring Stormtime, Telor takes us in his shuttle to the spaceport on Namhae. We report to the corvette *Cardis*, which will launch in six months. Captain Glenys is a cousin who graduated from Academy ten years ago. Lieutenants Barri of Hynafol, Betsan of Griffin, Deryn of Dolffin, and I will join others from eleven houses.

The *Cardis* is larger than the *Gorlassar*, whose destruction by the Adversary triggered the war. It is larger than the corvette whose launch Glint and I missed because we explored a lava-tube cave. *Cardis* carries two caravels and twenty fighters. The caravels have stardrive; the fighters have greater engine power and weapons than their predecessors; their torpedoes have fission warheads. We will escort a colony ship, the *Waldfa* in which five thousand people – both Res Publica and thralls – will be in cold sleep.

The *Cardis* and *Waldfa* use a still-secret stardrive that gives us a short-cut between universes. I spend a lot of time with

Uncle Grigor and Uncle Maddox learning about the drive and how to plot a ship's path through the non-space between realities.

~~~~~

The captain welcomes us aboard, and assigns a crewmember to show us our quarters. They are much like our rooms at Academy – bunk beds, small lockers for uniforms and possessions, a desk with a terminal, and chairs. Barri and Deryn will room together. Betsan will be my roommate. We drop our duffel and go to the bridge.

The bridge looks like a miniature house War Room. Six seats face panels of controls and display screens. The captain's chair sits behind and three feet above them. There are large screens at the front.

"Your position is helm," Captain Glenys tells me and gestures to a console. "You will also be primary for FTL comms. Become familiar with your station. You will spend a lot of time there." He assigns the others their positions – Betsan is Medico and in charge of environmental support – things like air, water, and the algae farm. Barri and Deryn control weapons.

I focus on the communication system since I suspect my tasks as helmsman will be little more than following orders. The comm system links us with the House Bleddyn War Room, the Council's Military Command, the *Waldfa*, and the two caravels.

In the remaining days, Captain Glenys holds training for the crew and drills us in our positions. He describes our first mission – to find a suitable planet for the *Waldfa* to colonize. "The first candidate planet is outside the range of the captured starchart. It is one an earlier ship of the house Bleddyn fleet identified as being seeded through Wave 4 but apparently abandoned after that. If it appears the Adversary has not revisited the planet, *Waldfa* will land and establish a colony. We will be in the vaward, first to penetrate and explore the target star system. *Waldfa* will follow only if we signal the system is safe."

The second part of our mission is to seek planets with sentient species abandoned by the Adversary and to recruit them to be allies. "This will be the most dangerous part of our mission," Captain says. "We will approach planets we know the Adversary has seeded through the final wave, planets on which their DNA may have become sentient primates – or cats." Despite the tension, the crew laughs. Everyone knows about the Planet of the Cats. "We will also visit habitable planets within the range of the starchart but which do not appear on the chart. We hope these planets were seeded but forgotten, overlooked, or abandoned by the Adversary."

The Captain does not mention the search for telepaths. Telepathy is still secret and not even the captain knows. Father set the Res Publica against an enemy of unknown strength. He hopes a telepath of House Bleddyn will learn our enemy's strength and his weaknesses and maybe find allies. My brothers Telor, Guffudd, Macca, Eurion, and Nephew Selwyn are telepaths. House Bleddyn has enough heirs to risk another one in space. Actually, I'm glad. I've had enough of planetary politics and vendetta.

The night before launch, the crew gathers in a private room where we swear by blood our obedience and loyalty to Captain Glenys. It is an oath that supersedes earlier oaths, and which will govern our behavior as long as we are on the ship.

After the ceremony, Uncle Madox hosts a supper for our closest relatives. Only five of my family attend – Father, Telor, Nana, and Rodric with Arawan. I'm glad it is they, and not disappointed others do not join them. It means I have more time for leave-taking. When I kneel to scratch the tips of Arawan's ears, I receive a distinct but puzzling image. It is of Arawan and me standing on a planet with a sun that is more yellow than World's and trees resembling giant ferns. I stare into Arawan's eyes, and think, *I will remember you wherever I go.* The wolf's usual snarky laughter is silent.

After the guests retire to their rooms, Uncle Madox speaks to me quietly. "You are going where Glint wanted to go. Perhaps you will see him." He turns and walks briskly away. He knows! He thinks I do not know and so he tells me. He believes friendship is stronger than oath, yet by telling me this way, and in private, he does not betray his oath.

The next morning, our AG engines lift us from the tarmac against the gravity of World. The *Waldfa* follows. Our sensors are at full strength and someone sits at each weapon console. Fighter pilots are in their fighters in the rotary launchers. When we reach an altitude of 500 kilometers, Captain orders the AG engines tuned to act against the vacuum energy of the universe. I steer us into an orbit around World. Again, the *Waldfa* follows, although more slowly. We spend two days checking systems before accelerating toward the cometary cloud.

Once clear of the cometary cloud, the captain orders me to compute our course for inter-universe travel. I have prepared for this. I know we must accelerate to near light speed upon entering the non-space between universes, and the velocity vector must point toward our target – or, where it will be when we reach it. I know how to do the calculations. "Aye, aye, sir."

I put data into the computer, hoping to complete the task without taking so long the captain becomes impatient. About halfway through, I realize the captain already prepared the solution. I resist taking the answer from his mind, complete my work, and display the course on the main screen.

"Very good, Mr. Bleddyn, send the solution to *Waldfa* and execute."

Before we enter the non-space between universes, I send an FTL message. It will be our last message until we pop back into our universe. No matter. There's nothing left to say.

Our first mission will take us past the farthest reaches of the Adversary's starchart and will require eighty-five years in cold sleep. One-by-one, we enter the canisters. I think about the *Kobaya's* crew, who entered cold sleep without knowing if they would ever be rescued. I shiver from more than cold when I lie in the canister and close my eyes. Each sound causes another shiver until I feel a jab in my arm. Then, I feel nothing.

~~~~~

I think I am in Father's den, standing with him in front of a fire crackling on the fire-wolves. My eyes snap open. I am not in Father's den, but in a cold-sleep canister whose lid is open. Warm air is blowing on my body. Betsan, because she is medico, wakened immediately after the captain and greets me. "We're here. Well, we're nearly here. How do you feel?"

"Sleepy?"

Betsan looks at my naked body and grins. "Get your cute butt out of bed. Captain wants a report sent to the War Room."

When we reduce our speed to 0.7 C, I send an FTL message.

<<Cardis and Waldfa nearing first mission point. Waldfa remains outside cometary cloud pending exploration. Initial indications are of no technology in system.>>

I sign the message, <<Garreth Bleddyn, Lieutenant, by direction.>>

Who will be on duty in the house War Room? What happened while we were asleep? Because we are moving so fast, it will take days for my message to be displayed at Fortress Bleddyn. By then, we will be slow enough the reply will be displayed instantly.

Several days later, my comm screen lights.

<<Garreth, so good to hear from you. Father is pleased, but no more than I. Telor>>

My brother lives. So must my father. Who else? I report to the captain. "Message received and acknowledged. Gens Bleddyn is still Gens. I mean … actually, I inferred that, but the message was acknowledged by—"

"Thank you, Lieutenant. No need for details."

Telor and I have time between official reports to exchange private messages. I learn Sister Bethan produced a dozen heirs for House Caerwyn. Her husband was declared Gens when his father was killed. Then, Bethan's husband was assassinated, probably by House Pugh, but no one is sure. Bethan is regent for her eldest daughter until she completes Academy and becomes Gens.

I do not need to ask before Telor contacts the offspring of Betsan, Barri, Deryn, and me, as well as the rest of the crew, and brings them to the War Room to exchange greetings.

When no official messages are being sent, Telor provides a news feed. Nothing surprising, actually, except that the *Kobaya* crew was rescued. Arawan died years ago but his offspring are breeding true, and nearly every scion of First and Second Rank of House Bleddyn has a companion-wolf. They cause quite a stir at festivals and stormtime gatherings, but – even after considerable pressure by Father – they are not permitted at Academy. Vendetta continues, but that is expected.

~~~~~

We do not find evidence the Adversary visited this planet in the thousands of millennia since the Fourth Seeding Wave. "Absence of proof is not proof of absence," Betsan reminds us. However, the colonists decide the absence of proof means the Adversary forgot the planet. They land and disassemble the ship for material to create their colony. They set up FTL systems and create links to their houses' War Rooms. The caravels and fighters take stations to become the nucleus of a planetary defense force. I send my last message.

<<Cardiff mission complete; departing system.>>

<<We'll talk again in five years.>> Telor sends.

Our next mission is to a planet seeded through Wave 5. One of our ships discovered it millennia ago. It is within the bounds of the captured star chart, but is not on the chart. The star is 30 light-years away, and our trip will last only five years. The subjective time is long enough we will enter cold sleep.

~~~~~

Again, Betsan wakes me. "We are close to our target system," she says. "Captain wants the command crew awake and alert." She rotates the rack. I grab a bar in time not to tumble onto the floor. Betsan grins and warms the next crewmember.

Less than a day later, sensors spot an Adversary ship. It is smaller than we are and moving toward the star that is our destination, and decelerating. "It is within torpedo range," Barri calls from his console.

"Fire!" Captain orders.

The Adversary reacts faster than expected with both torpedoes and masers. His masers intercept and destroy both our torpedoes. We intercept one of his torpedoes, but the second strikes us amidships. The *Cardis* breaks in two sections. The stern spins away and explodes before sending the tachyon signal. The bow holding seven crewmembers including me tumbles on its own path.

We have battery power to operate sensors and comms, and we see the Adversary ship match our course and run side-by-side. We know we face imminent death. I prepare a message for FTL transmission, but the system does not respond. My telepathy cannot cross the light-years that separate us from World. Father and Telor will not know I am dead.

My thought is interrupted when I feel someone enter my mind. *Who are you?* I ask.

I am Kendrick. I am on the Founder ship beside you. We can rescue you. Who are you?

I am Garreth, Helmsman of the Corvette Cardis of the House Bleddyn Fleet. Is your ship the one that destroyed mine?

Yes, I'm afraid so. But you fired first. I detect seven infrared spots. Are there seven of you? Is your captain among them?

Yes. There are seven of us on the bridge, and the captain is among us. He will kill himself and us rather than allow us to be captured.

What if it's not capture, but rescue? The voice in my head asks.

I don't know.

A few moments later, Kendrick returns to my mind. *My captain says if you and your crew offer your parole, we will treat you as guests and will do everything possible to return you to your people. However, we are subject to the authority of others and bound by universal constants that may make it difficult, perhaps impossible. All we can promise is we will try.*

"Captain, a message from the Adversary ship." I gesture to my console as if the message came from there. I relay the message to the captain, who rejects the offer. I watch him set the autodestruct timer. "You have a quarter hour to say your farewells," he announces.

At that moment, I feel a jab in the back of my neck. I turn and see Barri and Betsan through a haze. They catch me before I fall and carry me from the bridge. Captain sees them, and I dimly sense his approval. Deryn is waiting at a hatch. He and Barri strip off my jumpsuit and the slippers we wear aboard ship and shove me into a life pod. "There is only one undamaged life pod," Betsan says. She looks away. I sense her pressing buttons on the console. "The pod will seek the star we were approaching. It may take years, centuries to reach it. This is a long shot, but it's the best you have." She looks over her shoulder, turns, and disappears. I hear the clang of the pod door closing and feel a thump when the pod is ejected. Moments later, I feel the death of the captain, Betsan, Barri, Deryn, and the others. The pod's computer, programmed by – I remember, her name is Emlyn – puts me into cold sleep, and I see and feel nothing but darkness and dreams.

I am asleep when the pod seeks first the star and then a stable point in which to hide. I cannot know how long that will take; I cannot know how long it will take my people to find me. I cannot know if I will ever be found. I cannot even hope for rescue. I know nothing and hope for nothing for I am asleep. I may be asleep in a billion, billion, billion years when everything in the universe decays into nothing.

The End of this Book
The story will continue in Book IV
Working title: *Three Planets*

Radiation flares in the cold emptiness between stars. Ripples move through spacetime. Sub-atomic particles familiar only to a physicist – top and bottom quarks, Higgs bosons, mirror-spin particles, and others – appear, annihilate one another, and disappear in bursts of energy. After nearly two million years, E still equals MC^2. The energies fly away at the speed of light in a spherical wave. A starship of the Founders, Science Scout Cruiser SSC2200 Kendrick, pops into existence.

Around a nearby star, sixty degrees forward in the orbit of a gas giant, a life pod drifts from a stable point until drawn back by the unconquerable force of gravity. Inside the pod, a block of Element 90 decays to Element 82, releasing alpha particles, beta particles, and neutrinos. The alpha particles warm a thermocouple and provide energy to the pod's computer. The neutrinos are lost in the storm of their kind that permeates the galaxy. The beta particles, high-energy electrons, interact with shielding made of Element 74 that surrounds the block and produce x-rays with very short wavelength and high energy.

The energy created by the Founder starship's arrival in real-space triggers sensors on the life pod. The pod's computer wakes and compares three copies of its operating system and memory. Where quantum fluctuations created errors, the computer accepts two copies and overwrites the third. Then, it analyzes the energy signature of the starship. Strings race along algorithms' ternary paths. The computer wrongly judges the energy to have been created by a starship of the Res Publica. The computer modulates the x-rays, which move away at the speed of light.

~~~~~

Months earlier, the starship wakened and readied itself. It planted the first hydroponic cycle. It pumped warmed oxygen, nitrogen, water vapor, and trace gasses into passageways, laboratories, crew quarters, and the bridge. When the environment is stable the ship's voice wakes the sleeper.

"George? This is Kendrick. It's time to wake up." Kendrick's voice comes over speakers set in the ceiling.

In a 2.5-meter tube, about a meter across, a boy stirs. His eyes open, his hands press on the lid that covers the tube, he feels the warm air of the room. He turns and steps from the tube onto the floor. It's warm. The ship heated it for him.

"Kendrick? Where are we? Did we...?" I do not complete the question. I am not sure what the question is.

"George, you have been asleep for nearly a million years. Your memory will return.

"I do not know where we are. All sensors are operating properly, but I have heard no electromagnetic signals nor have I heard any telepaths. However, we reached our target – a spiral arm with many G-class stars. There will be time to plan when your memory settles."

~~~~~

I have been awake for a hundred days before my memories return. One of my memories is that we have no star charts. Neither Kendrick nor I know the location of our home planets. I'm sitting in stellar cartography, mapping stars and planning a search from star to star, when Kendrick's voice comes over the speakers and interrupts me.

"George, I received a modulated signal on a very short wavelength, what you call x-rays."

"Can you interpret the signal?"

"No, it's only twenty binary bits. The source could be dangerous."

297

"Twenty bits? Doesn't require a lot of power. Maybe a navigation beacon?"

"It's nothing like the Founders built."

"You said nearly two million years passed since we left Earth. It took us a million years to get lost, and another million to get back. Who knows what your people – or mine, or the Enemy – might have done? Was the signal aimed at us?"

"No. It was a spherical wave front. The source is near a G-class star that's very close to us." Kendrick puts a red circle around a star on my display.

"Then why are we sitting here?"

"I await your orders, Captain."

Kendrick calls me *Captain* to remind me although I gave him the universal unlock command and released all restrictions, he expects me to make decisions. "Okay, let's go there and do a check-it-out thing."

~~~~~

I elect not to go into an autodoc in suspended animation for this short trip, but am asleep in the captain's quarters when Kendrick wakes me.

"There is something interesting at the gas giant's $\lambda 4$ – Libration Point 4. It's one of the most stable—"

"Because gravity will pull things back into position if they drift," I interrupt. "What's there and why is it interesting?"

"Because of where it is and because I detect decay of a significant quantity of Element 90, what you call thorium. The object is small, a few meters long. It is symmetrical and artificial. It is probably the source of the earlier x-ray signal, but now it is emitting only un-modulated x-rays."

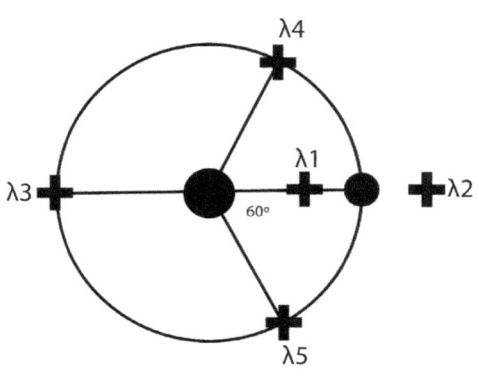

Libration Points (Lagrangian Points or Stable Points) in a two-body system (sun & planet or planet & large moon). Points λ4 and λ5 are stable without expending energy. A ship that drifted slightly away from one of those points would be pulled back into equilibrium.

"Thorium decay." I pull on a skin-suit with built-in boots. "If I wanted to build something with power for eternity, that's the element I would choose. The half-life of one isotope is, like, 14 billion years. Maybe somebody else had the same idea. Sounds more and more like a navigation beacon."

I add the collar that provides a force field, air, and communication – and weapons Kendrick has still not told me about.

Breakfast is fruit, cheese, and bread, made with ingredients from Kendrick's hydroponic gardens. His people didn't know coffee or tea, but I taught Kendrick to make tea from herbs. It is like the tea Mommy used to feed me and brings memories of her. I see her with a tray of food. She sits beside my wheelchair and feeds me, one spoonful or one sip at a time. She also changes my diapers, gives me sponge baths, powders my— okay, TMI.

~~~~~

One hundred eighty days later, we bring aboard something that looks like a capsule. Not a Mercury or Apollo capsule, but oval like a medicine one, except it is about three meters long and two meters in diameter at the waist. Kendrick puts it on the floor of an empty storeroom. After the capsule warms from the nearly absolute cold of space and Kendrick pumps the compartment full of an oxygen-nitrogen atmosphere, he signals it is safe for me to enter.

Before I can touch the capsule, Kendrick warns, "George! Machinery in the capsule activated. You must leave the room. Now!"

~~~~~

From the bridge, Kendrick and I watch someone crawl from the capsule. It is a human boy perhaps my age. He is naked and just under two meters tall. His bronze skin shines in the harsh lights. His black hair lies close to his skull. His ears are shells, not wrinkled like mine and I watch them twitch, trying to pick up every sound in the room.

He looks at the capsule, and then turns away, dismissing it. He looks around the room. It is empty except for him and the capsule. The door is pretty obvious and I'm not surprised when he turns toward it. The door does not open and he cannot find any controls. I sense his frustration and try to see into his mind.

He feels me instantly and his reaction shocks me. *Who are you?*

I am Captain George Morgan of the Science Scout Cruiser 2200. Who are you?

300

The boy stops moving around the laboratory. I hear, *I am Garreth, Helmsman of the Corvette Cardis.*

Kendrick's voice comes from speakers, and not into my mind. "George, I know his voice. I encountered him two million years ago and destroyed his ship. I did not know he survived."

See

Paul.Lentz.Author.com for information
on this and other books.

Words in quotation marks are the meaning of the entry in one of several ancient languages.

Abeam to port: Directly to the left middle of a ship.

Academy: Military school of the Res Publica. Entry is about age 12; survivors of the training graduate after six years or Forms. Cadets are assigned to elements of 18 boys and girls their age. Four elements of the same Form are aggregated into a group (72 cadets). Groups are aggregated into Squadrons.

Adrenaline: A natural hormone and neurotransmitter produced when a person faces danger or surprise. The current name on Earth Analogue III is Epinephrine. It triggers the fight-or-flight reaction, which draws blood to the major muscle groups and away from the face. It is one of the hormones the drugs in a vambrace moderates.

Adversary: Res Publica name for the Founders. See "The Stuff of Life: Books I and II."

Aelwen: Garreth's sister-plus-six. Assigned as instructor at Academy after graduation. "fair browed"

AG: Antigravity. Engines of floaters, shuttles, and starships that act against the gravity of a planet and the vacuum energy (dark energy) of the universe.

Alaw: Garreth's Sister-minus-three. "water lily"

Alexi: House Tarren soldier who offers his parole to Garreth.

Amino Acids: Natural organic compounds and the constituents of proteins.

An: Archaic form of 'if.' "An it please you" means, "If it please you."

Ancient Language: Language spoken until shortly after the War of Conquest. The language evolved over the next two hundred or so millennia. The ancient language is still used in formal occasions and oaths, and for names.

Andreas: Male member of Garreth's element, scion of House Tarren. "Andrew"

APC: Armored Personnel Carrier. Military vehicle with a battery-powered electric motor, an armored compartment with seats for sixteen soldiers, and a driver's compartment with bullet-proof windows and seating for two.

Apothecary: A chemist's place of business; a drug store.

Apothegm: An aphorism; a concise and often clever saying which might contain some truth.

Arawan [AIR ah wan]: Garreth's companion-wolf. "unrestrained wildness."

Arwel: Male member of Garreth's element, member of allied house Caerwyn. "prominent"

Astin: Lesser House, neutral.

Astronomical Unit (AU): The distance from a planet to its star, equivalent to one mean orbital radius. On Earth Analogue III, one AU equals about 150 million km or 93 million miles. The AU for the World of the Res Publica is somewhat larger. Their sun is hotter than Sol, and World's yearly orbit requires 595 days of approximately 25 hours each.

Atlatl: A device designed to extend the range and power of a spear.

Auroch: Ancestor of Earth Analogue III's cattle.

Baldric: a belt for a sword, an amanuensis's dispatch box, or other piece of equipment. Worn over one shoulder and reaching to the opposite hip.

Barri: Scion of House Hynafol. Member of Garreth's element at Academy. Element Commander, First Form. "summit."

Bastard: (1) A person not acknowledged by his or her father. (2) Any person of low status, often a person without house.

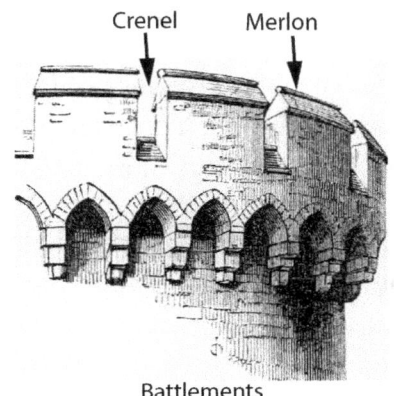

Crenel   Merlon

Battlements

Battlements: (1) The parapet at the top of a wall, usually of a fortress or castle with spaced openings ("crenels" or "embrasures") between raised "merlons." (2) The portion of roof enclosed by this parapet.

B.C.E. or BCE: On Garreth's World, **B**efore the **C**onquest **E**ra. Calendar years after the conquest of the Southern

305

Continent and the thralls. On Earth Analogue III, means **B**efore the **C**ommon **E**ra, roughly equivalent to B. C. (before Christ). (The BC/AD calendar of Earth Analogue III is at least four years in error. The Magi visit Herod whose life is well documented. It is also well documented that Herod died in 4 BC.)

Bedwyr: Member and one-time commander of Garreth's Academy element.

Bethan: A daughter of Gens Bleddyn, Garreth's sister-plus-15. "daughter of the Gens"

Betsan of House Griffin (unaligned): Female member of Garreth's Academy element; Garreth's second in Sixth Form. "Elizabeth"

Bleddyn: Greater House. Garreth's house and patronymic. "wolf." House colors: orange, black, and gold. House shield: *an escutcheon or, a wolf, proper, couped* (on a golden shield, the head of a wolf as if severed cleanly from the body, in profile and natural colors). Also, *a full moon tenné, a wolf couped sable* (on an orange moon, the head of a wolf). On banners, ancients, and flags, the wolf rampant or couchant may be used.

Bolas, Bola, or Boleadoras: A weapon consisting of three balls of steel tied together with wire, which are spun once around a hunter's head and released to wrap around the legs of prey.

Bo-taoshi: Battle game played at the Japanese Self Defense Force School, Earth Analogue III. Google "youtube bo-taoshi" for examples.

Book of Proverbs, The: A document which contains the wisdom (aphorisms, apothegms, stories) of both Geraint and Karmet.

Brân: Bastard whom Garreth meets when he runs away. "crow" or "raven"

Bräu: Male, scion of House Tarren. At one time, assigned to Garreth's element at Academy.

Brotherhood: The closest oath that can be made other than fealty. Brotherhood may be between boys, girls, or boys and girls.

Bryn: Member of Garreth's element at Academy.

Buzzer: Nickname for the small device used to check and adjust drug dosages of youngsters' medical vambraces.

Cach: "Excrement" in the old language. Used as an exclamation.

Cadre: Select members of a military unit or cadet corps charged with training new soldiers or cadets.

Caerwyn: House located on the central south coast of the Equatorial Continent. Blood-kin to House Bleddyn. "white fort" House colors are red and purple. House logo is a dragon.

Calendar: The year on world is 595 days long, and is divided into four quarters by the solstices and equinoxes. On Earth Analogue III these are December 21 and June 21, March 21, and September 21, respectively. On World, the New Year begins at the winter solstice, a custom established when the Res Publica were ignorant of science and believed that storms and the return of the sun after the winter solstice was the province of an imaginary, magical being. Academy years ("Forms") start just after Winter Stormtime (equivalent to late December in Earth's northern hemisphere). Twelve months of approximately 50 days each are marked by the phases of World's largest moon. Years are numbered C.E. for "Conquest Era," after the conquest of the Southern Continent by the Res Publica. B.C.E. is Before the Conquest Era.

Humans (members of the Res Publica and thralls) mature physically and mentally at about half the rate of humans on Earth Analogue III. Therefore, age as noted is comparable to the age of a person from Earth Analogue III. (Slow growth in childhood and adolescence is thought to be one reason for their millennium-long natural life span.)

The half-life of Thorium in Earth years is 14 billion; in Res Publica (World) years, it is 7 billion.

Call to the Field: Phrase meaning to challenge to a duel.

Camalos: An ancient soldier of House Bleddyn whose courage and loyalty are invoked by that house in ceremonies to induct new soldiers and in brotherhood rituals.

Cammies: Nickname for camouflage uniforms, usually jumpsuits in jungle or desert colors and patterns.

Cams and nuts: Devices that can be wedged into cracks in a rock to support a climber.

CAP: Combat Air Patrol. Tactic for positioning shuttles, floaters, or fighters high above a battlefield.

Caravel: Small, fast starship used for scouting and exploration. One or more caravels may be carried on a corvette or other larger starship.

Cari: Scion of House Merrick. Member of Garreth's element at Academy. Female. "friend."

Cardis: Corvette (starship) of the House Bleddyn fleet. Garreth's assignment after graduation from Academy.

Catrin: Female member of Garreth's element.

C.E.: Conquest Era (see Calendar).

Ceirois: [say ROY] A girl, one of Garreth's companion-playmates. "cherry"

Chancellor: The most senior official on the staff of a Gens (house leader). Duties are administrative (e.g., presiding over meetings of the Privy Council not attended by the Gens) and diplomatic (e.g., serving as emissary to other houses).

Chang sa jin (also Jang sa jin): Long snake formation. A line of soldiers or ships pointing to the enemy to minimize exposure, attacking one at a time then turning, retreating to rearm, allowing the next soldier/ship in the line to attack. A tactic used by Admiral Yi Sun-sin (Earth Analogue III); see the bibliography.

Charge block: A battery holding power for an energy pistol, rifle, or laser-tag weapon.

Chemical determinism: The tendency for certain compounds to form in ways that minimize bonding energy. This phenomenon is a part of the hypothesis underlying the natural formation and evolution of life.

Chemist: A pharmacist, a dealer in drugs of all kinds.

Chojeom (초점): "Focal-point." Similar to the Earth Analogue III German, Schwerpunkt. The literal translation is "main focus, main emphasis, or focal-point." In military parlance, a Schwerpunkt or *chojeom* attack means "striking the enemy at a point that is both vital and weakly defended." Chojeom is one of the most common attack strategies of *Bo-taoshi*.

Cislunar Space: The space between a planet and the orbit of its primary moon.

Cledwyn: Male member of Garreth's element. Scion of House Caerwyn. "a river"

Clowder: (Earth Analogue III) A noun of venery (a collective noun) for cats. Compare to a "pride of lions" or "a congress of baboons."

Cold sleep: A period of suspended animation at very low temperatures used by the Res Publica to extend the lifespans of their starship crews. (Hyphenated when used as an adjective.)

Colonizer: A class of starships carrying c. 5,000 colonists in cold sleep. May also carry shuttles, fighters, and caravels.

Cometary Cloud: Like the Oort cloud believed to surround the solar system of Earth Analogue III, World's cometary cloud is a bubble of icy debris (comets, planetoids, dust) that surrounds the sun at a distance of between 5,000 and 100,000 of World's orbital radii. [See "astronomical unit (AU)."]

Comfort Zone: A band around a star in which a planet is close enough for liquid water to exist but far enough away the water doesn't boil off. On Earth Analogue III, call the "Goldilocks zone" (not too hot, not too cold, just right).

Commander: The military title of a Gens within his Home Guard.

Compact, First: The agreement among the houses created after the king, Gens Triumph Tarren, was overthrown and the Council was established. Originally, the Compact only set up the Council of Gens of the Greater Houses as the government of the Res Publica and the first mission of the Council, which was the conquest of the Southern Continent. Additional provisions were made over the millennia, including rules for vendetta, enforcement of an agreement banning nuclear fission, abolishment of primogeniture (more honored by some in the breach than in the observance), the abolishment of slavery, creation and maintenance of the tachyon signaling system, and rules for the operation of Academy.

Companion: A friend or someone in a more formal relationship.

Companion-Guard: A formal relationship that exists between a scion of a Greater House and older relatives and members of sworn houses who are charged with the scion's safety. Sometimes shortened to "guard."

Companion-Playmate: A formal relationship that exists between a scion of a Greater House and close kin or members of sworn houses of the scion's age who are fostered to the Greater House. Sometimes shortened to "playmate," "schoolmate," "companion," or "mate."

Companion-Student: A formal relationship that exists especially among cadets assigned to the same Academy element and group. It requires a degree of amity and courtesy, and (in theory) excludes vendetta.

Conquest, War of: The war in which the Res Publica conquered the people of the Southern Continent about 200,000 years before this narrative.

Consort: A respected companion of a person (male or female) whose spouse is away on duty.

Corvette: A class of starship. Corvettes normally carry twenty fighters and two caravels. Newer corvettes may carry as many as a hundred colonists in cold sleep.

Corundum: Aluminum oxide (Al_2O_3) which may have traces of iron, titanium, and other minerals. Forms the gemstones ruby and sapphire. Ruby was a critical component in early lasers on Earth Analogue III.

Cos: Male corporal in the Mountain Company of House Bleddyn's Home Guard. A tutor of Garreth Bleddyn.

Council: Ruling body of the Res Publica comprising the patriarchs and matriarchs ("Gens") of the thirteen Greater Houses.

Council House: Complex of buildings on Mesa where Council meets and the Res Publica conducts business.

Crenel: See "Battlements."

Curtain wall: The outer wall of a fortress, usually connecting towers or barbicans.

Cytgord [SIT gord]: An open city within the territory of Gens Bleddyn, location of a mercenary auction. Inhabitants are both thralls and members of Res Publica. Anyone entering the town must agree to a truce. "harmony, concord"

Cythrual [KITH rowel]: Greater House sworn to House Tarren.

Daffyd: A son of Gens Bleddyn, Garreth's elder-by-twelve-years brother.

Dagger: A knife, usually thin, with a blade of up to 45 cm and a simple hilt often topped with a house's symbol.

Dark Energy: The universe comprises ordinary matter, dark matter, and dark energy at approximately 4%, 23%, and 73%, respectively. While dark matter seems to exist (mostly) in a "halo" around the edges of galaxies, dark energy pervades the entire universe. Its presence is thought to be uniform throughout the universe. Same as "vacuum energy."

Davit: A small crane aboard a ship, including the pairs of cranes from which pinnaces and lifeboats are often suspended.

Dawn Horse: A horse similar in size and characteristics to the American Quarter Horse of Earth Analogue III, but with a larger and more blocky head. [Because the DNA of the Res Publica was included in early seedings, they began their evolution already more advanced than many creatures on Earth Analogue III, which is why the ancestors of Dawn Horse, pterodactyls, saber-tooth cats, and other seeming anachronisms co-exist with them.]

Delwyn: Garreth's eldest sister-plus-twelve. A twin of Daffyd. "pretty"

Deri: Male member of Garreth's element. "oak"

Derog: Boy of House Hynafol who meets Garreth at a Fall celebration. "obstinate one"

Deryn: Of House Dolffin. Member of Garreth's element. "falcon"

DNA: Deoxyribonucleic acid. The molecule present in almost all living organisms and which carries the genetic code.

Dobok: [DOUGH bock]: Uniform worn when practicing martial arts. Same as "gi."

Dojo: A gymnasium dedicated to the martial arts and related gymnastics.

Dolffin: Lesser House subject of a history story by Gens Bleddyn. Ally with blood ties to House Bleddyn. The Gens has been for millennia a woman.

Duck Walk: Walk with knees bent and body close to the ground to minimize exposure and take advantage of cover.

Dŵr y bywyd: Five-times distilled and 1000-year-aged liquor drunk only for ceremonial purposes. "water of life."

Element: (1) A squad of eighteen soldiers usually commanded by a Sergeant with a Corporal as second. (2) Eighteen Academy cadets of the same age who train together. Supervision is provided by Tactical Officers ("Tacs"). Leadership is provided by age-group peers. (3) A flight of two or three starships of the Res Publica that operates under a single commander.

Element 82: Plumbum (lead).

Element 90: Thorium.

Element 92: Uranium.

Elevation: The ceremony at which the child is acknowledged as legitimate and presented to family or to the Council of the Res Publica.

Elfyn: Boy, one of Garreth's companion-playmates. "bard or poet"

Elint: Electronic Intelligence. Information gathered about an enemy's radar and similar detection systems.

Ellis: Lesser House aligned with House Tarren during Garreth's youth. House shield: *a hart, proper, accorné gules* (a deer in its natural color with gold antlers). House colors: brown, white, and gold

Emlyn: Thrall child whom Soosong meets in Cytgord [see "House of Wolf"]. Later, employed by Uncle Madox in House Bleddyn's spaceport. "industrious"

Empath: An individual who can sense and emit emotions and images, but not read thoughts. See also telepath.

Emrys: Greater House; neutral.

Endorphins: A class of hormones and other chemicals created naturally by the central nervous system and the pituitary gland which relieve pain, reduce stress, and boost happiness.

Energy weapons (pistol, rifle): Weapon based on laser technology and powered by a replaceable magazine (charge block).

Entrée: The right to enter or join a group, house, sept, element, etc.

Equatorial Continent: The main body of land inhabited by the Res Publica. Approximately 4,500 miles wide, 2,500 miles from N to S.

Eryr [EYE are]: Lesser House allied with House Tarren until the Gens allies with House Bleddyn. "eagle" Nickname of house: "Mountain Eagles."

Ethanol: Ethyl alcohol – C_2H_5OH.

Eurion: Garreth's brother-minus-nine. "golden"

Fast-rope: "Fast Rope Insertion-Extraction System" by which troops can deploy from a shuttle when the shuttle cannot touch down. The soldier who fast-ropes down breaks his or her fall without carabineers, but only with gloves.

Fauna: Comprehensive term for all animal life in a location or on a planet.

Flèche: A move in fencing when a person lifts his rear foot while lunging forward on his forward foot with sword pointed toward his opponent's breast. Risky, but effective if well executed.

Fender: First Cousin of Garreth Bleddyn, Lieutenant in the House Home Guard, and commander of Garret's companion-guards.

Field Marshall: The highest rank (other than the Gens) in a house's Home Guard. The Gens rank is Commander.

Fighter: One of several types of shuttlecraft. Until c. 200,365 C.E., fighters were merely armed shuttlecraft with engines capable of operation in a planet's atmosphere or in cislunar space. Around 200,365 C.E., House Bleddyn designed and built fighters more streamlined, with less room for crew but more powerful offensive arms, stronger armor, more powerful, and capable of longer-range operation.

Fionn: Female member of Garreth's element; replaced Cari in Forth Form. "foxglove flower"

Fire-Wolf (Fire-Wolves): Andirons, sometimes called "fire dogs," that hold wood above the floor of a fireplace ensuring a draft to encourage burning. They are usually of wrought iron, and may have fanciful images.

Floater: Any of several models of anti-gravity sleds, shaped something like a toboggan, usually less than three meters long and a meter or so wide. Most are designed for one person, lying prone and with legs and torso clamped into a cradle, facing down into a display from a forward-looking camera and other sensors. A transparent windscreen provides some protection from wind. Two-person models are used for training and transport.

The military floater is capable of an altitude of perhaps 500 meters and a speed of more than 100 kilometers per hour. Its display includes visual and radar sensors, a satellite location system, and targeting systems for its armament. Floaters used in mock combat may have paintball guns and may be equipped with laser-tag lasers and sensors. Floaters used for military operations are usually equipped with rocket grenades. Floaters used by exploratory vessels may be larger and have a greater cargo capacity. The basic civilian model is limited to an altitude of 100 meters above ground level and a speed of 50 kilometers per hour.

Flora: Comprehensive term for all vegetation in a place or on a planet.

Footy: A game resembling soccer with teams that change composition as players are forced into time-out after scoring, and as new players enter the game.

Forensic: As used herein, forensics is the application of science to crime investigation.

Form: A year at Academy. Enrollment last six Forms (years). Forms begin immediately after Winter Stormtime (q.v.) and end just before the next Winter Stormtime. Membership in an element may change during the first two Forms, but usually stabilizes by the beginning of Third Form.

Founders: Their own name for the people whom the Res Publica call "Adversary." See "Stuff of Life: Book I."

Four-leg: Herbivorous animal, ancestor of modern deer of Earth Analogue III. See the Wikipedia article on "Deer," and scroll down to "Evolution."

Froward (FRO ward): An English word from Earth Analogue III meaning "difficult to deal with." It is related to "**toward**," pronounced "TWO ward," as in "to and fro." A toward child is tractable and obedient; a froward child is contrary. Something toward is appropriate; something froward, inappropriate.

FTL: Faster Than Light. Refers to both a communication system and starships' drive.

Γ: The Earth Analogue III Greek letter "gamma."

Garreth: Tenth child (ninth in line of succession) of Gens Bleddyn. "brave and modest"

Gavan: Member of Garreth's element in Forms Five and Six. Scion of Eryr. "white hawk"

Gawain: Son of Gens Dolffin, about Telor Bleddyn's age. "courteous"

Gens: Title of the leader of a House of the Res Publica. Plural: Gens. Singular and plural possessive: Gens.

Geraint: A historical figure and philosopher known for his wisdom. A great teacher whose name is invoked in rituals binding protégés and mentors. Considered to be a pacifist, he lacks the respect of the more militant members of the Res Publica (see "Karmet). "old"

Glint: Garreth's cousin and later, sworn brother. From Namhae.

Glenys: Captain of Corvette *Cardis* and cousin of Garreth Bleddyn. "riverbank, shore"

Gordan: One of Garreth's companion-playmates.

Gorlassar: Corvette of the House Bleddyn fleet and mother ship of the Caravel *Kobaya*. The *Gorlassar* was destroyed in the first documented encounter of the Res Publica with the Adversary. "above the sky"

Grace knife: A long, thin blade used to administer the final blow to a wounded enemy, a comrade wounded too badly to survive, or one's self if disgraced or captured. From "coup de grâce." See also, "Leave no companion behind; never become a captive."

Greater House: See House.

Greensward: Grass-covered ground outside the walls of Fortress Bleddyn. A lawn.

Griffin: Lesser House, unaligned. "king's hand"

Grigor: Uncle of Garreth who is expert in quantum mechanics, co-discoverer of the third-generation stardrive.

Group: Four Academy elements (i.e., 72 cadets) of the same age (Form) who attend class and engage in other activities as a unit.

Guffudd: Garreth's brother-plus-nine. "the Gens strong grip"

Gwaethafwyr ("Gwen"): Member of Garreth's element. "pessimist"

320

Gwenallt: Name given to Soosong by Telor Bleddyn upon her adoption into House Bleddyn.

Gymnosperm: "Naked seed." A tree, such as a pine whose seeds are usually carried on the wind.

Hectare: A measure of area equal to 10,000 square meters or about 2.47 acres.

Hemocyanin: Copper-based chemical in blood used to transport oxygen to the cells and carbon dioxide back to the lungs. Compare to "hemoglobin," below. On both Earth Analogue III and World, hemocyanin-based blood is found in snails and certain mollusks.

Hemoglobin: Iron-based chemical in blood used to transport oxygen to the cells and carbon dioxide back to the lungs. Common among most creatures on Earth Analogue III, but only among the "beasts of field and forest" on Garreth's World.

Haft: *n.* the handle of a knife, spear, or ax. *V.t.* to attach such a handle.

Hagik-jin: Crane-wing formation. A semi-circular formation of soldiers or ships that creates a killing zone in the middle. May involve luring the enemy into the killing zone. After formation used by Admiral Yi Sun-sin in the Battle of Hansan (Hansando), 8th Day of 7th Moon, 1592 C.E., Earth Analogue III.

Halee: Female scion of House Itan, member of Garreth's element in Sixth Form.

Helygen: Greater House allied with House Tarren. "willow"

Hide-and-find: A children's game, similar to "hide and seek" on Earth Analogue III. Hiders have tokens that earn points for the seeker if he or she finds the hider, or for the hider if he or she is not found. Since children often bet their desserts on the outcome, the game can become very serious.

Home Guard: A house's private army. Subject to being ordered into action by the Council, for example, to put down a rebellion among the thralls or, in extreme circumstances, to stop a war between rival houses.

House: An extended family related by blood and fealty, ruled by the senior patriarch or matriarch who is addressed as "Gens." The thirteen original houses (the Greater Houses) trace their origin to antiquity. The Lesser Houses were formed following dynastic wars within Greater Houses.

Hubris: Overwhelming pride, considered by the Greeks of Earth Analogue III to be a grave sin, marking a person for destruction by the gods.

Hynafol: Greater House. Allied with House Bleddyn. "ancient"

Ilja-jin: One-line formation. A tactical formation consisting of lines of soldiers or ships. It allows volley fire but sacrifices maneuverability. Used effectively by Admiral Yi Sun-sin, Earth Analogue III.

Ilym: Male member of Garreth's Academy element until Fourth Form.

Infiltration Element: Strike teams of usually eighteen soldiers trained to operate independently, live off the land, strike from concealment, and conduct guerilla warfare. Created by House Bleddyn c. 100,000 C.E. in response to House Tarren's creation of large land armies.

Infirmary: A medico's clinic. More than an examination room; less than a hospital.

Isca: Male member of Garreth's Academy element. "Fortress."

Isotope: A variety of an element with the same atomic number but additional or fewer neutrons, giving it a different atomic weight. "equal place"

Itan: Lesser House. Unaligned until 200,367 when it aligns with House Bleddyn.

Jang sa jin* (long snake formation) See also *Chang sa jin: A line of soldiers or ships pointing toward the enemy to minimize exposure. The force elements will move forward and attack one at a time before turning, retreating to rearm, and allowing the next force element to attack. Based on a strategy employed by Admiral Yi Sun-sin, Earth Analogue III.

Jaryeondo (자련도/自鍊道): Literally, "self-training-way," meaning a method of training and discipline. It is the name of the martial art that Garreth and others of the Res Publica study.

Jumpsuit: Any of several varieties of one-piece garments that cover the torso, legs, and maybe the arms. May have integral webbing to attach gear and weapons. Usually includes a belt. May be in camouflage pattern, house colors, or plain. May include flashes of rank and patches with house shield, unit insignia, etc.

Kaetween [kate wean]: Ancient house destroyed c. 20,000 B.C.E. by all other houses, united, after employing a nuclear fission weapon in combat.

Karmet: An ancient philosopher whose art of war resembles that of Sun Tzu of Earth Analogue III. See also "Geraint."

Kata (plural, Kata): A system or series of choreographed training exercises for practitioners of martial arts including *Jaryeondo*, q.v. The term also applies to formal Japanese rituals (Earth Analogue III) including the tea ceremony and theatrical Kabuki.

Kendrick: Starship SSC2200 of the Founders' Fleet; see "The Stuff of Life, Book I." Related to the ancient name, Cynwrig "having the quality of a leader or hero."

Kilogram: A measure of mass equivalent to 2.2 pounds.

Kith: Usually used in the phrase, "kith and kin" meaning friends and acquaintances as well as blood kin.

Knap: To shape a stone such as flint into a knife, arrow or spear point, etc.

Kobaya: A caravel which survived an early encounter between the Res Publica and the Adversary.

Koje Island: Southwestern-most large island of the five House Bleddyn islands, southeast of the Equatorial Continent.

Kosong: House Bleddyn island located off the eastern edge of the Equatorial Continent.

Lagon: Greater House, which historically maintains a neutral position.

"Leave no companion behind; never become a captive." Res Publica expression of what is known on Earth Analogue III as "The Hannibal Directive." See the bibliography.

Lebensraum: "Living room." Room in which to expand. From the German of the late 1930s, Earth Analogue III.

Lesser House: See House.

Libration point: A point in space where the combined gravitational forces of two large bodies, such as World and its largest moon are equal to the centrifugal force experienced by a much smaller body. This interaction creates a point of equilibrium where a spacecraft may be secured. Only two of the points are stable without any expenditure of energy. On Earth Analogue III, these are more often called Lagrangian points.

Life pod: A one-person lifeboat carried aboard larger starships of the Res Publica. A capsule about three meters long and two meters in diameter at the waist. Pods have a computerized autopilot, a small ion engine, and thermo-electric power supplied by Element 90 (called Thorium on Earth Analogue III).

Life span, life-extension treatment: Normal life span of the Res Publica is about one millennium. Early life extension involved modification of the DNA, especially the Master Genes, the telomeres at the end of DNA strands, and editing genes and RNA. This gives the already long-lived people of World life spans of scores of millennia of life (if they're not assassinated of killed in vendetta). More recent treatment includes injecting nanobots to repair damaged cells and tissues, treatment which may result in near immortality.

Light-year: The distance light travels in one Julian year of 365.25 days on Earth Analogue III (about 9.46 trillion kilometers). On Garreth's home planet, which has 595 days of about 25 EAIII hours, this would be significantly longer.

Lilith: Girl of House Cythrual, in Garreth's group, Second Form of Academy. Challenges Garreth to a duel. "witch"

Llywelyn: Garreth's brother-plus-18. "lion"

Lowri: Female member of Garreth's element. A bastard.

Macca: Garreth's brother-minus-six. "hammer"

Maddy: Male member of Garreth's element. Replaced Mawrith in Fourth Form. "good fortune"

Madox: Glint's father; Garreth's uncle. "champion"

Maelon: Gens allied with Gens Tarren. "a follower"

Mammal: A class of vertebrates usually distinguished by hair, three middle ear bones, a neocortex, and females with mammary glands. On Earth Analogue III, mammals include whales, dogs, and humans. On Garreth's world, where evolution was modified by the Adversary, other mammals include the saber-toothed cats and mastodons, *inter alia*.

Marredudd: Greater house, aligned with House Bleddyn. "great lord"

Markham: Woman; member (later Sergeant) in Gens Bleddyn's Praetorian Guard.

Marwin: Son of Gens Dolffin. "sea hill"

Maser: "Microwave amplification by stimulated emission of radiation." A device to excite atoms to generate a coherent beam of electromagnetic radiation of a single frequency. Precursor of the laser, but operating in the microwave band.

Master-genes: The genes that appear to turn on and off other genes especially during gestation of an embryo. Also associated with senescence. Known as "HOX" genes on Earth Analogue III.

Mawrith: Scion of Eryr. Male. Member of Garreth's element. "of the sea."

Medico: A doctor of medicine.

Melatonin: A natural hormone produced by the pineal gland. It regulates sleep and wakefulness.

Memory Stick: a finger-sized chip for holding data. Think, "flash drive."

Merlon: See "Battlements."

Merrick: Lesser House aligned with Gens Tarren.

Methane: Main component of natural gas. CH_4OH. Created by the decomposition of organic matter. A greenhouse gas. When methane burns in air, it produces two other greenhouse gasses: carbon dioxide and water vapor. ($4CH_4OH + 7\,O_2 \rightarrow 4CO_2 + 10H_2O$)

Millennium: A thousand years.

Mufti: Non-uniform clothes or "civilian" clothes when worn by a soldier.

Myrmidon: (MUHR mi duhn) Name of Academy Provost from 200,365 until 200,384 C.E. From Greek mythology, Earth Analogue III: "one who unquestioningly follows orders."

Namhae: Island off the southeast coast of the Equatorial Continent of World. Site of House Bleddyn's spaceport.

Nana: Nickname from infant's speech of Garreth's surrogate.

Nanobot: Microscopic robot.

Naphtha: More accurately, benzene. C_6H_6. Flammable liquid distilled from methane, which is captured from sewer gas and vegetation rotting in compost piles. The only high energy density fuel available to the Res Publica, it is reserved for fighters to supplement their anti-gravity engines, and for emergency lighting and heat.

Nudd: Male scion of House Eryr. Member of Garreth's element at Academy. "fog."

Objective time: See "subjective time."

OCD: Obsessive-Compulsive Disorder. See "vambrace."

Open City: Specified locations such as the cities of Aberwith and Cytgord in which a truce of non-violence holds.

Orbit: (1) the path taken by one body around another dictated by mass and gravitational attraction. (2) The distance from the sun to World, used as a measure of other distances in World's solar system. For example, the cometary cloud is between 5,000 and 100,000 orbital radii from the sun. See also "Astronomical Unit (AU)."

Panspermia: Hypothesis that life (which had to originate somewhere) was spread through the galaxy on comets, meteorites, dust particles driven by solar winds, etc. Or, in this particular reality, by seeding ships of the Founders.

Peace Bond: Agreement or oath to not use weapons, engage in vendetta, etc. which may be applied to persons entering an open city (q.v.). May be symbolized by colored yarn wrapped around hafts of swords and through trigger guards.

Phalanx: A group or body of soldiers who may be in any of several formations. See, for example, *chojeom*, the focal-point attack formation.

Pinnace: A small, light boat carried aboard a larger ship and used as a tender, scout, or captain's lighter.

Pitch: Any sports field may be called a "pitch."

Pogrom: Earth Analogue III Russian, "to wreak havoc or destroy violently." Used to describe attacks on Jews in the Russian empire and elsewhere by non-Jewish populations. A harbinger, perhaps, of the Holocaust. Used to describe similar excesses by soldiers of House Tarren during the wars with the Southerners.

Pole pull-down: See *Bo-taoshi.*,

329

Praetorian Guard: Soldiers selected for ability and loyalty to guard important people including a Gens. They may also act as secret police. From the history of Rome, Earth Analogue III.

Primate: A mammal of the order that includes monkeys, apes, and humans.

Progenitor: The biological parent of a House. In pre-history, it was common for the male house leader to be the only male to father children. When one house defeated another in battle, it was common for all males of the losing house to be killed and the females impregnated by the winning house's progenitor. When birth by surrogate became possible, a female house leader might be the only one whose eggs were fertilized. These customs largely fell out of practice c. 50,000 C.E..

Provost: A senior administrative officer of a school. From Earth Analogue III Latin, *praepositus*, "head, chief."

Pseudaelurus: (Earth Analogue III name) Hypothetical ancestor of the common bobcat of North America; lived around 9-20 million years B.C.E.

Pterodactyl: (tere dakt'l), occasionally shortened in speech to 'tero. ('terō or 'terah). A flying reptile with leathery wings and a long beak. Flourished in Earth Analogue III's late Jurassic period (roughly 150 B.C.E.) but contemporaneous with humans on World.

Publican: One who operates a public house, such as a cafe or ale house.

Pugh [PEW]: Greater House aligned with House Tarren. "son of Hugh"

Quark: A sub-atomic particle carrying a one-third electric charge and one-half spin. The building blocks of protons and neutrons. The types of quarks are up, down, strange, charm, bottom, and top. Protons have two up and one down quark, and "gluons" that bind them together. A neutron has two down and one up quark.

Rain-shadow Desert: An arid region created downwind of a mountain or mountain range which blocks the prevailing winds that carry moisture, forcing the air upward where moisture condenses and falls as rain or snow on the windward side of the mountain(s) leaving the leeward side desert.

Reaches: The borderlands of a territory. Those parts of a house's territory that might be challenged by a neighboring house.

Reese: Lesser House, aligned with House Tarren. Territory consists of several large islands to the east of the Equatorial Continent. One island holds the shipyard and spaceport used by House Tarren and its allies. "enthusiasm"

Remembrance: A ceremony conducted after someone's death during which friends and family express their grief at the person's passage, share stories of his or her life, and experience catharsis.

Res Publica: World's dominant civilization; from the Earth Analogue III Latin: *common good, commonwealth, body politic.*

Reshot: "Resistance shooter" which propels a small piece of rock or metal using elastic bands; a slingshot.

Rhiannon: Garreth's horse.

Rhingyll [RING ill]: Master Sergeant and Company Commander of House Bleddyn's Mountain Company. He is the only non-commissioned officer to command a company, and has repeatedly refused promotion to officer grade.

Rigor mortis: Stiffening of a body that occurs a few hours after death and which may last a day or more. Caused by chemical changes in the muscles. Decomposition usually begins four-five days after death, causing the muscles to relax.

Rodric: Garreth's brother-plus-three and after this brother's death, Garreth's new brother-minus-fifteen.

Rocket grenade: Short for "rocket-propelled grenade." A weapon consisting of a warhead and a solid-fuel rocket propulsion system. Used to attack a crowd of people, an armored vehicle, a floater, a shuttle, or a fixed structure. Different versions and sizes may be fired from a corvette, shuttle, floater, over-and-under slug rifle, or hand-held launcher.

Sally Port: An opening or gate in the wall of a fortress through which troops can "sally forth" to battle.

Sangtae: Coastal city on the Southern Continent.

Sani: Member of Southern people, thrall in the employee of Gens Bleddyn, second mentor to Garreth. "old one"

Sarcopterygian: The Sarcopterygii are a class of bony fishes of which, on Earth Analogue III, the coelacanth is the only living related fish, the others having become extinct during the Late Cretaceous period.

Scion: A descendant of a noble family, usually a son or daughter, sometimes a niece or nephew.

Second: (1) Short for "second in command." (2) The person who stands with a participant in a duel until the duel begins. These seconds are armed with only grace knives. Since all adult duels are to the death, the seconds of adult combatants have the responsibility to kill the combatant to whom they are seconded should the combatant be wounded too badly to continue to fight.

Sehwa: House Bleddyn island nearest the equator. Location of a hospital.

Selwyn: Son of Telor Bleddyn and Gwenallt. "friend"

Senescence: Deterioration of the body and brain that occurs with age.

Sept: A branch of a larger house. Recognized as part of the house but not entirely integrated with it.

Shield: Most often, used to mean the symbol of a House. May be a stylized letter from the alphabet, an animal, or other figure. The shield of Gens Bleddyn is a "wolf rampant" which may appear in two or three dimensions (on a document or badge, or at the top of the haft of a dagger, for example).

Shuttle/Shuttlecraft: An AG-powered vehicle about 8-15 meters long and 5.0-7.5 meters in cross section. Larger versions are used as troop transports and to carry freight. Racing shuttles are capable of speeds 3.2 times the speed of sound (Mach 3.2 or about 4,000 kilometers per hour).

Soando: Volcanic island off the southeast coast of the Equatorial Continent. Location of Gens Bleddyn mines, a military garrison, and a population of thralls.

Solar plexus: A complex network of nerves located just below the sternum. A blow to this spot can cause the diaphragm to spasm and cause difficulty in breathing – "getting the wind knocked out of you."

Soldiers' Oath: "I swear always to live by honor, to be valorous in battle and loyal to my Gens, house, and the Res Publica." This is often abbreviated as "Honor, valor, loyalty."

Songbaek: Island slightly southwest of the Equatorial Continent in House Dolffin territory. Home of House Dolffin's school and Fortress Dolffin.

Soosong: Academy cadet, assassin. "a humble person of low status or class"

Southern People, Southerners: The thralls. The same species as the Res Publica, but whose evolution diverged slightly only by skin color when the southern and equatorial continents were separated by tectonic plate movement. At one time enemies, the Southerners were defeated millennia before Garreth's birth and are often servants or employees of the Res Publica.

Spindrift: Spray blown by wind from the crest of waves.

Squadron Phoenix: The Academy squadron into which Garreth's element is inducted.

Stardrive: Same as faster-than-light drive.

Status quo: "that which is" or "that which was." For example, *status quo ante bellum* means "the way it was before the war."

Stormtime: The period of extreme weather at the winter and summer solstices and the spring and fall equinoxes. The storms may be called "solar storms." Much of the equatorial continent is shut down and people seek shelters for about fifteen days during stormtime.

Subjective time: Onboard a starship traveling near the speed of light, time passes much more slowly than time outside the ship. Subjective time is the time within the ship; objective time is time as measured by observers outside the ship.

Suppression Fire: An infantry tactic in which soldiers take turns firing weapons in single shots or short bursts to conserve ammunition while hoping to keep the enemy's heads down.

Surrogate: A child's birth mother and usually Nurturing Mother during childhood.

Tac: Short for Tactical Officer. Adult military officer who supervises an element at Academy. The Tac is not the Element Commander although his or her orders are to be obeyed.

Tachyon: A hypothetical particle that can travel (and carry information) faster than the speed of light.

Tardigrade: Also called "water bear." Microscopic aquatic animals that can survive extreme conditions including complete dehydration and ionizing radiation. See the bibliography.

Tarren: Greater House. Historical enemy of House Bleddyn. "burnt lands" House colors: black and gray.

Tarmac: A paved area that may be a road, an airport, a runway, or a spaceport. Technically, a tarmac consists of crushed rock mixed with tar. On World, a tarmac may be native rock.

Telor: Son of Gens Bleddyn by a consort. "Singer." Eldest of the children of Gens Bleddyn. Member-by-blood of the House. In line of succession after siblings born of Gens Bleddyn's seed and his wife's eggs.

Temperature: The Res Publica temperature scale is identical to the Centigrade/Celsius scale on Earth Analogue III: 0 is the freezing point of water; 100 is the boiling point. On EA III, this presumes a sea-level atmospheric pressure, which is lower than the sea-level pressure on World.

Ternary: Base 3 arithmetic. Compare to base 10, common on Earth Analogue III, and base 2, often used in computer logic.

Terrwyn: Lieutenant and commander of the Prime Element of Gens Bleddyn's Praetorian Guard. Cousin of Garreth. "brave"

Tetrapod: Early evolutionary ancestor of amphibians, reptiles, birds, and mammals.

Time (Clock): Day and night are broken into hours. There are twenty hours in one solar day. The first hour is that which begins at dawn. At one time, day and night were divided into ten hours, each, which meant that winter day hours were much shorter than winter night hours, and summer day hours were much longer than summer night hours. As the Res Publica civilization developed, this custom was abandoned for the timing of atomic clocks.

To the field: A "call to the field" is a challenge to a duel. Duels between adults are always to the death.

Triage: A field medical procedure in which casualties are assigned degrees of urgency based on wounds and likelihood of survival.

Triumph: Name of an ancient, despotic, and psychotic Gens of House Tarren.

Tywyll: Captain in House Bleddyn's Home Guard. Formerly Commander of a guard detachment on Soandyo Island ("House of Wolf"); later, Commandant of Cadets at the Dolffin school.

Ultraviolet: Light shorter than visible light (shorter than 390 nanometers – nm) to humans of Earth Analogue III. The eyesight of the Res Publica and thralls can detect shorter light waves, something that began as a survival characteristic during the coldest years of the Res Publica's evolution.

Untoward: See "Froward."

Vacuum Energy: Same as "dark energy," q.v.

Vambrace: Traditionally, a piece of armor that protects the lower arms. It may be made of metal or leather. It may cover part of the arm and be held on with leather straps or completely encircle the arm. The vambraces worn by younger members of the Res Publica completely encircle the arm. They contain sensors that monitor blood chemistry. Drugs are injected to maintain specified blood chemistry. The vambraces monitor the hormones and electrochemicals associated with Attention Deficit Disorder/Attention Deficit Hyperactivity Disorder (ADD/ADHD), Obsessive Compulsive Disorder (OCD), Bipolar syndrome, and Mood Disorders that affects all people on World (Res Publica and thralls) from about the onset of puberty until about age eighteen.

Vaward: The front of an attack formation.

Vision (eyesight): The vision of the Res Publica evolved during major fluctuations in the temperature of World, during ice ages. They can see through the near infrared to the far ultraviolet. Like birds of Earth Analogue III, they have four types of cones in their eyes.

Vole: A small rodent, related to the mouse. Unlike the mouse, they usually live in the wild. They damage grass, tuberous plants, and tree and plant roots, and are considered pests.

Waldfa [WALD fa]: Colony ship of the House Bleddyn fleet, accompanied by Garreth Bleddyn on his first space mission.

Wall hammer: A hammer often with a short head used by a climber to drive pitons into rock. Google "climber's hammer" for examples.

Warner: Private in Gens Bleddyn's Praetorian Guard.

338

World: The common name for the planet of Garreth's people, the Res Publica.

Year: World circles a young, hot, blue star at an average distance of 218.5 million km. Its year is 590 days. Days are a bit longer than those on Earth Analogue III.

Your Grace: Formal term of address for a Gens, especially Gens of the Greater Houses.

ACKNOWLEDGMENTS

Except where indicated otherwise, all persons and sources are from Earth Analogue III, the one in which you are reading this.

I am especially indebted to beta readers Lani Clancy, Charles Robinson, Charlotte Robinson, Robby Viens, and Michael Weinstock. Their thoughts were invaluable in the creation of the final version.

Many of the early chapters were reviewed by The Peachtree City Library Writers' Circle, which included David Allman, Alexandria Bolden, Pat Butler, Patricia and Chuck Cruzan, Petra Engish, Sharon Marchisello, Mark Myers, Delayne Ryms, Susan Samson, Robin Strickland, and Rebecca Watts (at that time, the Writers' Circle Leader and Facilitator).

A number of the battles were drawn from accounts of the life and career of Korean Admiral Yi Sun-sin (1545-1589 C.E.).

A young friend and linguist, Shi Ho Kim, was very helpful showing me how to modernize the spelling of historical locations in Korea which allowed me to track Admiral Yi's battles. Shi Ho also created the name of Garreth's martial art (*Jaryeondo*), using his knowledge of Korean, Chinese, and English.

The connection between Garreth and his Companion-Wolf, Arawan grew from a discussion of empathy with Debbie Berry.

I am especially grateful to the Korean Spirit and Cultural Promotion Project for their generous donation of the books on Korean culture and history listed in the bibliography.

The stories of the wolf and the pterodactyl, the boy who carried the flag of House Dolffin, the saber-tooth cat and the wolf, and probably some others were transmogrified from various editions of *Aesop's Fables*. The moral of the wolf and pterodactyl story as Sani presented it, "Live and work for the benefit of all," is an expression of the philosophy of *Hongik Ingan*, and is the unofficial motto of South Korea. See the bibliography.

The aphorism, "Wars are fought with weapons, but they are won by men," is attributed to General George Patton, US Army.

The aphorism, "You will never do anything in this world without courage. It is the greatest quality of the mind after honor." is attributed to Aristotle. He lived c. 384-322 B.C.E.

The expression, "All we have to fear is fear itself" is from US President Franklin Roosevelt's first inaugural address.

The question, "is it better to be honorable and thought to be a scoundrel, or to secretly be a scoundrel and be thought honorable" is based on both Plato's question to Glaucon and ideas from "The Righteous Mind." See the bibliography.

The expression, "If you want a boat, do not order your people to build one, but lead them to the sea" was inspired by Antoine de Saint Euxpéry's "The Little Prince."

Cledwyn's words, "He who does not fear death will live; he who seeks to live will die. If a solitary defender stands watch at a strong gateway, he may drive terror into the hearts of an enemy numbering in the thousands," paraphrases Korean Admiral Yi Sun-sin addressing his forces c. 1595 CE.

Telor's lesson to "doubt everything, for doubt leads to questioning and only questioning leads to truth" is a simplistic form of the first of Peter Abelard's most famous injunctions. The others are (again, in simple terms): use language with precision and demand precision from others; be aware of propaganda and attempts to distort the truth; question even the most sacred texts.

The ancient command, "Leave no companion behind; never become a captive," is based on the Hannibal Directive of the Israeli Army. See the Bibliography.

Other quotations from the Res Publica's *Book of Proverbs* were taken in large part from the writings of Machiavelli, Aristotle, Plato, Sun Tsu, Von Clausewitz, Yi Sun-Sin, William Shakespeare, Benjamin Franklin, and other figures from Earth Analogue III.

Gwen's battle as element commander with pirates is based on Admiral Yi Sun-sin's Battle of Hansando, 8th of the 7th Moon, 1592 C.E.

The phrase, *"Extraordinary claims require extraordinary evidence"* echoes something said by Carl Sagan, and is known as the "Sagan Standard."

Nudd's conundrum, presented at the café just before Sixth Form, is based on the writings of Admiral Yi Sun-sin.

Garreth's element's graduation exercise was inspired by experiences of Sergeant Lawrence M. Lentz, United States Marine Corps, who led a six-man Battalion Reconnaissance Team which was cut off in al-Kafhji by Iraqi forces during *Gulf War I*. Although given the option by their command to flee, they elected to remain and spent four days concealed on a rooftop, surrounded by the enemy. About 2200 hours on 29 January 1991, the Iraqis launched an attack that lasted some 40 hours. Sergeant Lentz called for artillery fire on his own position to persuade the Iraqis to call off a search of the area. The team later escaped in a HUM-V with flattened tires.

Telor's lesson, "As far as fear and courage go, you come out of Academy the way you came in. The only thing is, you are smarter," and Garreth's thought about exercise planning, "This is in every way a joint operation. No hierarchy, no [excrement], just ideas about the best way to succeed," are also attributed to Sergeant Lentz.

BIBLIOGRAPHY

Good science fiction is based on good science – perhaps taken farther than its originators believe possible. Here are some of the articles and books that inspired this story and others in "The Stuff of Life" tetralogy. This book is not a research paper, and the format of this bibliography would probably get it a failing grade in any high school or college writing course.

_____, *Admiral Yi Sun-sin: A brief overview of his life and achievements*. Diamond Sutra Recitation Group. Undated. [Some of Garreth' battles are based on Admiral Yi's defense of Korea in the 1590s of the Common Era.]

_____, CWRU [Case Western Reserve University] researchers discover brain waves may spread by weak electrical field," The Daily, 2016-02-24. [Telepathy]

_____, *The Practice of Hongik Ingan: Lives of Queen Seondeok, Shin Saimdang and Yi Yulgok."* Korean Spirit and Cultural Project, published by the Diamond Sutra Recitation Group, March 2011.

Diaz, Jesus. "…a wearable device for kids with ADHD." *Fast Company.* 2015-09-31. [Vambrace]

Haidt, Jonathan. "The Righteous Mind: Why Good People are Divided by Politics and Religion." Kindle Edition, 2012.

Hawking, Stephen, and Mlodinow, Leonard. *The Grand Design*. Random House Publishing Group, 2010. Kindle edition.

Jeong Byeong-Jo. "Master Wonhyo: An Overview of His Life and Teachings," Korean Spirit & Cultural Promotion Project, 2010.

Journal of Neoroscience, March 2016, "Propagating Neural Source Revealed by Doppler Shift of Population Spiking Frequency" See also the popular article on the Case Western Reserve University web site, "…brain waves may spread by weak electrical field" 24 February 2016. [Telepathy]

Logsdon, John M. *et al*, "Origin of antifreeze protein genes: A cool tale in molecular evolution." Proceedings of the National Academy of Science, April 15, 1997. [Cold sleep]

Machiavelli, *The Prince*.

"Extremotolerant Tardigrade Genome…Tardigrade-Unique Protein" in "Nature Communications," 20 September 2016. [Genetic modification for protection against radiation]

Mingming, Zhang *et al*. "Propagating Neural Source Revealed…", "The Journal of Neuroscience, 2016-03-21. [Telepathy]

NOVA, "Einstein's Quantum Riddle" (video) 2019-01-19 (may require a subscription)

Plato, The Republic

Sun Tzu, The Art of War

Von Clausewitz *On War*

Wipperecht, Anouk. "…a brain computer interface for tackling ADHD…." "IEEE Spectrum." 2019-05-24 [Vambrace]

Yi Pun, "Biography of Admiral Yi Sun-sin," quoted in other documents, above.

Yi Sun-sin, Admiral. *War Dairy (Nangjung Ilgi)* 1598. English edition. Translated by Ha Tae Hung, Edited by Sohn Pow Key. Published by Yonsei University Press, 1977

Yi Sun Sin, Admiral. *Memorials [Memoranda] to the Court.* Translated by Ha Tae Hung, Edited by Lee Chong Young. Published by Yonsei University Press, 1981

Story of Camalos: www.PaulLentzAuthor.com on the "Son of Wolf" stories page.

CRISPR and DNA Editing: https://en.wikipedia.org/wiki/CRISPR (and follow the links)

Dark Matter and Dark Energy: Start with Wikipedia, including the Λ-CDM model (Lambda-Cold Dark Matter) article and follow the links.

Faster than Light (FTL) Communication, Spooky Action at a Distance, Entangled Pairs, Wormholes, and more

"Towards quantum Internet: Researchers teleport particle of light six kilometres" http://phys.org/news/2016-09-quantum-internet-teleport-particles-kilometers.html

https://gizmodo.com/100-000-video-game-players-helped-scientists-prove-eins-1825935176 https://blogs.scientificamerican.com/critical-opalescence/how-to-build-your-own-quantum-entanglement-experiment-part-1-of-2/?redirect=1

Genetics: Dsup (Damage Suppressor) Protein: http://www.bbc.com/news/science-environment-37384466 "Survival secret of 'Earth's hardiest animal' revealed." Downloaded 21 September 2016.

http://www.nature.com/ncomms/2016/160920/ncomms12808/full/ncomms12808.html "Extremotolerant tardigrade genome... tardigrade-unique protein." Downloaded 21 September 2016.

Hemocyanin. https://blogs.biomedcentral.com/on-biology/2015/03/18/blue-blood-on-ice-blood-pigment-helps-octopods-sustain-oxygen-supply-at-freezing-temperatures/

Specific effects of thiosulphate and L-lactate on hemocyanin-O_2 affinity in a brachyuran hydrothermal vent crab: http://link.springer.com/article/10.1007%2FBF00347269

Octopuses Survive Sub-Zero Temps Thanks to Specialized Blue Blood, Harmon, Katherine. Scientific American blog, July 13, 2013. http://blogs.scientificamerican.com

Boleadoras (Bolas), Making and Throwing: https://www.youtube.com/watch?v=3ef0swCXmoU; https://www.youtube.com/watch?v=JSPft-I1lIM

Hannibal Directive: 2016-06-29 telegraph.co.uk. "Israel ends the 'Hannibal Directive' – military policy to kill your own troops rather than let them be captured."

https://www.usnews.com/news/world/articles/2018-03-14/israels-hannibal-directive-criticized-in-official-report

http://www.foxnews.com/world/2018/03/14/israels-hannibal-directive-criticized-in-official-report.html

https://en.wikipedia.org/wiki/Hannibal_Directive (and follow the links)

www.ingramcontent.com/pod-product-compliance
Lightning Source LLC
Chambersburg PA
CBHW062008170626
46813CB00001B/78